"Noah?" Jasmine's heart skipped a beat and she froze in stunned silence. Was this some kind of a cruel joke? "You . . . can't be. He's dead."

"If you open the door and look, you'll see that I'm very much alive."

"Her entire body shook. She said nothing.

"Did you really think I was dead?" he pressed.

"No." The single word escaped her mouth before her brain could even register it. Keeping the chain lock engaged, she opened the door partially and stared at the man standing the hall. Even in the dim lighting, there was no denying it was Noah. He seemed a lot taller than she recalled, but then she had never seen him out of bed before.

"Why are you here?" The question sounded oddly stupid but it was all she could think to say.

"If you let me in, I'll try to explain."

Jasmine reached for the chain, then hesitated. Despite her extraordinary past relationship with him, she still didn't know anything at all about the man. He was mysterious. He could be a murderer, a rapist. *He could kill her.* Wait a minute—*how* could he kill her? In a figurative sense, she was already dead.

She swung the door open wide.

DAWN'S HARBOR

KYMBERLY HUNT

Genesis Press, Inc.

INDIGO LOVE SPECTRUM

An imprint of Genesis Press, Inc.
Publishing Company

Genesis Press, Inc.
P.O. Box 101
Columbus, MS 39703

ISBN: 13 DIGIT : 978-1-58571-271-7
ISBN: 10 DIGIT : 1-58571-271-X
Manufactured in the United States of America

First Edition

Visit us at www.genesis-press.com
or call at 1-888-Indigo-1-4-0

DEDICATION

This book is dedicated to the memory of two little NYC girls named Elisa and Nixzmary, and to all the children whose knights in shining armor didn't show up on time.

ACKNOWLEDGMENTS

Even those of us who tend to be introverted realize that humans were not created by God to be solitary. Therefore, I gratefully thank the Creator for readers who still enjoy romantic stories with an inspirational twist, my supportive family, and the many friends, real and imagined, who have inspired my writing.

In this story, Cielo Vista is a fictional country but it is based on the combined history and geography of many similar countries in Africa. The Baka people really do exist and their beliefs are typical of those described in the novel.

PROLOGUE

Enough! Jasmine stormed into the room and halted abruptly beside the bed where her slumbering sister lay curled up in sloth-like oblivion. The covers concealed most of Natalie's face and exposed only a few frizzy braids. Hovering over her, Jasmine clenched and unclenched her fists in an attempt to get her temper under control. She really wanted to strangle Natalie, but ethically and morally speaking, that was not an option. Instead, she squeezed her eyes shut, counted to ten and opened them again.

The view did not improve. Her once immaculate, inviting guest room was now a disaster area. Children's toys were all over the floor, the rug was askew, and horror upon horrors, little Dawn's artwork in fluorescent orange marker glared back at her from the wall. The crib in the corner held Natalie's second creation, a six-month-old cherub who was now screaming his tiny head off. All the commotion was no deterrence to Natalie's slumber.

"God help me," Jasmine seethed. She grabbed the covers and yanked them completely off the bed. "Nat, get up right now!"

Startled, Natalie sat bolt upright and stared at her with the wild-eyed expression of a snared animal. "What!" she screamed.

"What do you mean, what?" Jasmine shouted back, towering above her sister with her hands on her hips. "I have to leave for work in less than ten minutes. The baby is screaming and Dawn's alone in the kitchen eating peanut butter and corn flakes. Just when do you plan on getting up and taking care of your kids?"

Natalie, having partially recovered from the shock, rolled her bloodshot eyes and grappled for the non-existent covers. "All right already. You don't have to be such a drama queen. I'm getting up now."

Before she did the unthinkable, Jasmine spun around on her heel and marched out of the room. She entered the room that served as her office, snatched up her briefcase and locked the door with a key, having recently installed the lock in order to keep the children away from the computer, which was used primarily for business.

She had to give an important presentation before the board at work. As the only African-American and female member of Spherion Architecture, Inc., she seemed to fall under an unwritten rule that said more was expected of her than the others. She had stayed awake all night, arranging and rearranging the computer graphics for the slideshow portion of the presentation, accompanied by the baby's crying, Dawn's tantrums and the visit from her sister's latest boyfriend.

Natalie had abandoned the youngest child's father because of what she said was an abusive relationship. It had been the same scenario with Dawn's father. She hadn't married either of them and claimed that she couldn't go back to stay with her foster mother, who lived in Indiana, because she would lose her job in Manhattan. Now Natalie was living in Jasmine's suburban New York townhouse and had conveniently lost her job anyway.

Jasmine was furious at herself. She'd agreed for her sister and the kids to stay for two weeks only. Yet she'd allowed the time to stretch to two months. Natalie had always been irresponsible, and having young children to care for had not changed her in the least. In fact, Jasmine had found herself playing mother to both Natalie and the kids. It wasn't that she didn't love her little niece and nephew, but she had chosen a career and her own personal space over being a mother, and at this point in her life she wasn't ready to change that. She wasn't really sure what a mother was supposed to be because most of her childhood had been spent in one foster home after another with no privacy and no space. She didn't want to live like that again. Enough was enough. She needed to reclaim her life.

On her way out the door, she threw a glance back as Natalie dragged into the kitchen. Two-year-old Dawn was running in circles around her high chair, banging on the table with a wooden spoon, her thick, curly hair framing her head like a lion's mane.

"Natalie, I'm dead serious this time. I can't live like this anymore. You're going to have to find another place."

"You're throwing us out?" Natalie turned from the refrigerator, clutching a bottle for the baby. Her expression was so melodramatic that had it been a different situation Jasmine would have found it comical.

"We'll discuss this when I get back," Jasmine replied sharply. She did not want to argue in front of Dawn, even though the child didn't seem to be paying the slightest bit of attention.

"You're being totally selfish," Natalie said. "Can't you see I have a problem here?"

"I think you better do a reality check, Sis. You're the one being selfish."

Jasmine hurried out to the driveway where her SUV awaited and paused for a moment. The sky looked jaundiced, and in the distance she heard the muted rumble of thunder. The air was laden with humidity, and she shuddered as a bizarre sensation of being transported somewhere else overwhelmed her. The foliage of the trees seemed much thicker and greener than usual and the chirping of the birds sounded too exotic for the region's usual robins and sparrows. In the distance she could hear the rushing sound of a river running through a rainforest.

A jagged bolt of lightning split the sky, shaking her out of her trance. She rushed to the safety of the car, took a deep breath and looked around again to confirm that there was nothing strange or exotic at all. Her eyes focused on the same old driveway and the shrubbery along both sides of it . . . shrubbery that needed trimming. She shook her head and laughed out loud.

"Girl, you're losing your mind," she muttered aloud. A vacation was long overdue.

Thunder rumbled again, and she groaned. It was going to be a rough commute into the city and, thanks to Natalie, she had already lost valuable time. She turned the key in the ignition; the engine responded sluggishly at first, then caught on. That was another thing that would have to be checked out. The stupid car was only a year old, and it definitely shouldn't be sounding as if it were ten.

Muttering angrily, she flipped the gear into reverse and the vehicle jolted backwards violently. She floored the brake to halt the unwarranted momentum and simultaneously heard, as well as felt, a soft, resounding thud.

"Oh, please . . . don't do this to me. Not now," she muttered aloud, thinking that Natalie's kid had left her tricycle in the driveway again.

She got out of the car just as the heavens unleashed a torrential downpour. Bracing herself against the monsoon, she rushed to the rear of the car and then froze. Lying there on its back, with its arms spread like angel wings, a porcelain doll with glazed eyes stared up into the stormy sky. The doll was wearing pink pajamas and had thick, tangled hair. A small pool of dark red blood was forming a halo above its head.

"Dawn!" Jasmine's scream rattled the heavens and lightning ripped across the sky in torment.

CHAPTER 1

A year later

The trash had been emptied, the furniture dusted and the bathrooms thoroughly cleaned. Jasmine gave an obligatory glance around the echoing corridors of the hospice to make sure she wasn't being observed and she slipped quietly into the stark bareness of room 23. No flowers decorated the bedside table, no cards from family members. There was no visible evidence that anyone cared about the person who occupied the room. She pulled up the orange visitor's chair that would have collected dust had it not been for her nightly visits.

"Well, Noah, here I am again," she said, and laughed ironically that she was on a first name basis with him. "What's going on with you tonight? Nothing, you say? I guess it's no surprise. It doesn't matter to people like us because we're both just breathing and little else." She rubbed her eyes wearily. "Actually I'm getting really tired of this . . . I mean it's worse for me. I still have to get up every day, work, pay bills, and pretend to live, but you, you can just stay asleep until your heart stops beating. There isn't much pain in that, is there?"

She sighed deeply, flicked back a stray braid, and studied the Caucasian man who lay stretched out on the steel-framed bed before her. He wore a faded blue hospital-issue gown that stripped him of any dignity he might have had in his conscious life. Mercifully, the lower half of his body was concealed by blankets, which hid limbs emaciated by disuse, as well as the intravenous tubing and other necessary apparatus.

He was young, compared to the rest of the residents of the hospice/nursing home who were slowly, painfully whiling away their final hours. Even in his sallow-skinned comatose state, he was a handsome man with finely chiseled features, raven-black hair and darkly arched eyebrows. She focused on the shadows beneath his closed eyes and the long eyelashes fanning them.

On the first day she had started working at the hospice, she'd learned from a chatty nurse's assistant that the man's name was Noah Arias and he had been in a car accident, which had left him in his present state. Initially he'd been on life support for a month, but after the doctors declared the coma to be irreversible, his family had requested the respirator be shut down. Surprisingly, he'd continued to breathe on his own, and apparently not knowing what else to do, the family had condemned him to Glendale Hospice, where he had been for the last two years. Alive but dead.

Jasmine squeezed her eyes shut and continued to talk. "Do you remember what I told you last night about the little girl in the apartment next door? Well, it's true she really does like me. Imagine that. I don't want to encourage it for obvious reasons, but she's an unusual kid. She likes to play with her dolls in the hallway just outside my door. She used to run away when I opened it, but yesterday she just stayed there."

Tears welled up in her eyes and she allowed them to fall. It amazed her that she could cry so much when she was alone with him, yet at the most tragic and poignant moments in her adult life she rarely shed tears. Maybe it was because talking to Noah was only one step up from talking to herself. He never gave the slightest indication of hearing anything and he certainly didn't see her, which was probably a good thing because her appearance—no makeup and unkempt braids emanating from her scalp like writhing snakes—would probably repel anyone.

She had been indulging in the one-sided conversations for nearly six months, long after having stopped the recommended therapy sessions, which had done little to ease the crushing guilt over her niece's death, guilt that was still devastating her own life.

"I don't know how she could come from that family," Jasmine rambled on. "She doesn't look or act anything like those other wild brats. And the mother . . . well, I've only seen her a few times but I'll bet she's an alcoholic or drug addict or something."

Her attention drifted toward the window. The drawn shades were lightening, telling her that in a short time a new day would dawn. She remembered the pleasure of watching the sun ascend over the Hudson River during early morning jogs through the nearby park when she used to live in the suburbs. She recalled the laughs she used to share with her childhood friend Valerie as they ran, talking about work and the impossible men in their lives.

Valerie wouldn't even recognize this Jasmine, who lived in self-imposed exile on the twelfth-floor of a run-down Brooklyn housing project and paid for her meager existence with her earnings as a cleaning lady. During the day she spent most of her time escaping into the benign world of sleep, shutting out all the obnoxious sounds of the city and its people.

The truth was, since her termination from her position as a partner at Spherion Architecture, she didn't recognize herself anymore. Initially she had been crushed by the unfairness of the dismissal. The senior partners had been sympathetic to her grief at first, but they simply had not given her enough time to pull herself together. Now she realized that they probably had had no choice except to let her go because she had started over-medicating on prescription drugs for depression, which left her in a useless haze. To add to that, she had become so traumatized by flashbacks that she could no longer drive and had sold her SUV, forcing herself to rely on public transportation, which always made her late for crucial client meetings—when she remembered them at all. Even when she was present, her mind had been elsewhere.

Jasmine glanced down at her watch and back at Noah's emotionless face. "I guess I've bored you enough for the night," she said, starting to stand. "It's time for me to leave."

"Don't go."

Jasmine froze between sitting and standing. She dropped heavily back into the chair and stared at the man. "Did . . . did you say something?"

There was only the usual silence, punctuated by his breathing and her own heartbeat pounding in her ears.

Jasmine laughed and held her hand over her forehead. "Oh, God, this is it. I really am insane."

"No, you're not."

The voice was raspy and barely audible, but his eyes were open and they seemed unnaturally illuminated in a mysterious shade of gray. The electric eyes were focused exclusively on her. Jasmine jumped up, nearly knocking the chair to the floor.

"I'm not imagining this. You really are speaking!"

"Yes."

"Oh, my . . . this is . . . this is weird. Please stay awake. I'm going to get the nur—"

"No!" he interrupted in a loud and commanding tone, which caused her to stop in her tracks. Instantly his voice dropped five decibels back to the hoarse whisper. "Please don't."

"But . . . but why?" she stammered, feeling light-headed. "You've been unconscious for a very long time. People have to know."

"Don't want to talk to anyone. Just you. Could you . . ." He struggled for the right word. "Sit. Please . . . didn't mean . . . to scare you."

"I'm not scared," Jasmine said. "I'm just shocked."

She sank back into the chair, resisting the urge to flee, because she still felt she was imagining the whole bizarre scene. It was a good thing she wasn't the fainting type or she would have passed out by now.

"The little girl . . ."

"Little girl?" Jasmine repeated, staring at him with dazed eyes.

"Yes. The little girl you . . . talk about."

She swallowed hard. A man who had been in a coma for over two years was miraculously out of it and only interested in talking about some little girl who really had nothing to do with either of them.

"You *remember* what I was talking about?"

"You talk . . . a lot."

Considering the circumstances, she knew she wasn't completely justified to feel annoyed, but nevertheless the comment irked her. She tried to control her inner impulses.

"How long have you been awake?"

"Don't know." He took a deep breath before he spoke again. "I've heard . . . your voice . . . for a very long time. Do I know you?"

"Actually you don't know me at all. I'm just the cleaning woman. I do your room every night."

"You called me Noah."

She shifted uncomfortably in the chair. "Well, that's your name, isn't it? It's on your wrist tag."

His eyes shifted downward to study the plastic tag.

"You don't remember your name?" she asked.

"I remember." He took another deep breath. "What happened? Where am I?"

"I've been told that you were in a car accident, and this is Glendale Hospice in Manhattan. You've been in a coma for just about two years." She stood up again and started backing away. "I really have to go get the nurse.

I'm no expert on things like this and someone else will be a lot better at answering your questions. They'll be able to call your family and . . ."

Her voice trailed off as she noticed his eyes were fixed in a glassy unfocused gaze toward the ceiling. She rushed back to his side.

"No! Please . . . please don't go back to sleep."

She gripped his shoulder and shook him desperately. There was no response. He seemed to have drifted back off into unconsciousness. Fighting against the familiar wave of despair, Jasmine tried to think. If she went and told the nurses now, what good would it do? Who would believe her? The nursing staff in general treated her as if she were invisible unless something needed cleaning.

It occurred to her that maybe if she stayed a little longer and continued to talk he would return. It was a long shot, but definitely worth a try.

She sat back in the chair. "I think the little girl's name is Morgan, at least that's what I heard the other kids call her. She's very pretty. She has long, curly black hair and the biggest brown eyes you've ever seen. She looks . . . she looks kind of the way I would imagine Dawn would look if she'd lived to be six or seven."

"Eerie," he said.

Jasmine's heart pounded with relief and exhilaration upon hearing his response, but she didn't trust it to last. As much as she wanted to change the subject, she continued out of fear of losing him.

"It is eerie, and I'm not sure I like it," she said.

His eyes shimmered. "Signs, you have to . . . read the signs . . . may be a reason why this is happening. Divine inter . . . inter—"

"Divine intervention?" she interrupted his stammering. "I don't see anything divine about it. I think it's cruel. Dawn is gone and now I have to see her in some stranger's child."

Noah attempted a smile. "Maybe it's a sign that Dawn forgives you . . . wants you to move on."

"That's ridiculous."

"Is it?" His voice became stronger and clearer. "What happened to your daughter . . . was a tragedy, but it was an accident. You can't bring her back . . . have to forgive yourself . . . go on. No point being alive if you don't."

"She wasn't my daughter. She was my niece," Jasmine replied sharply. "And if you're going to remember every detail of my whining sessions at least get the facts straight."

He chuckled. "No need to get hostile."

"I'm not hostile. I just don't enjoy talking about this and I can't imagine why you do. It's crazy for me to go on and on about myself when you obviously have your own health issues that need to be dealt with."

A silence fell over the room as Jasmine became even more aware of the intensity of his strange, mesmerizing stare. His eyes were like smoky cut glass with dazzling beams of sunlight piercing through, both unsettling and alluring at the same time.

"You're right," Noah said slowly. "Don't remember much."

Jasmine evaded his gaze and stared at the window. The shadowy residue of night had faded from the curtains. Daylight was rapidly approaching and she knew she had to leave before someone came in and questioned her awkward presence in the room. Yet she hesitated, trapped between her own desire to just walk out and never look back, and the urge to tell the nurse for his own good, whether he wanted her to or not. He didn't seem capable of preventing the latter, since he had made no attempt to sit up or even change positions.

"Need your help," Noah said.

"I hope you're going to ask me to get the nurse before I leave."

"No. Not that." His voice was barely a whisper now. "Please, just listen. Need you to call somebody for me. I remember his number. . . ."

How could he remember something as specific as a telephone number and little else, she wondered, but she picked up a pen and a notepad from the nightstand, realizing for the first time that there was no telephone in the room. She almost laughed. Of course there wasn't a phone, a person in a coma would have no need for one. He gave her a number and she wrote it down.

"Know this sounds crazy," Noah whispered urgently, "but I'm . . . in danger. Call Aaron. Please. Tell him I have to see him . . . soon."

He's delirious, Jasmine thought. "Is that it? You don't want me to say anything else?"

"No."

She sighed. "Whatever you want. Goodbye, Noah, and good luck." She moved quickly to the door, still feeling the smoldering heat from his eyes.

"Jasmine," he said.

She paused without looking back.

"The kid next door . . . be friendly. Dawn might like it."

By the time Jasmine had made the tedious journey on the foul-smelling elevator to the twelfth floor and her Brooklyn apartment, she realized that the number he had given her wasn't even a local one and the charge was going to be her responsibility. She dialed anyway, half expecting it would be incorrect or that no one would even answer. It rang. She waited.

"Hello," a voice responded. It was masculine with a touch of a foreign accent she couldn't quite place.

"Am I speaking to Aaron?"

"Yes."

"My name is . . ." She hesitated. *What difference does it make what my name is?*

"Your name is . . . ?" he repeated.

Irritated, she ignored the question. "I have a message from Noah. He wants you to come see him as soon as possible."

There was a slight pause. "Message received. Thank you," he said.

She heard the phone click on the other end. That was it. No questions asked . . . nothing. She shook her head and put the receiver down. What was all the mystery about? Who was Aaron anyway? Were the two involved in a same sex relationship? The thought disturbed her more than it should have. But it couldn't possibly be true, because even though Noah had seen her in a most unattractive light, there was something about the way he looked at her that conveyed with no uncertainty that he was a man who had, and always would, appreciate women.

Is any of this supposed to matter? Jasmine thought. *As soon as he reconnects with his past, he won't even remember me. Why should he?*

She glared at the clock. It was almost seven A.M. and normally she would have been showered and peacefully tucked into the cocoon of her bed. She had just started her preparations when a familiar sound made her stop. She heard the apartment door next to hers open, followed by a deafening blast of hip-hop music. The door slammed shut again, muffling the music, but it was still loud. A few minutes later she heard someone brushing against her door, then the familiar child's voice talking to her family of dolls as if she really expected them to answer back.

School was out for the summer; it was way too early for children to be up and out of the house. She had a good mind to walk next door and tell the mother that she should be taking better care of her daughter. It was something she definitely would have done in the distant past, but instead Jasmine leaned against the door listening.

"I want to stay with you, Daddy." The child's tone of voice was high-pitched, pleading. Then it quickly deepened into a mock imitation of a man's voice. "I'm sorry, princess, but you just can't go with me. There's no place for little girls up here."

Jasmine quietly slid the bolt and chain mechanism down, unlocking the door and opening it slightly. The child looked wide-eyed up at her from her cross-legged position on the floor. Her hair was in a messy ponytail and she wore a wrinkled green T-shirt that was much too big, and grimy, untied sneakers. She held a doll in each hand. One of them was a tiny naked girl and the other, a shabby-looking Ken.

"Hello," Jasmine said.

The girl studied her anxiously. "I'm not being bad."

"Of course you're not, but wouldn't it be more fun if you played in your room instead of in the hall?"

"But I don't have a room."

"Well, I'm sure your mother would like it better if you at least played inside your own apartment."

"She yells at me when I'm there. And there's too many of them."

"Too many of who?" Jasmine asked.

"Too many kids."

The answer amused Jasmine a little, even though the child didn't realize it.

"You mean you have too many brothers and sisters?"

The big dark eyes lowered as she avoided eye contact. "They're not my brothers and sisters. They're just kids. The social lady said I have to stay with them because my daddy's dead and Grandma's sick."

Jasmine sighed. Another foster child case. She knew all too well what that was like. She didn't want to remember her own early years spent being shuttled back and forth from one foster family to another, and finally being placed in a state-run facility for orphans. The memory was too painful, so she didn't pursue it.

"What's your name?"

"Morgan."

"Princess Morgan, that's very pretty. I like it."

Morgan's face brightened. "My daddy named me. He called me a princess, too."

"Your daddy was right. You are a princess."

"I like you," Morgan said. Then she added anxiously, "You're not really a crazy lady, are you?"

Jasmine's eyebrows rose. "A crazy lady? What makes you think that?"

"Oh . . . I know you're not. It's Tasha and Bobby. They said that you're crazy and ugly 'cause your hair looks funny and you don't talk to people and stuff."

Jasmine flinched. So she had never been invisible to the so-called neighbors after all. She took a deep breath and swallowed her pride. She was, after all, talking to a child, and children were usually tactless but sincere. "Who are Tasha and Bobby?"

"The kids," Morgan replied. "They're really mean and I hate them. Tasha looks like a gorilla and she's got bumps all over her face and ugly hair, and Bobby's lots bigger than me, but he wets the bed like a baby."

"I know how you feel, Morgan, but you shouldn't hate them. Tasha and Bobby don't know any better. They don't realize it's not right to say nasty things about people they don't even know. I'm glad you're so much smarter."

Morgan beamed. "When I lived with Grandma I was in second grade already . . . and I'm only six. But when I came here, I had to go to first with the babies again 'cause nobody thinks I'm smart."

Jasmine was seeing too much of her past in the child—a past she so desperately wanted to forget. Though part of her wanted to invite Morgan in and continue the conversation, she knew she was not ready. The logical choice was to retreat.

"It doesn't matter if other people don't think you're smart, as long as you know it yourself. Well, I have things to do. Goodbye, Morgan. Have fun playing with your dolls."

She struggled to ignore the child's disappointed look because it made her feel cold and heartless; still, it was not her problem. She was only one person and she couldn't be expected to bleed over and over again for the millions of children around the world who felt unloved and insecure.

"Bye," Morgan said.

Jasmine took a deep breath behind the closed door. However, it did not block out the mechanical sounds of Morgan's chatter, which had resumed as though never interrupted.

"I know there's not s'posed to be little girls up there, Daddy, but couldn't you just ask God for me? Maybe He might change His mind."

CHAPTER 2

Noah was drifting in and out of reality. There was no one in the room to keep him focused, and his brain seemed to be detached from the rest of his body. In his mind, he was walking out of the room and moving in a direction where he felt totally relaxed and at peace. The place was very familiar with brilliant sunlight in a clear blue sky.

He could hear palm trees gently rustling in the warm island breeze and the melody of frothy waves caressing the sandy shore as he strolled hand in hand with a woman who had a distinctly mesmerizing voice, but strangely enough, possessed two alternating faces. The first face reflected an almost surreal beauty with sea-foam eyes, porcelain skin and golden sun-kissed hair; then the face evolved into another with equally stunning, but more natural, beauty with gold-flecked brown eyes, raven black hair and a creamy, caramel-colored complexion.

He felt serenity and peace all around him, until the wind suddenly shifted and grew malevolent. The sky darkened and the waves surged forward with storm-tossed fury. The woman beside him became faceless and vanished into the swollen sea. He distinctly heard the sharp cracking of gunfire, followed by moans and cries, voices and explosions. He heard his name being called by many people. But he did not listen; instead, he ran, half-crouching, half crawling, toward the distant mountains, hoping they would conceal him.

Footsteps echoed from far off, and the visions dissolved into a vaporous haze. Alarmed, he remembered where he was and stared at the grayish white ceiling of the room. He quickly closed his eyes. The footsteps grew nearer. They were different, unlike the whispery, hurried ones he associated with Jasmine, or the dutiful stride of the nurses. These footsteps were brisk, purposeful and they were coming into his room. Relief flooded over him. Jasmine had kept her word. How could he have doubted her?

"Well, look who's back," Aaron said, towering over him. "It's about time."

Noah laughed. He wasn't sure why, but he did.

Aaron pulled up the chair and sat down. "Do you remember anything?"

"I remember you," Noah said.

"From where?"

Noah hesitated. "Israel."

"You were never in Israel that I know of," Aaron said bluntly. "But if you really do remember me, then you must remember more."

Noah's voice tightened with frustration and impatience. "I remember my name and a woman named Jasmine. She's the one who called you."

Aaron stood up again and paced around as though deep in thought. "It's okay," he said finally. "It might take some time, but I'm sure your memory will come back."

"Jasmine told me that I was in an accident. Can you explain the rest?"

"I will, but later. The most important thing is to get you out of here and back to Mariel's place as soon as possible."

"Who's Mariel?"

"Your mother."

There was another long silence. Obviously if this Mariel was his mother, he certainly should remember her. He tried to conjure up an image but his mind drew a blank. Intense anger that he'd been trying to deny bubbled over, and the tall brooding man looming over him became the target for it.

"Any fool should remember his own mother," he snapped, "but the simple fact is I don't! Do I have a wife, too? Kids? Are they dead?" The mounting rage increased. "Why are you looking at me like that? Tell me more."

Aaron didn't even blink. He pulled the chair up closer and sat down again. "Noah, calm down. I know this is tough, but you're just going to have to trust me. I can't tell you anything more until you are back home and—"

"Well, I can't just get up and walk out of here," Noah interrupted.

"Just let me finish. I'm taking care of all the arrangements. You don't have to do anything except continue to play dead for at least today. You will be out of this place by tomorrow."

Noah stared directly into Aaron's eyes. They were as focused and unyielding as his own disturbingly selective memory recalled them to be. He was just going to have to rely on a gut sense of friendship and loyalty, even though he couldn't remember when and how the bond had been forged. In either case, the "playing dead" part wasn't going to be that difficult because he had been out of the coma for some time and no one realized it. Now, uncertain about what lay ahead of him, he wondered if he had made a mistake in asking Jasmine to call Aaron.

"Where is home?" he asked quietly, resigned. "You can tell me that, can't you?"

"Right now home is in South Carolina."

At that point, Noah shut down mentally. Whatever had to be done would be done. He didn't want to hear Aaron's voice or his silence anymore. The only voice he wanted to listen to was Jasmine's, and it didn't matter that she was only the cleaning woman with no connection to his past. He wanted to shield himself with her existence. He wanted to continue to block out everything he didn't remember from his own life because her life seemed a lot more tangible and possibly salvageable. He wanted to see her smile.

In a flash, he recalled the vision he'd had earlier, and it dawned on him that the second woman's face had been Jasmine's without the unkempt braids. They had been replaced by dark, shining ripples of hair, and she had been radiantly happy.

Jasmine could not sleep. Normally, regardless of daylight and other outside stimuli, it took her about fifteen minutes after tumbling into bed to blank out the world. Not this time. She tossed and turned, feeling the steamy effects of the mid-June heat wave. She found herself staring intensely at the flaking paint on the ceiling and then at the window. Not even one tiny breeze stirred the filmy yellow curtains. The traffic down below seemed amplified a hundred times.

"Shut up!" she yelled, seizing the pillow and pulling it over her face.

It didn't help. In her mind she kept playing over and over again what had happened a few hours ago. That moment when Noah had ceased to be her sounding board and become a real person. She was happy for him—or was she? He would eventually rediscover his life, barring any setbacks, and he would return to it. She, on the other hand, had spent months exposing herself to him. If he had retained even half of what she had revealed, the humiliation would be unbearable. She never wanted to see him again. The thought echoed in her mind as she finally drifted into a fitful, dream-plagued sleep.

It was late in the evening. She was nine years old, waiting in a busy bus terminal, hanging on to the hot, sticky hand of her three-year-old sister Natalie, who had a bad cold and was alternating between crying, whining and coughing. Jasmine was trying not to cry herself. Their mother had told them to sit on the benches with the luggage while she went around the corner to the ladies' room, but she had been gone for a very long time.

"I want Mommy," Natalie whined.

"We have to wait here 'cause someone might steal the suitcases," Jasmine said for the tenth time. Natalie started crying loudly.

Jasmine wanted to slap her, but knew it would only make things worse. "Shut up! She's gonna be back soon."

Natalie's coughing was worse. Jasmine was not only scared but angry as well because she didn't think it was right to be getting on a bus and traveling far away with a sick kid. Her mother's ideas were always crazy. Why couldn't she be more like the mom of her best friend Lisa? Lisa was probably home in bed asleep in her own room right now. She would wake up in the morning and her mother would be there to take care of her and her little brothers.

It wasn't fair that she had to be here at a bus station waiting to go to Florida and playing mother to a screaming kid. She didn't want to go. The whole plan was stupid because soon this guy—her mother's latest boyfriend— would get sick of them all and throw them out.

"I wanna go home," Natalie wailed.

Jasmine wanted to go home, too, but she wasn't sure where home was anymore. Her mother had said that they had been kicked out of their apartment in Queens and maybe other people had moved in already.

"But why were we kicked out? Didn't you pay the man?" she had asked.

"That fool wants too much money for this dump and I ain't got the money," her mother had answered.

"But what about your check in the mail? Isn't that s'posed to pay it?"

"Never mind about that check. It ain't nearly enough to pay the bills and feed you and your raggedy little sister, too."

But you don't always feed us, Jasmine thought. A lot of times she and Natalie went to bed hungry while their mother was out partying with some of her men friends. Jasmine knew better than to mention that, though. If she did, she would probably get slapped.

"But what are we gonna do now?" she asked.

"Worry, worry, Jasmine, you're just like a little old lady. We're going to Florida to stay with Uncle Tyrone for a while. He won't mind."

Jasmine flinched. She had every right to worry. Tyrone was not her uncle. She didn't even remember him because there had been so many men in the past. She didn't even know which one of them had been her father or Natalie's.

"Jasmine, I don't feel good," Natalie whined, tugging at her arm.

Jolted back to the present, Jasmine made her decision. "Let's go get Mommy," she said. "I don't care about the suitcases."

The ladies' room was dimly lit and foul smelling. A homeless woman dressed in dirt-encrusted rags stood at the only working sink with the water running full blast. She turned and smiled at them, displaying two missing front teeth; the remaining few were rotten and fang-like. Trembling, Natalie clung tighter to Jasmine, who deliberately ignored the woman and ran farther down to where the eight stalls were. Three of them had no doors.

"Mom," she called.

"Mommy," Natalie whimpered.

She was not there.

There were shuffling sounds and Jasmine looked back to see the homeless woman moving toward them. "I been here in this room a while now and ain't seen nobody come in," she said.

"Are you sure?" Jasmine's voice trembled as she struggled to lift Natalie, who was about to scream.

"Don't worry. I help you find your momma." She advanced closer, beckoning with bony fingers that looked like twisted tree branches.

Natalie let loose a deafening scream and Jasmine, half carrying and half dragging her, bolted clumsily past the woman and didn't stop running until she was right back at the bench where the suitcases remained. She dumped Natalie on the bench and tried to figure out what she should do next. Maybe her mother had gone to another bathroom. In a place as big as this there had to be more than one. Maybe they should keep walking and looking around. Maybe.

Huddled on the bench, near panic and trying to think, she observed hundreds of strangers passing by. Mothers were wheeling their babies around in strollers and others were holding the hands of little kids Natalie's age. All of them knew where they were going, and none of them were as frightened and invisible as she and Natalie were.

Natalie wasn't crying anymore. In fact, she wasn't saying anything. Jasmine bent over her and shook her. "Nat, wake up. You can't sleep here."

Natalie was not asleep. Her eyes were open, but they were unseeing. Suddenly her arms and legs started twitching and she began making horrible choking sounds.

"Natalie!" Jasmine screamed.

She couldn't be faking. She was really sick. "Help!" Jasmine yelled to passersby. "Please help my sister."

A lady wearing a fur coat and a tall man with silver hair came over. The man said he was a doctor. The woman talked softly, trying to calm her down. Everything else was a blur. The next minute she and Natalie were in an ambulance, heading for the hospital.

Jasmine sat up in bed, wiped the perspiration from her face, and stared once more at the tauntingly motionless yellow curtains. She might as well forget about sleeping. Trapped in the sweltering jail of a room and remembering her mockery of a childhood left her with a dazed, sickening feeling.

She remembered Natalie's recovery from the seizure, which had been caused by a fever and double pneumonia. After that, both of them were placed in a state-run facility for homeless children and they never saw their so-called mother again. Despite charges of child abandonment and a police investigation, no one ever found her and the case went cold. It was as if the woman had vanished off the face of the earth.

Later a couple from Indiana, who could take only one child, adopted cute little Natalie. Jasmine remembered well what it was like to be completely abandoned and shuttled from one foster home to another. She remembered the one home she'd definitely wanted to remain in; it had been only temporary because the foster mother was almost eighty and too old to keep her.

Ida Gordon, a widowed, retired teacher, had been the kindest, most inspiring woman she'd ever met. It was Ida who first recognized Jasmine's intelligence, encouraged her love for learning, and who had been behind the scenes motivating her and cheering her on through all her middle-school and high school years, even up to the time of her winning a scholarship to a prestigious college in Connecticut.

More importantly, Ida had been the one who had introduced her to spirituality. There had been no end to Mrs. Gordon's faith. "Nothing God can't do" had been her mantra. Jasmine recalled her twelve-year-old self praying and actually believing that God cared about her as an individual.

Mrs. Gordon had kept in contact with her even after she had been permanently placed in a Catholic-run institution for homeless children. The friendship, and her bond with God, had lasted until Mrs. Gordon died when Jasmine was eighteen and about to go out on her own to college. At that time, being a good christian had clashed with her newfound freedom and her worldly ambitions.

The things she had learned about having faith seemed even more mocking now because God had not prevented Dawn's death. It was fair enough if he wanted to punish her for turning aside from his commandments, but why did an innocent child have to die?

CHAPTER 3

Apprehensively, Jasmine approached room 23 and hovered outside the door. Death rattle snores reverberating like a jackhammer in her head confirmed that Noah was no longer there, but she peered in anyway and observed, under the dim nightlight, a slumbering elderly woman with waxy, wrinkled skin and wild, white hair. The orange plastic chair was gone, replaced by a more comfortable one with cushions and an afghan spread over it. There were cards and flowers on the nightstand.

Someone cares about this woman for now, she thought. *But after a while, if she stays alive too long, there will be no more gifts, maybe no more visitors.* She felt rage mounting within her, not justifiable rage over the plight of the abandoned elderly, but stupid, senseless anger and childish jealousy because her personal sounding board was no longer there and this woman had so quickly occupied his space. She turned away.

It's sad how nutty I've become, she thought. Any normal person would be happy that he'd been moved to a rehab center. She, on the other hand, had deliberately, guiltlessly called in sick for two days just to avoid him because she didn't want the embarrassment of having to deal with what else he might remember about her personal life. And now that he had moved on, she was upset anyway.

As she went through the motions, mopping floors, dusting furniture, she kept telling herself there was no point in dwelling on Noah's recovery and her feelings, but the repercussions continued to disturb her. Where was all the fanfare? Wasn't it even newsworthy that a man who'd been expected to die after being in a coma for over two years had suddenly returned to life? She was a hermit, but she did listen to the news, and there had been no mention of it at all. The nurses on the floor were all going about their usual business as if nothing had happened. Could such a miracle have been forgotten in two short days?

Jasmine returned some cleaning equipment to the storage closet and walked toward the unit secretary at the nurse's station. The dour-looking woman, whose name she did not know, had just hung up the phone and evaded eye contact upon her approach.

"Could you tell me what happened to the patient who used to be in 23?" Jasmine asked.

The secretary focused on her computer. "He passed away," she said nonchalantly.

Jasmine's heart missed several beats, the room lurched and, for a split second, she just stood there with her mouth open. "Passed away?" she repeated. "That can't be true. Are you sure? His name was Noah. Noah Arias."

The woman finally made eye contact, nailing her with the kind of expression one might use to address an imbecile. "I know which patient you mean. Mr. Arias died. They all do. Just takes some longer than others."

In complete denial and not wanting to display her true emotions, Jasmine glared venomously at the secretary, turned abruptly and walked back down the hall. It was all she could do to keep from collapsing in a heap. Died? How could he have passed away? She had spoken to him two nights ago and he'd been very much alert. He was heading for recovery. He had told her to contact his friend. How could it be? The secretary was lying.

She had had enough. She stepped into the supply closet, shut the door and dropped down on a step stool. This was her last night at the hospice. She would find the housekeeping supervisor and inform her that she was leaving. What she was going to do after that, she didn't know, but she knew she couldn't stand another moment at Glendale.

Jasmine dialed the number Noah had given her two nights earlier. She didn't know exactly what she was going to say, and she doubted she'd get any information from the mysterious Aaron. The phone rang but no one answered it. She allowed it to ring for a long time, hoping an answering machine would kick in. Finally, she banged the receiver down and threw the number into the trash.

There was no logical reason why anyone would lie about Noah's supposed death, and the odds were against his still being alive, but Jasmine had a strong vibe going. She knew in her heart that he was still in existence. She could feel his presence—hear him breathing, even— somewhere out there beyond her grasp.

Of course she also realized that her vibe could just be her own madness, derived from depression and self-imposed isolation, that was making her feel that way. In either case, regardless of whether Noah was alive or dead, she would have to start dealing with her own situation, which meant finding another job.

Another job to sustain this miserable lifestyle? she thought. A part of her wanted desperately to leave the hideous apartment, leave Brooklyn and return to being an architect and having a life again.

How had she allowed herself to sink to this low point, anyway? Weren't there less extreme measures to atone for her guilt? The thought alone made her feel ill, because she knew the answer, and it didn't take a high-priced therapist to tell her that it all went back to her humiliating beginning. This was the life she had known, her mother's legacy to her. If she had never tried to escape it through higher education, she probably wouldn't even have owned a car and Dawn would still be alive. Because of her, an innocent little girl would never grow up, would never get to be anything. What right did she have to selfishly pursue her own goals as if nothing had ever happened?

She would get another job, another one that she was overqualified for. But it was not urgent. She needed time to think, to get over the loss of Noah. There were still savings left in the bank, and she planned on dipping into them for a while.

It was well into the night, two A.M. The building seemed unusually quiet. Were the obnoxious residents away, or actually sleeping like normal folk? Jasmine was not tired at all and she knew she would never be able to sleep if she went to bed. She paced around the living room, turned on the television, and was rewarded with an old black and white Cary Grant movie. Bored, she left the TV to babble on and went to stand near the door. She pressed her cheek against it.

The painted steel surface felt like prison bars against her face, locking in the coldness that had crept into her soul. She squeezed her eyes shut and listened to the silence until she became aware of something strange going on out there, something beyond the chilling quiescence. The door inhaled softly on the other side. At any moment it was going to swing wide open and some mysterious presence was going to enter.

A breathing door? She flung it open abruptly and her eyes dropped down to a bundle of rags huddled at her feet.

"Great!" she fumed aloud. As if life wasn't unpleasant enough, now people were throwing garbage at her door. She stood there for a few moments, preparing to kick it away, and then she stopped short and sucked in her breath. The bundle of rags was a sleeping child. She knelt down and gently tugged away the raggedy blanket.

"Morgan," she called.

The child sat up abruptly, clutching at the blankets, eyes still heavy with sleep.

"No. Don't be frightened. I'm not going to yell at you. It's way past midnight . . . why are you out here in the hall?"

"I sleep here a lotta times." Her voice was slurred. "I . . . I didn't know you was home."

"But why here in the hallway like this? Don't you have a bed?"

"Tasha sleeps in it."

"This is totally unacceptable," Jasmine said aloud, but more to herself. "You're coming with me, young lady."

Morgan didn't respond right away, so Jasmine gathered her and the blankets up in her arms, ignoring the fact that the child was heavy, and moved around the corner to the neighbor's door. She kicked it loudly with her foot. The door did not open immediately, but when it did, a teenage girl with curlers in her hair peeked out.

"Is your mother home?" Jasmine asked.

"Oh, you found her," the girl said, acknowledging Morgan with a yawn.

"Is your mother home?" Jasmine repeated.

"No. She's out." The girl opened the door wider, allowing her to enter. "I'm sorry if Morgan did something crazy. You can just leave her here."

Jasmine was appalled. "Did something? She was sleeping right outside my door."

The girl merely shrugged. "That kid does weird stuff all the time."

The apartment was dimly lit, smelled like burnt toast, and was in total disarray. The teenager cleared a space for Morgan on a couch cluttered with newspapers, comic books, dirty clothes and children's toys. Still reeling from the scene, Jasmine gently lowered the child onto the couch. Morgan immediately curled into a fetal position and covered her face with the blanket.

"Would you mind telling me where her . . . your mother might be?"

"She's just out," the teenager replied testily. "She'll be back soon."

"Well, I'm going to talk to her when she gets back."

The girl shrugged. "Whatever."

"Hey, Tamara, who's that?" Another girl, who looked to be about ten or eleven years old, appeared in the room, shadowed by a slightly smaller boy. They were both in pajamas. The two stared at Jasmine, exchanged glances with each other, and then broke into giggles.

"Y'all shut up and get back to bed!" Tamara shouted.

They retreated and Tamara turned back to Jasmine, who had pulled the blanket away from Morgan's face and was feeling her forehead.

"It's okay," Tamara insisted. "The kid's not sick. She's just crazy, that's all."

Jasmine straightened up "Well, I wouldn't call her that. People usually have reasons for doing what they do. I'm leaving now. Please don't let her outside again. She could get hurt. It's not safe for children to be outside alone at night."

"I'll watch her," the girl said.

Jasmine left, refraining from slamming the door. *Idiots!* she thought. Where was the mother, anyway? Out partying with friends? In a bar? Doing drugs in some place even sleezier than the building they lived in?

She returned to her apartment and slammed her door. The sound reverberated in the hall. "Imagine that, Noah," she declared. "Morgan sleeps out in the hall. I don't even know how long she's been doing it. She could just walk out by herself again. What am I supposed to do about it? What would you do?" She stopped talking and laughed to stifle the scream that was about to come out.

She abruptly went to the bathroom and switched on the light. The bare ceiling bulb reflected her image in the cracked mirror. She hadn't worn makeup in about a year. Her long, cornrowed hair had not been redone in just as much time. Rows were knotted together in a nappy, dead-looking crown on top of her head and a ponytail contained a swarm of dangling braids. Her cheekbones, once considered a virtue, were now too prominent in a face that was hollow and gaunt. She removed her owlish glasses and saw dull eyes highlighted by raccoon-like circles.

"No wonder those brats laughed at me," she murmured aloud. "Here I am looking like Frankenstein's bride, worried to death about someone else's child, and instead of talking to God, I'm talking to a man who is supposed to be dead. Why can't I stop this?"

CHAPTER 4

Frustration, determination, and what could only be called rage lifted him out of the bed and forced his weak, emaciated legs to carry him across the room. Every muscle screamed in agony just from those few steps, but he made it to the window and stood there gripping the window frame with sweat trickling down his face. He pulled up the shade.

The scene outside, with blinding sunlight filtering through towering, moss-draped oak trees, registered nothing in his memory. All he knew was that it had to be hot and steamy, even though the air-conditioned interior of the house disguised it well. Noah turned away from the window and literally groped the walls to make it to the doorway. He succeeded, but his energy was drained away.

Now what was he supposed to do? It was pretty obvious he couldn't leave the house without assistance, let alone catch an airplane and head back to find Jasmine Burke in New York. He laughed sarcastically and turned around to contemplate the distance back to the bed that beckoned to him and repulsed him at the same time. His body refused to move and he was forced to stand still, hanging onto the door, while his brain tried to comprehend and come to grips with the events of the last few days.

Mariel, the woman who claimed to be his mother, had told him that this was the same room he'd had as a twelve-year-old. He didn't remember it, or anything else about the house in South Carolina. But on a nearby bookshelf, there was a gold-framed photograph of a five-year-old boy with his father and mother. The black-haired, gray-eyed child definitely could have been himself at that age, and there was an eerie resemblance between his present self and Diego Arias, the man in the portrait who was supposed to be his father.

Mariel had also told him that the picture had been taken during happier days in Cielo Vista, the small country off the coast of Africa where he'd been born and where his father had been proclaimed president for life. She'd told him that she and his father had divorced after seven years of marriage due to his father's bizarre belief in polygamy, and that she'd married a Nigerian-born lawyer and gone to live in the United States, leaving him in his father's custody.

Five years after the divorce, when Noah was twelve, Diego Arias, his political allies, and most of his family were assassinated late at night during a bloody coup at the presidential estate. It was explained that he, the vice president's daughter Isabella, and his half-brother Rafael narrowly escaped the same fate by being spirited off the island with the help of his father's confidante Aaron Weiss. Isabella was sent to relatives in Spain and he and Rafael were taken to live with Mariel and her new husband in the United States.

As an adult, he'd earned a bachelor's degree in economics and a master's degree in political science at an acclaimed Boston college. Then he'd strangely ignored the years he'd put into formal education and attended a local flight school, where he learned to pilot commercial jets. After a year of flying for a major airline, he'd formed a business partnership with his longtime friend Aaron. They jointly owned Avian International, a private cargo jet company which transported goods all over the globe.

At some point during the career juggling, he'd married his childhood sweetheart, Isabella, who he now learned had abandoned him soon after the car accident and, shockingly, returned to Cielo Vista.

Mariel had given him a lot of information, but he sensed there was even more being withheld, and as much as he hated to admit it, her decision to hold back was wise. He was having a hard enough time just getting past the revelation that his wife, the so-called love of his life, had been so quick to abandon him. In his vulnerable emotional and physical state, there wasn't much more he could handle.

His grip on the door weakened. His eyes were so leaden it was difficult to keep them open. He tried to call for help, but no words came out. *Maybe I'm about to lapse back into unconsciousness again,* he thought. The idea actually appealed to him. Maybe if he passed out and woke up again he would be back in the hospice waiting for the only person who made any sense to come talk to him again.

"My goodness, Noah, what are you doing up?"

Mariel, tall, olive-skinned and regally attractive, circled her arms protectively around him, as though she were positive she could keep him from falling. He caught the faint citrus-scent of her perfume, and it struck him suddenly that at least the scent was familiar.

She called for Miguel, the hulking but surprisingly agile aide who had been hired to attend him. The man entered and escorted him to the bed, supporting almost all his weight, but sparing him the indignity of being carried like a child. The next thing he knew he was lying on his back, staring up at the ivory-colored ceiling and its dormant ceiling fan.

His eyes shifted downward abruptly and focused on a delicately pretty young girl who'd appeared in the doorway with a concerned look on her face. The girl, he'd been told, was his half sister.

"It's okay, Gianna," Mariel said. "He'll be all right."

The girl wavered in his vision for a moment and then seemingly dematerialized into the atmosphere.

Mariel pulled up a chair near the bed. "Please don't try to get up again without help." Her voice was Spanish accented, pleasant, but tinged with a taut urgency in the tone. Noah turned his head away from her, desiring only silence, and watched the bulky form of Miguel exit the room.

Mariel did not leave. She placed her hand on his shoulder. "I understand how you must feel. You are doing phenomenally well, all things considered. But you're trying too hard. I don't want you to have a setback."

Noah's voice returned, and it sounded as bitter as he felt. "You can't possibly understand. I am here in your house. I'm supposed to be dead, and I don't even remember you, this whole family, or any of the bizarre stories you've told me. Maybe it would have been better if I actually had died."

"My son would never say such a foolish thing!" Her voice rose in indignation. "You are not *that* kind of self-pitying coward. God allowed you to come back to us for a reason . . ."

"Maybe I'm *not* your son," Noah interrupted.

She gripped his shoulder tightly as if trying to ward off some demon that might have possessed him. "Listen to me, Noah. Right now you have some obstacles to overcome, but you are very much alive and we plan to keep you that way." Her voice lowered again and her fingertips stroked the side of his face. "You will remember everything, but it's not going to be overnight. You have to be patient with yourself. You've only been here a few days."

Noah took a deep breath. Maybe the person he was supposed to be was no coward, but the shell of a man he was now certainly felt like one. He wanted desperately to be back in a euphoric state at the hospice, awaiting Jasmine's nightly visits. He yearned for the whispery sound of her voice, for the smooth sensation of her hand touching his. But that was not going to happen. Not now, anyway. Resigned, he made eye contact with Mariel.

"Where's Aaron?"

"He had to leave the country, but he'll be back soon. He said he would come to see you."

"I don't recall saying anything about wanting to see him."

"Maybe not, but you asked about him," Mariel said. "It's a good sign that you do remember him somewhat. He *is* your business partner."

"So you've told me. He also is extremely charming and likable," Noah retorted sarcastically.

"Aaron has always been a man of few words, but many deeds. A lot of people don't quite know how to take him, but you've never had any problems understanding him," Mariel said.

Really? Noah thought, silently cursing the only person he vaguely remembered. If Aaron really was such a great friend, he would have put him out of his misery. Why on earth had he asked Jasmine to call him?

The frustration was too great, and he realized he couldn't keep dwelling on his disabilities and his lost memory. Mariel was right about that. He had been unconscious for a long time and it wasn't possible to immediately return to normalcy. He closed his eyes and tried to relax.

As he mentally escaped the house in South Carolina, his thoughts returned to Jasmine. What was she doing right now? Was she at the hospice? It made him cringe to think that that intelligent and potentially beautiful woman, who had apparently been abandoned and betrayed by her own family, was reduced to mopping floors and emptying trashcans for a living. He hated that she was still blaming herself for the tragic death of a child and, in so doing, dishonoring the child's memory. He hoped she had at least followed his suggestion and decided to befriend the little girl who lived next door; if nothing else, it was a diversion from her own isolation. Right before he drifted off into an oblivious sleep, a thought of great personal significance struck him—did she miss him as much as he missed her?

Jasmine's day started with a persistent banging at her door and a rather husky sounding female voice calling her. She opened the door and confronted a tall, thin, brown-skinned woman with boyishly short auburn-dyed hair. The woman's large eyes were fixed and piercing, framed by brows knitted together in a permanent scowl. An intense odor of cigarette smoke emanated from her.

"I'm Rachel," the woman declared. "My daughter said you was going to come over and speak to me about Morgan. Well, I gotta be somewhere in a hour . . . so start talking."

Not exactly surprised, but a bit taken aback by Rachel's stance, Jasmine hesitated for a second. "Yes, I do want to talk . . ."

"I know what you're thinking," Rachel interrupted. "You think I'm an evil person and a terrible mother. You already got me tried and hung."

"I can only reach a conclusion by what I see," Jasmine stated. "The little girl you're supposed to be taking care of is obviously being neglected."

39

"That little girl is my daughter. Did she tell you that she was a foster kid or something?"

"Well, she didn't exactly say. I kind of reached that conclusion." Jasmine glared at the woman impatiently now. "But whatever the relationship, it's beside the point, isn't it? You're the adult and she's a child. Do you really expect me to just close my eyes and pretend I never saw a little kid sleeping in the hallway?"

Rachel drew herself up haughtily. "Most people in this building know they don't own the hallway."

What an idiot, Jasmine thought. "Am I hearing you correctly? You're going to argue about a hallway? Would you have preferred that I call the police?"

Some of the defiance evaporated from Rachel's eyes. She wrung her hands together. "Look . . . I don't want no trouble. I know it's annoying and I'm sorry about what happened. She won't do it again."

"Listen." Jasmine could not contain the sharpness in her voice. "I'm not telling you this just because I'm annoyed. I'm telling you because I'm concerned about Morgan."

The woman's body twitched in agitation. "You're concerned because Morgan's a pretty little kid, aren't you? People tell me that all the time just 'cause her daddy was Puerto Rican and she look like a Latin doll, but the kid's not right in the head. I got four kids and one grandbaby. She's the worst one. She don't get along with the other kids. She sneaks out of the house at night when she's supposed to be asleep, and all she does is talk to herself and tell lies. The girl lies so much you can't believe a word she says. Truth is, I don't know what to do about her."

Jasmine's frustration grew. The cynical part of her really did not want to know all the details, but she felt compelled to ask. "Has she always been that way?"

"Probably. I don't know. Her father had custody of her until he died. She been with me for about a year now."

"Was she close to her father?"

"I suppose. He and his crazy mother spoiled her rotten. Gave her everything she wanted and they wouldn't even let me see her. His mother would still have her if she wasn't so old and sick."

Jasmine took a deep breath and tried to focus on what she had just heard. She did not really know Rachel, and even though her impression of her was definitely negative, she didn't want to be overly judgmental. It sounded like a tough situation for everyone involved.

"If you don't mind my asking, what happened to Morgan's father? Had he been ill or did he die suddenly?"

Rachel's full lips curved into a sarcastic, gap-toothed smirk. "He was a fireman . . . one of New York's bravest. He died in a fire when the roof collapsed on him."

"How *tragic*." Jasmine paused for a moment, feeling sympathy for the child. "And the grandmother?"

"That witch is sixty-nine and in real bad health."

Jasmine shook her head in dismay. "Poor Morgan. She's lost both of the people who raised her. Did you take her for counseling and . . ."

"Counseling? I ain't got money for no shrink. My other kids been through some pretty bad stuff, too, and they ain't crazy like her."

Jasmine flinched at the redundant use of the word crazy, but she stifled the urge to lash out at the woman. "You know, I'm not working right now. Maybe I can help out with Morgan sometimes. When I'm home, of course." Her throat constricted. She couldn't believe the words that had spilled out of her mouth.

The woman blinked. "I don't got money for no babysitter, either."

"I'm not asking for money."

"That's real nice of you." Rachel hesitated, as if waiting for Jasmine to retract the offer. When she didn't, she continued, "Morgan and two of my other kids gonna be spending a couple of weeks this summer with my sister in Newark, but I would really appreciate if when they get back . . ." Rachel stopped in mid-sentence and made direct eye contact. "Wait. How do I know you ain't some kind of pervert or something?"

Jasmine fought back the urge to laugh. This woman claimed to be unable to prevent a six-year-old from wandering around at night in a building that was infested with drug dealers, addicts and who knew what else, and suddenly she was worried about perverts?

"Do I look like a pervert?" Jasmine braced herself for the response.

"No. I s'pose not. But girl, you need to get a life, and you sure need to do something with that hair."

CHAPTER 5

The fleeting summer days slipped into fall, and no one was more aware of the time passage than Noah. Despite having been told a lot more than he wanted to know about his previous life, he still didn't remember much of it and the blanks only made him even more desperate to get back to New York.

He was physically able to leave now. He considered this as he completed his daily regimen of isometrics and calisthenics, which included sit-ups, pushups and weight lifting. Months of supervised therapy sessions and his own intense workouts had been grueling but had paid off. His once-emaciated body had been transformed into a lean, sinewy, functioning machine, which was almost fully capable of performing whatever he asked of it. Not bad for a thirty-four-year-old who'd lost over two years of his life and couldn't even remember his own family.

Noah peeled off his damp T-shirt, mopped the sweat from his face with it, and exited the library that had been temporarily changed into a gym. He nearly collided with his teenage sister, the offspring of his mother's second marriage.

She gaped. "Wow, Noah! You look hot . . . I mean, you look exactly like you used to."

Noah managed a tight smile. "I'm sorry for walking around half-dressed. I was just going to my bedroom. Didn't know anyone was in the house."

"I . . . I got out from school early. You really don't have to apologize. This is your home too."

Gianna's earlier exuberance had switched to vague disappointment, Noah observed. The young girl had been very kind and helpful to him in the past few months, and she wanted desperately for his memory to return. He sensed that they'd once had a close relationship. Of all the people in the family, he resented not remembering her the most.

"I really do appreciate the compliment," he said.

"I was being silly," she said, blushing.

"Hey, I mean it, Gazelle." He reached out and gently tugged a few strands of her waist-length dark hair. "You're the only one here who I actually feel a bond with, even if I don't remember. It takes a real idiot not to remember a great little sister like you."

"You *do* remember some things, I mean, you still call me Gazelle just like you used to. I just know you're going to remember everything. It's just taking longer than I wish." Gianna's large, honey-colored doe eyes shimmered as she looked up at him.

She was such a sweet kid, small and petite with light tan skin and an enchanting smile. He impulsively hugged her, and she responded warmly.

"You're right, he said. "I will remember. I just have a few very important things to take care of first."

It was close to midnight, a bone-chillingly cold September night with torrential rain and strong winds that almost swept Jasmine down the city streets as she returned home from her current cleaning job at an office building in Manhattan. She ducked into the vestibule, tossed her ruined umbrella into a trashcan and pushed the button for the elevator. No response. She waited. Nothing. Darn! The thing was broken again.

Taking a deep breath, she scanned the corridor to make sure that no predators lurked in the shadows. Resigned, she pushed open the heavy door to the stair-well, gagged at the urine and cigarette odor and stepped inside. The feeble amber lighting that illuminated the litter-strewn steps did little to allay her safety concerns. However, it certainly wasn't the first time she'd had to scale the entire twelve flights.

Her legs and calves burned by the time she reached the ninth floor. As she stood on the landing for a few moments to catch her breath, she became aware of footsteps below. They were approaching rapidly.

No, she did not want to have an encounter with a stranger in a dim stairwell, particularly a male one. More angry than afraid, she reached into her bag for the never-before-used can of mace and began to sprint up the remaining flights. Upon reaching the twelfth floor, she raced around the corner to her door, where she fumbled for her keys with her free hand and then dropped them.

The stairwell door banged shut. The person behind her had also emerged on the twelfth floor. She quickly picked up her keys and stabbed at the lock. A shadow loomed in the distance.

"Hello?"

With her finger pressed threateningly on the mace spray trigger, Jasmine looked up at a tall man approaching—a tall white man. What was a white man doing in this building after midnight? Wait, maybe he was Dominican or Puerto Rican. "Don't come any closer," she hissed.

The stubborn door yielded and she quickly stepped inside her apartment, slamming the door behind her and locking it.

"Jasmine?"

How on earth did this stranger know her name? Was he a cop? Her hands were shaking as she double-bolted the door and slid the chain mechanism.

"My God, what on earth is wrong with you?" she muttered aloud. She had lived here for a while now, and for the most part the goings-on in the building had annoyed but never terrified her. She'd maintained a persistent "I don't care" attitude and found that the more negative she felt about herself, the less likely anyone was going to threaten her. No man ever preyed on an invisible woman.

"Jasmine, is that you?" the voice outside the door persisted. "I didn't mean to fright—"

"Who are you and what do you want?" she demanded.

"Look, I know it's after midnight and I apologize, but my plane got in late because of the weather. Jasmine, it's me . . . Noah. You remember me from Glendale Hospice?"

"Noah?" Jasmine's heart skipped a beat and she froze in stunned silence. Was this some kind of cruel joke? "You . . . you can't be. He's dead."

"If you open the door and look, you'll see that I'm very much alive."

Her entire body shook. She said nothing.

"Did you really think I was dead?" he pressed.

"No." The single word escaped her mouth before her brain could even register it. Keeping the chain lock engaged, she opened the door partially and stared at the man standing in the hall. Even in the dim lighting, there was no denying it was Noah. He seemed a lot taller than she recalled, but then she had never seen him out of bed before.

"Why are you here?" The question sounded oddly stupid, but it was all she could think of to say.

"If you let me in I'll try to explain."

Jasmine reached for the chain. She hesitated. Despite her extraordinary past relationship with him, she still didn't know anything at all about the man. He was mysterious. He could be a murderer, a rapist. He could kill her. Wait a minute—how could he kill her? She was already dead in a figurative sense. She swung the door open wide.

Noah entered, bringing in the intoxicating scent of rain, wind, and man. His close-cut black hair was slick with moisture, his face sculpted and sun-tanned. He wore beige khaki pants and a black leather jacket with beads of water glistening on it. His alluring gray eyes were very much focused on her. Painfully so.

"You look pretty much the same," he commented.

She flinched involuntarily. "You look . . . um . . . healthy."

"It's been a long struggle," he said. "I'm still not quite where I want to be physically, but I'm okay for the time being."

Frustration and impatience collided. "Why are you here?" she repeated.

His eyes sparkled. "Maybe you can tell me."

"That's *not* a good answer."

"Give me a better one."

He stepped farther inside, glancing into the living room. "This is cozy. Much too small, but at least it's neat."

"Are you here to make fun of me?"

"No. There are a lot of interesting things about you, but I've never really found you funny."

Still breathing hard from the walk up the stairs, she attempted a combative, fierce expression. "So here you are back from the dead after two . . . no, three months, and that's all you have to say? I let you in for that?"

"Why did you?"

"Why what?

"Why did you let me in?"

"Because I'm insane, but that's an understatement. Obviously, I'm not the only one." She gestured dramatically. "Come on. Start talking."

He sat down on the sofa without being asked. "I will if you stop waving that can of mace around. It probably doesn't work anyway."

"Maybe I should test it." She banged the can down on the bookcase. "Who are you, Noah Arias, and what do you want?"

"The sad truth is that I *still* don't know. I've been living in South Carolina with these people who claim to be my mother and younger sister. They've told me a lot of stuff about . . ."

"I'm sure they did," Jasmine interrupted. "But before you get into any of that, I think you should tell me why you came back to see me. How did you know where to find me?"

"You told me."

"I *told* you my address when you were unconscious, and you remembered it?"

"Yes. That, plus a little detective work."

"What an amazing mind you have," she said sarcastically, turning away from his gaze, pacing the floor. "But . . . but why? I'm certainly not your family. I'm nobody to you."

His eyes narrowed. "That's not quite true. We have a unique bond between us. Are you going to tell me it's all my imagination?"

Jasmine hesitated. She was tired and still trying to recover from the shock of not only seeing him, but also having him sitting in her living room. In some ways, he had never really gone away. She'd spent the past few months still talking to him like a child with an imaginary friend.

"We do have a bond," she admitted.

"Good. Is it okay if I spend the night here? I didn't have time to book a hotel room."

Dazed, Jasmine shook her head. "I'm not prepared for a guest."

"I'm not a guest." The quirky curve of his mouth widened into a blazing smile. "I'm your innermost thoughts. I'm your muse."

"My muse?" Jasmine echoed and then laughed. Realizing that laughter was probably inappropriate, she bit her lip and frowned. "Noah, this is just too strange. I have a headache and I'm really not in the mood for my muse or my innermost thoughts tonight. So, if you don't mind, I'm going to my room." She reclaimed the can of mace. "Feel free to do whatever you please—alone." She made direct eye contact with him. "I don't want my innermost thoughts interfering with my space or my privacy right now. Is that understood?"

"Perfectly."

"The bathroom is down the hall," she recited almost mechanically. "After the kitchen, it's the first door on the left. Goodnight."

"Goodnight, Jasmine."

He sounded as if he were getting ready to laugh. He probably was. She didn't want to think about it, couldn't think about it. Maybe if she went to her room and came back out in the morning, he would be gone. Maybe she had completely lost it and was imagining the whole scene.

The alarm clock erupted, piercing the silence, awakening her abruptly and further distorting her fragile sense of reality. The illuminated dial was blinking 7:00, reminding her that soon Morgan would be knocking at the door and she would have to be up to make sure the child was dressed and ready for school.

Knotting the frayed belt of her faded robe, Jasmine stepped out of the bedroom and into the hall where she immediately caught the strong scent of coffee mingled with bacon and something else. She stopped. Noah was watching her from the kitchen while seated at the table with a newspaper.

It had not been a dream. He was still there, larger than life. Simultaneously intrigued and outraged by his insolence, she scowled and patted at her unruly hair. Why hadn't she at least put on something more presentable?

"I hope you're feeling better than you look," he said on cue.

"No one's forcing you to look at me," she retorted. "If I look that hideous, you can go find a better view elsewhere."

"I didn't say you were hideous." He took a sip of coffee from a paper cup. "I stopped by the deli while you were sleeping. Want a bagel?"

The food smelled delicious, which annoyed her because she was tempted to accept his offer. "No, I don't want a bagel."

"Don't you ever shop?" he asked. "I checked out the fridge and *nada* . . . nothing. People are supposed to eat, you know."

"I'm not running a diner."

"You're not running a home, either."

She glared at him. "You didn't look hard enough. There's milk in the refrigerator, and if you'd checked the cabinet, you might find . . ."

He stood up—all six feet plus of him—and flung open the cabinet. "Aha! Frosted oats with marshmallow bits." He waved the brightly colored cereal box in the air. "Now that's what I call real food."

Jasmine bit her lip to keep from laughing. "Morgan likes it."

"Morgan? Well, what do you know? There has been some progress after all. You're feeding your neighbor's kid."

"It was your idea."

"I never said you had to feed her."

Jasmine flung up her hands in frustration. "Just stop it, Noah. This . . . this whole conversation is totally ridiculous, and it's about time for you to start really talking about who you are and what you're doing."

He opened his mouth, but before any words escaped, there was a gentle tapping outside the door.

Noah smiled mockingly. "That must be your little friend."

"And just how am I supposed to explain you?"

"Do you have to explain?"

Ignoring him, she opened the door.

"Jasmine, can I . . ." Morgan rushed in, stopped short and froze when she saw Noah in the kitchen. Her eyes widened.

"It's okay, honey," Jasmine said. "This is Mr. Arias. He's just visiting."

"Oh." Morgan looked skeptical.

Noah turned to smile at the little girl. "*Buenos dias, señorita.* Jasmine has told me many good things about you. What a beautiful little lady you are."

Morgan looked at Jasmine and then back at Noah. Sensing that he meant no harm, she started to smile, but quickly positioned her hand over her mouth to conceal it.

Noah's eyes glistened. "Don't cover your smile. A princess should never do that."

"My smile's ugly," Morgan said.

"It is not," Jasmine said, drawing the girl closer to her. "You have a very beautiful smile."

Morgan hung her head shyly.

"She's six, and she recently lost her front tooth," Jasmine explained to Noah.

"People laugh at me," Morgan said.

"That's nothing to worry about at all," Noah said. "It happens to everyone. Come here and I'll show you."

Morgan looked at Jasmine again.

"You can go to him if you want to," Jasmine encouraged. "He's a friend."

Morgan came to Noah, who held her gently at arm's length.

"Put your finger right there where your tooth used to be," Noah said.

Morgan's nervousness abated. She obeyed.

"Does it feel hard?"

She slid her finger over the surface. "Uh huh."

"What you're feeling is your new tooth getting ready to come in. In a few weeks you'll actually see it, but you can't keep looking in the mirror and worrying about it because if you do it will take a long time."

"Why?"

Noah smiled again. "Because when you keep waiting for something to happen it seems to take forever."

"Like waiting for my Grandma to tell me I can come back home?"

"Morgan, do you realize what time it's getting to be?" Jasmine interrupted, saving both herself and Noah from replying to the question. "Come here so I can fix your hair."

Distracted, Morgan turned away from Noah and followed her down the hall to the bedroom. The room had become very familiar to the child because Jasmine had purchased a cot for her that was positioned alongside her own bed. Morgan occasionally spent the night there when her own family neglected her.

"Let's see, you've got your yellow sweater and plaid skirt. You look fine, except for your hair."

Morgan nodded and knelt down on the floor while Jasmine sat on the bed and brushed out her matted, curly hair. Rachel had told her that doing the child's hair was a real pain in the neck, but Jasmine always used a children's spray detangler on it to make the job easier. In fact, the long hair wouldn't even be a problem at all if Rachel would just braid it at night so it wouldn't tangle.

"Jasmine?"

"Yes."

"Is Mr. Arias your man?"

Jasmine pretended not to hear. "Is he what?"

"Your man . . . you know."

"No, he's not my man. He's just a friend, that's all."

Morgan seemed relieved. "Rachel's got a man. He's mean."

Jasmine banded Morgan's hair into twin ponytails. "Does he yell at you?" she asked worriedly.

"Sometimes. I don't like him 'cause he's mad all the time. He doesn't smile like Mr. Arias."

Jasmine was disturbingly aware that a certain Victor Morales appeared to have moved in with Rachel and her children, bringing two of his own kids along with him. Morgan wasn't exaggerating; Morales did not appear to be a very pleasant person. He always seemed to have a snarl on his face and he never even said as much as good morning when their paths crossed in the hallway. To make matters worse, she suspected he was doing drugs.

Rachel had had only a few redeeming qualities to begin with, but lately even those qualities were eroding. Before Morales entered the picture, the woman used to stop by to chat and express appreciation for her taking care of Morgan, but now everything just seemed to be taken for granted and Jasmine couldn't help feeling a little resentful. It was true she enjoyed her time with the little girl, but Morgan was not supposed to be her total responsibility.

"There you are. All set," she told the child. "Hurry now, so the other kids don't leave without you."

"But I want them to leave without me. I want to walk with you," Morgan said.

Jasmine sighed. That was another imposed duty that never should have gotten started. "I'm sorry, honey, but I really can't walk with you every day. You'll be okay with your big sister and the other kids."

Morgan was not happy. When Jasmine escorted her back to her own apartment, she was literally dragging her feet and sulking. It made Jasmine feel bad, but their relationship needed limits and right now she had a more pressing issue to deal with.

Noah was pacing the living room like a caged panther when she returned. "How about going for a ride while we talk. I have a rental car that's parked a few blocks away."

Jasmine collapsed on the couch. "You're stalling again. Why is explaining yourself so difficult?"

His eyes twinkled. "Who's stalling? I was prepared to tell you last night, but you didn't want to hear it."

"That's right, blame me for everything."

"I'm not blaming you. Actually you're telling the truth. It *is* difficult to talk about myself since I don't remember much." He glanced down at the floor. "I'm only going to be repeating what others have told me."

Jasmine sighed. She did empathize with his situation. It had to be disturbing and frustrating not to remember one's own past, even if that past left a lot to be desired. But stuck here in her cloistered territory, she found herself focusing more on his manly physique than on what he was about to discuss. It didn't help either that Noah's pacing and his relentless gray eyes seemed to consume everything in the tiny room, including the oxygen.

She stood up abruptly. "Maybe going out is a good idea. I've suddenly got a terrible case of claustrophobia."

He jingled the keys in his pocket. "I'm glad you agree. The weather looks nice enough."

She glanced at the sunlight streaming through the window. "It does. Wait just a second while I go change."

She hurried to the bedroom and searched for and found a brand new turquoise sweater and a pair of jeans that actually fit. Painstakingly, she smoothed back her puffy braids as best she could, banded them into a ponytail, and studied her reflection in the mirror. She didn't look as pathetic as usual, but more was needed. Rummaging through drawers, throwing clothes on the floor, she actually came upon her long abandoned makeup kit. From it, she extracted a tube of dusty-rose lipstick and with shaking hands, applied it to her mouth.

"Let's go," she said, rejoining him.

"Nice sweater," he commented. "Turquoise looks great on you."

She winced, preferring him to say nothing at all about her appearance because she knew she was still a long way from looking her best, and for some irrational reason that bothered her.

CHAPTER 6

The exceptional warmth of the morning embraced them. Birds twittered from the treetops and fat clouds floated lazily in the blue canvas sky. The serenity belied the fact that they were meandering through a run-down park, which had once been a shady oasis amidst the Brooklyn streets. Now the cracked stone pathway sprouted weeds, and most of the benches were badly vandalized and coated with graffiti.

Noah stood before an old, vine-choked fountain featuring a headless cherub whose stone hands were raised piteously toward heaven as though in a silent plea for mercy. He touched the moldering basin sympathetically. "Whose garden was this?"

Jasmine scanned the park and rested her eyes on the tortured cherub. "I don't know, but it's a shame what happened here. It must have been beautiful once."

"Have you ever been here before?" he asked.

"No. I've passed it often, but this is the first time I've actually gone in. It's not very inviting."

His eyes twinkled ever so suggestively. "Maybe not, but I do find it intriguing. With a little time and loving care it could be restored to its former beauty."

A lengthy silence followed. She hoped he wasn't going to use the glaring metaphor as another opportunity to analyze her life.

"Have you ever heard of a place called Cielo Vista?" he asked, dispelling her fear.

"Geography was never one of my strong points," she said, trying to think. "Isn't it a small country in South America?"

"Well, it *is* a small country, except it's not in South America, but off the coast of Africa."

She shrugged. "And?"

"Hang on. I'm getting to the point. I was born there."

She smiled. "Somehow you don't look very African to me."

He returned the smile. "No. I guess not. My ancestors were from Barcelona. Cielo Vista was one of very few African countries claimed by Spain back in the eighteenth century. It's independent now, since 1976, and while the majority of people are native Africans, it still retains a large Spanish population and Spanish is the official language spoken there."

He went on to tell her what he had been told about his earlier life, including his father's presidency, his parents' separation, and about the coup that had taken the lives of his father, stepmother and their political allies.

He appreciated the way Jasmine listened attentively, searching his soul with velvet brown eyes, gilded gold by the sunlight. Her hand had brushed against his and their hands had automatically clasped together. He was acutely aware of how natural it felt because he remembered having held her hand many times when he'd been light years away from reality at the hospice.

She finally spoke. "That's quite a story." Then she hesitated for a few seconds. "It must be painful to reflect on it. You don't have to answer this, but you did say you were around twelve years old at the time of the coup. Were you here in the United States with your mother when it happened?"

Noah shrugged. "Don't worry about my feelings. I'm pretty detached from the whole thing. I guess I forgot to mention that my father had custody of me. I was living at the presidential estate on that night, and apparently I missed my appointment with destiny because I had snuck off the grounds to be with Isabella, my girlfriend." The fact that he flinched upon mentioning her name didn't go unnoticed by Jasmine. "My older half-brother, Rafael, escaped, too, because he was out spying on us, probably with the intention of tattling. We were kind of young to be dating."

Jasmine gripped his hand tighter. "But I don't understand why they would have wanted to kill you and your brother. You were children."

"I was supposedly the heir to the so-called kingdom," Noah said dryly. "They wanted us all wiped out."

"You were heir? Doesn't that right usually go to the oldest son?"

"Apparently my father chose me. I'm not really sure why."

A brief chill passed through her and she shuddered. "Who were the people behind the coup? Are they still ruling the country?"

"The main person behind it was my father's brother, my uncle Alejandro, and yes, he is still ruling."

"My God . . . your father was murdered by his own brother." She searched Noah's eyes for some emotion, but his expression was as blank as though he were reciting from a newspaper.

"Noah, what happened when you returned to the estate that night?"

He leaned casually against the fountain and squinted up at the blazing sunlight, and she was struck by his sculpted profile and exquisite Latin features. She moved closer.

"I've been told that we found the bodies and realized what had happened. Somehow we managed to escape the estate without getting caught, and we ran for the mountains."

She shuddered at the thought of young people discovering the massacred bodies of their parents, but Noah still showed no trace of emotion. "How did you end up in the United States?"

"It seems I had a lot of allies among the African natives who lived in the jungles and mountains. We found refuge with them for a couple of weeks until we were rescued by a family friend who managed to slip us out of Cielo Vista."

"Who was this friend?

"Aaron Weiss."

"So that's the person I talked to on the phone," she murmured half to herself.

"What?"

61

"Nothing. I was just thinking out loud." She took a deep breath. "Weiss sounds like a Jewish name. What connection did he have to Cielo Vista?"

"Aaron was a former Israeli citizen," Noah said. "Anyway, he was forced to live in Cielo Vista for a few years before moving to the United States. This was while my father was still president."

Her questioning eyes told him she wanted to know more, so he continued. "When Aaron was young, he had quite a presence in the Israeli Air Force until he did something that caused him to fall out of grace with the military and he got deported from his own country. My father offered him asylum in Cielo Vista for a while because of a longtime friendship he had with Aaron's father."

"This Aaron person seems really important to you. Is he something of a father figure?" she asked. "I mean, he must be quite a bit older than you."

Noah laughed. "There is at least a twelve-year age difference between us, but, no, he's hardly a father figure. Why *are* you so curious about Weiss?"

Jasmine shrugged. "I don't know, maybe because he's the only person you seemed to remember when you came out of the coma."

"Good point." He stared blankly into space for a long time, and then refocused his attention. "Anyway, Aaron took Isabella, Rafael and me to the United States when we were kids."

"To be with your mother?"

"Yes.

"How?"

"How what?"

"How did he get you all out of Cielo Vista without being caught?"

A disturbed expression crossed Noah's face. "I . . . I don't know. It was a warm night and there was this white crescent moon." He rubbed his forehead. "The stars were glittering like diamonds. I believe we swam. I think Aaron had some kind of boat waiting."

Jasmine felt her heart skip a beat. She was standing so close to him that she could feel his pulse racing. "Are you remembering?" she asked anxiously.

"It does kind of sound like that, doesn't it?" He looked baffled. "The sea was pitch black. It—" He frowned, rubbing his eyes in pained frustration. "No. I don't remember any of this, but what I do know is that I'm getting a headache. It seems to happen whenever I try to recall."

"I'm sorry," she said, concerned. "Maybe we should stop talking about—"

"It's all right," he interrupted, squeezing his eyes shut and opening them again. "I still want to talk." He drew in a ragged breath. "Rafael and I came to live with my mother and stepfather in South Carolina. She took us both, even though Rafael wasn't her biological son." He continued to fill in the statistics about his adult life, but he did not feel inclined to mention his marriage to Isabella.

"What happened to Isabella?" Jasmine asked on cue. "Who took her in?"

He hesitated. "She . . . well, with both parents gone, she was raised by an aunt in Spain."

Jasmine noticed a tiny flash of emotion. It seemed to happen only when Isabella's name was mentioned.

She shook her head incredulously. "Your life has been not only tragic, but complicated as well. I realize you're only repeating what you've been told, but except for when you were talking about the sea . . . and Isabella . . . you don't seem to have any emotion at all. Doesn't knowing all this make you feel angry . . . bitter?"

His eyes met hers with unyielding intensity. "I wish I did feel something, but I don't. I don't even know if I'm being told the truth."

She exhaled deeply. "Can you think of any possible reason why your family would make up such a story?"

He shook his head. "No. Not really."

"Then it must be true. Have any of them suggested you might be in some kind of danger now? I mean, what's with all the secrecy? Why was I told at the hospice that you were dead?"

"Technically speaking, I am dead." He reached in his pocket, removed a wallet and showed her his driver's license. The photograph was definitely of him, but the name beside it was Daniel Viera. "Only you and my family use my real name now."

Overwhelmed, Jasmine unconsciously ripped a trail of clinging vines away from the decaying fountain. "Are you in a witness protection program or something?"

"Not exactly, but there are certain individuals other than friends and family who seem to be very interested in keeping me alive. I can't go into great detail about this, but I will tell you a little." He hesitated as though trying to decide what to filter out and what to reveal. "Aaron has ties to some pretty powerful people in the government. A doctor friend of his signed my death certificate, and I was removed from Glendale while faking my own death. I even had a phony obituary and a funeral in New Jersey, where I was living right before the accident."

"But why such extreme measures? Does all this still have to do with Cielo Vista? Why would some . . . some crazy dictator half a world away still be trying to kill you? It's been what . . . twenty or so years? You don't even have anything to do with that country now. You're a citizen here. Unless . . ."

"Unless what?"

"I hate to suggest this."

"Say it."

"Unless you were plotting to take the country back and someone found out."

Noah's eyes narrowed. "Maybe that *is* what I was doing before the accident."

She closed her eyes. "This gets worse and worse. Does that mean the car accident might not have been an accident at all?"

"Aaron doesn't believe it was."

"What *does* Aaron believe happened? And why, why would you have wanted to go back to that country when you had so much going here? You were a successful businessman."

Noah stared distantly up at the clouds. "You're right. It doesn't make a bit of sense. I'm thirty-four years old. If

I intended to avenge my father, why would I have waited so long?"

She felt dazed. "This is actually very scary. Did Aaron tell you who he thinks was behind your accident?"

"Enough." Clasping her hand, Noah moved away from the fountain, towing her gently but firmly along with him. "There are other things to be concerned with, perhaps more tangible things."

"But what could be more important to you than your own life . . . getting your memory back?

"How about *your* life and getting you back."

He walked swiftly, fluidly, buoying her along as if she were an extension of his own body.

"I should have known you would take this opportunity to shut down and focus back on me," she babbled, aware that he didn't seem to be paying attention. "My life, or what's left of it, isn't so significant any more. It's not like I'm the only one suffering here."

"The part about you not being the only one suffering is true," he said when they were back in the car. "The rest of what you said is not. Your life is very significant because you remember it. Maybe you wish you could shut out the bad parts, but you can't. That doesn't mean all is hopeless. You have to be able to at least remember your life before you can salvage it."

He shifted the rented SUV into gear, checked the mirror and pulled out into traffic.

"Where are we going now?" she asked, feeling confused and at a loss for words.

"You're going back to your place."

"And you?"

"I'm not sure, but I'll probably be around the city for a while."

He double-parked in front of her building. She did not want to get out. The ending of the conversation seemed too abrupt, and she was concerned about him.

"Noah, don't you think it would be better if you returned to South Carolina? Your family must be worried sick about you. Do they even know where you are?"

He laughed. "I'm a grown man. They can't keep me a prisoner there. Besides, I have a gut feeling that I'm more likely to get my memory back by being away from them."

She shook her head. "I don't understand the logic in that."

"You don't have to. It makes sense to me."

She hesitated. "Well, if you don't go back there, you still shouldn't be here all alone. What if you get sick, or have a relapse?"

"Where should I be?"

The question hung on the air for a split second. "You could stay at my place." She sucked in her breath upon realizing the possible implications of what she'd just suggested. "I . . . I mean as a friend, of course. You'd have to sleep on the couch in the living room like you did last night. . . ."

He smiled disarmingly and his eyebrows arched in both a charming and somewhat mocking manner. Sunlight and shadows collided and danced in his eyes.

"That's a tempting offer, at least it started out to be . . . before you threw in the part about the couch, but no thanks. I was serious last night when I told you about wanting to be your muse. A muse is a source of inspiration, or creativity. It's not someone you're supposed to worry about or feel sorry for."

But she *didn't* just feel sorry for him. Forget about the couch. She wanted him, and had the feeling that he knew it. She wanted to hold him close enough to feel his heartbeat, close enough to consume her pain and erase her memories, and close enough that she would even forget about questioning her own sanity.

"Are you working tonight?" he asked.

The unrelated question jarred her.

"Yes."

"Where?"

"I'm cleaning an office building in Manhattan."

"Still cleaning buildings instead of creating them? I see I've got a lot to do to get you back on track," he said.

Exasperated, she glared at him. "I'm perfectly satisfied with what I'm doing at this point, and I'd appreciate it if you'd stop with the games. I know way too much about you now to participate in this ridiculous muse charade of yours."

His eyes twinkled. "Believe me, you still don't know even half as much about me as I do about you."

The words stung. *Ouch*, the embarrassing things she had told him when he was supposed to be comatose. Just one of those embarrassing things was talking to him about her past relationships with men who'd betrayed her. He probably remembered that well. Irritated, she got out of the car and slammed the door.

He opened his door, "Wait, I'll walk you up."

"Don't bother," she snapped. "I've been doing it for a year. I don't need Mr. Macho Muse to protect me."

"This isn't over," he called. "I'll see you soon."

"Whatever."

She walked swiftly up the stairs toward the lobby, hoping he wouldn't follow her. He didn't. And she was disappointed.

CHAPTER 7

It was late at night when Noah tumbled, exhausted, onto the bed in the small hotel room. After parting with Jasmine, he had driven out to Kennedy Airport to watch the planes take off, hoping, always hoping, that he would remember something. After all, how could he have once piloted the giant steel birds and now feel disconnected from the whole concept of flight? The end result had been disappointing because he had felt nothing.

Still, he refused to be discouraged. Maybe if he were actually inside the cockpit of a plane the pieces would start to come together. It had to be like riding a bicycle. Once you learned how, you never forgot. He was going to have to take a trip with Aaron on one of their cargo jets.

His mind drifted back to Jasmine. He was annoyed with himself. He'd told her entirely too much about his alleged past, but the words had developed a will of their own and had gushed out of his mouth in torrents and waves. He knew everything had gotten out of control because he had been captivated by the way she had looked at him and the way she'd held his hand as he talked. Though knowing that she was worried about him was somewhat disturbing, he was secretly pleased he had affected her in that way.

He hated being alone in the empty room; he would have loved to be with her. In a recurring fantasy, he could see them lying together, their bodies warmed by the morning sunlight and the afterglow of love. He sat up abruptly. Afterglow? Love? He couldn't even remember his own family, yet he was savoring feelings of a more sensual nature.

And it felt as real as though it had actually happened. But Jasmine couldn't have been part of the past. The intense feelings could only be attributed to Isabella, the woman who had once been his wife. Why had she left him? Maybe he should disregard all the warnings and return to Cielo Vista to find out.

Shifting positions, he reached into his pocket and removed his wallet. He thumbed through various documents and came upon the picture of a golden-haired woman with eyes as blue as an unpolluted sky staring dispassionately back at him. She was beautiful—so beautiful that she was agonizing to look at. He flipped the wallet shut and closed his eyes.

His head ached and his neck was still stiff from sleeping on the couch at Jasmine's hovel. He'd started to get up to take some prescribed medication when the phone rang. He picked it up.

"Had enough of the city yet?" Aaron asked.

"No, but it won't be much longer."

"I'm still watching your back, Noah. Remember that."

Noah grimaced. "How can I forget when you won't let me?"

"I'm not the enemy, *comprende?* Don't forget that either."

∼⦿

"Catch me, Aunt Jammin!" Dawn shrieked.

"Dawn, where are you?"

"Find me."

"I can't. Please don't do this to me. Be a good girl and come back."

"No. You gotta find me."

Jasmine parted the clinging vines and pushed her way through the teeming jungle. Foreign birds shrieked in the blood-red sky and the acrid scent of sulfur permeated the air. The ground, soft and loamy, sprang sponge-like under her feet.

"Dawn!" she screamed. Shafts of sunlight penetrated the trees and she caught a glimpse of the child running nymph-like. She was barefoot, dressed in something gauzy and gown-like, her hair wild and flowing. Jasmine ran swiftly, sprang forward and caught her by the arm. She gaped. Dawn was a lot bigger than she had been.

"Let go," the child said. "It's just a game, Jasmine. It's like hide and seek. You were s'posed to find me."

Jasmine continued to hold her arm, dazed and puzzled, until it dawned on her that the girl was taller because she wasn't Dawn at all. She had transformed into Morgan.

"Morgan, what are you doing here? Where is Dawn?"

Morgan yanked her arm free, giggled, tossed back her hair and started to run again. Jasmine ran after her, the branches and foliage slapping at her face. She reached a clearing filled with the shrieking of birds. Lying at her feet was the inert body of a toddler dressed in pajamas, staring blankly up into space, crimson soaking the ground under her head. Jasmine screamed.

"Dawn! No! Oh, my god. Dawn!"

Jasmine sat bolt upright, shaking violently, her heart pounding. She stared at the dark walls of her bedroom. A dream. Nothing but another stupid nightmare. She staggered out of bed in her child-like cat pajamas, went to the bathroom and splashed her face with cold water. After that, it was difficult to go back to bed so she paced the living room, her heart still pounding, trying to get her bearings.

She thought about Noah and wondered where he was and what he was doing. She wondered how much of what he had told her about Cielo Vista had mixed with her own emotional baggage and gotten into the dream. Why on earth would she have been running in a jungle chasing after Morgan? Or had it been Dawn? She was completely confused and she wanted to tell him about it. But hadn't she told him enough? She shuddered.

His subconscious mind was so amazingly disturbing. He seemed to recall every detail and nuance about her, but when it came to himself, he could only quote what others had told him. Why had he bothered to return? Was she really so memorable . . . so pathetic that a man with his own traumatic issues would feel compelled to help her?

Jasmine drifted toward the telephone. She had the strong urge to pick it up and call her friend Valerie. The urge got stronger. After more than a year, Val would be shocked to hear from her. She picked up the receiver. What would Val think about Noah? Wait a minute— what was she thinking? It was after midnight, too late to call anyone, and for that matter, maybe Valerie didn't even want to reconnect with her. She put the receiver down.

Her thoughts shifted abruptly to her sister and her little nephew. Damon, Natalie's baby, was now about the same age Dawn had been, and it hurt to realize that she would probably never see him again because Natalie had made it crystal clear that that was the way it would be.

Jasmine sat down on the couch and buried her face in her hands until muffled thumping sounds at the door forced her to look up.

"Jasmine, let me in. Pleeease." Morgan's voice sounded weak and teary.

Abruptly, Jasmine sprang to her feet and opened the door. The child bolted in, barefoot, dressed only in a pair of pink panties and a raggedy undershirt.

Jasmine gaped, catching her. "Morgan, where on earth are your clothes?"

"She locked me out. She wouldn't let me get them," the little girl wailed, clinging to her.

"Who locked you out?"

"Ra . . . Rachel did. I didn't mean to break it, honest, I didn't. It kind of fell."

"Come to the bedroom. You can borrow one of my T-shirts. You can tell me what happened."

"I wanted to talk to my grandma, and Rachel wouldn't let me," Morgan said, once she was sitting on the cot opposite Jasmine's bed, wearing a long T-shirt.

"Your grandmother called you *this* late at night?" Jasmine asked.

"Uh huh. She wanted to talk to me, but Rachel said no and she kept pushing me away."

"What did you do then?"

"I screamed real loud and I . . . I kind of kicked her. The devil made me. He just grabbed my legs and made me."

"You *kicked* your mother?"

"She's *not* my mother!" Morgan shrieked, on the verge of hysteria.

"Okay, okay. What happened next?"

"She . . . she hung up the phone and she threw me out of the room. I was screaming and I was mad. The lamp got broke and Victor woke up. He . . . he started yelling that he was gonna throw me out the window and that he was gonna beat the cra—"

"Shhh. It's okay," Jasmine interrupted, seething. "I get the picture." She wanted to march over to that apartment, tell Rachel off once and for all and call the police. But what good would that do? There were no obvious signs of physical abuse on the child's body, and a lot of people in the building were always threatening their children verbally without actually doing what they said. She and Natalie had been victims of similar treatment when they were growing up and they had survived . . . barely.

She sat on the cot next to Morgan and hugged her tightly. "I'm sorry about what happened, baby. I know how much you wanted to talk to your grandmother, but you should never have kicked Rachel or broken the lamp."

Morgan hung her head. "I'm sorry."

Jasmine held her tightly in her arms, rocking back and forth.

"I don't want to live there anymore," the child sobbed. "I want to go home. I want Daddy. I'm gonna run away."

Jasmine felt like screaming. She really didn't know what to do, and she hated being forced into playing the role of the insensitive, logical adult when she totally empathized with the child.

"I know this is hard for you, Morgan. I know. When I was a little girl, bad things used to happen to me too, but you can't run away. If you do, then it will be even worse."

How could it be worse? she thought. *My, how ridiculous I sound.*

Morgan was crying outright now, the tears streaming down her face.

"Morgan, listen to me. I'm going to try to help you see your grandmother."

"You are? Really?" Morgan rubbed her eyes with both fists, and then stared up at her as though she'd suddenly transformed into a beacon of light.

"I can't promise, but I'm going to talk to Rachel."

"She's gonna say no."

"We'll see. Sometimes it helps when another grownup talks, but right now it's late. You need to get some sleep."

"I don't have to go to school. Tomorrow's Saturday," Morgan said.

"I know, but you still have to sleep. Here, slide under the covers, I'll tuck you in."

Morgan obeyed. It was obvious that she was exhausted because, despite all the drama, her eyes were shut even before she was completely tucked in.

Sighing, Jasmine paced around. She glanced back at Morgan's sleeping form and then she quickly changed into a pair of jeans and a T-shirt and impulsively left the apartment, assured that the child would not wake up.

She pounded on Rachel's door. The door opened and Rachel stood there, over-exposed in a flimsy nightgown with one strap hanging off her shoulder. Bloodshot eyes and wild hair completed her drug-induced look. A peculiar smoky odor wafted from the apartment.

"Oh, it's you."

"Who did you think it would it be? Why did you lock Morgan out of the house, and where are the other kids?"

Rachel looked puzzled at first, and then she scowled. "The other kids are staying with my sister."

"Why isn't Morgan with them?"

"Because my sister can't put up with her retarded crap, and neither can I. So don't you come here with no attitude asking about that brat. I'm not letting that little demon back in this apartment tonight. No way. She attacked me and she was screaming her little fool head off. She broke my good lamp. I'm surprised you didn't hear all the noise. She's possessed, I tell you. Never seen no kid act like that before, and Victor ain't either."

"You've been smoking something, and I know it's not cigarettes," Jasmine said bluntly, hands on her hips. "You have some nerve calling that little girl a demon. Look at yourself. What kind of mother . . . what kind of person are you anyway?"

"You just mind your business, Miss Weirdo, high and mighty. You don't know the half of it. The devil is always changing into an angel of light, and that's what you seeing when she comes to you. But she's far from an angel. She's not even a real kid. If you saw some of the stuff she does you—"

"Forget it!" I'll talk to you when you're sober!" Jasmine snapped.

She left the strung-out woman standing in the doorway, talking to herself.

Early in the morning, Jasmine found a note from Rachel under her door. The barely legible chicken scratch stated that she had to go out of town for the weekend and she would like her to take care of Morgan. She also offered a vague apology for last night and mentioned that there was a suitcase outside with the child's clothes in it.

Jasmine rolled her eyes and let the scrap of paper flutter to the floor. She mechanically stepped out into the hall and retrieved the suitcase. When she stepped back inside, the phone rang. Quickly, she picked it up and was greeted by a now-familiar voice.

"Noah?"

"Are you doing anything today?" he asked. "I was wondering if you'd like to come for a ride with me out to New Jersey. I'm going to visit my old house in the Ramapo hills. It might jog my memory."

Her pulse quickened in anticipation and then she groaned. "I'd really like to, but I can't."

"Why not?"

"It looks like I've got Morgan for the weekend. She's asleep in my room."

There was a silence. "Is she okay?"

"Physically, yes."

"She's not a problem. We can take her with us."

"I don't know. She was really upset last night, and I'm kind of thinking that I might try to find her grand-mother today. Morgan's mother told me that the grand-mother was sick, but how can I believe anything a drug addict tells me? This whole thing about keeping them apart doesn't make any sense. Surely she can't be crazier than Rachel is."

"Does Morgan know her grandmother's address?"

"She might. I do know she lives out in Queens. I'll have to ask her when she wakes up."

"You never told me you had a car."

"I don't. I sold it two years ago. I haven't driven since . . ." She stopped as Dawn's name was about to escape.

"So how do you plan to get to Queens?"

"The same way I get around everywhere else in the city—taxis and subways."

"Jasmine, I'm coming over. I'll do the driving."

"But . . ." Jasmine stopped short. He had made the offer, so what reason was there not to accept. "Thank you," she said almost in one breath, hoping he didn't detect how invigorated she actually felt. Maybe it would be a pleasant and productive weekend after all. She needed the change, and so did Morgan.

CHAPTER 8

When Jasmine rang the bell of the well-maintained Tudor-style duplex in St. Albans, Queens, a petite, dark-skinned woman wearing a nurse's uniform opened the door.

"Can I help you?" she asked.

"Yes, my name is Jasmine Burke. Would it be possible for me to see Mrs. Garcia?"

The nurse glanced back over her shoulder to the interior of the house, then back at her. "I'm afraid that won't be possible. Mrs. Garcia is very ill. She had a rough night and she's just now getting to sleep."

Jasmine took a deep breath. "Is there any chance at all? I'm coming from Brooklyn and I have her little granddaughter with me. She's waiting out in the car."

The woman's eyes lit up immediately. "You have Morgan!" she cried. "Of course you can see her. Mrs. Garcia will be so happy. She's been trying so long to get to talk to her—even called late last night. I don't understand what's going on." She stopped abruptly. "Are you Morgan's mother?"

"Me? Oh, no. I'm just a friend who's trying to help out."

"Oh, but this is such a blessing. Mrs. Garcia doesn't have much time. This is just what she needs. Please tell

Morgan to come in. My name is Helen, by the way. I'm a private duty nurse."

Jasmine hesitated. "Helen, I'm afraid I know very little about the condition of Morgan's grandmother. Could you tell me before I let her in, so I can prepare her?"

"Of course." Helen's voice dropped to barely a whisper. "Mrs. Garcia has a malignant, inoperable brain tumor. She's already had two strokes and there is nothing the doctors can do for her. Basically, she has only a few weeks to live. The end could come at any time."

Jasmine felt her mouth go dry. "That's *horrible.* I'm so sorry to hear . . ."

"That's life and death," Helen interrupted. "It is sad. I've grown very fond of her myself, but she has accepted the reality of her situation. The thing troubling her the most is Morgan's welfare. You know the child's father is gone and that woman who's supposed to be her mother leaves a lot to be desired."

"Yes, that part I definitely know," Jasmine admitted. "Doesn't Mrs. Garcia have any other children . . . family?"

"Her younger son was with her all last week, but he's in the service and he had to go back to where he's stationed in Europe. There is no other family, only friends."

"I—I'll have to tell Morgan," Jasmine said. "Can Mrs. Garcia talk? You did say she had a stroke."

"The stroke left her partially paralyzed on her right side, but she can still talk and she is still in her right mind at this point. I'll go tell her that Morgan is here." She hesitated. "I'm so sorry to have to tell you this bad news."

"It'll be all right, we'll just have to deal with it," Jasmine said. "At least Morgan already knows that her grandmother is sick."

Feeling disheartened, Jasmine returned to the SUV where Noah was trying to contain Morgan. She was grateful that he was with her. How much more depressing this whole situation would be had she and Morgan been alone.

"What took you so long?" Noah asked. "Princess Morgan can't contain herself much longer."

"I'm contained," Morgan said with a giggle. "Can I go in now?"

"Yes, but you have to know that your grandmother may not be exactly the way you remember her."

Morgan looked puzzled. "What do you mean?"

"Well, people change when they're very sick. They . . ."

"Oh, I know that," Morgan said, springing from the car. "Grandma had a stroke and she's got brain cancer."

Noah gazed directly at Jasmine, surprised at Morgan's reaction. She was struck once again by the disconcerting radiance of his gray eyes.

"Who told you that?" she asked Morgan.

"Nobody. I heard Rachel talking about it when she thought I wasn't listening. I looked it all up in the medical 'cyclopedia."

"Do you know what cancer and stroke mean?"

Morgan nodded her head solemnly. "It's real bad, but Grandma's not scared. She's not scared of anything."

Jasmine gave an audible sigh of relief. "You're a very smart girl, Morgan."

There was no point in questioning her any further. She had learned from past observation that Morgan was an exceptional reader for her age and she didn't doubt the child's ability to understand what she read.

Noah waited in the car while they returned to the house. Inside, the shades were drawn and it was a bit dark, but the living room was very neat and cozy. The television was on because Helen had probably been looking at it. She escorted them down a short hallway.

"That's my room," Morgan announced, opening a door on the left. Jasmine glanced quickly inside to see a girly-pretty lavender room with a ruffled canopy bed, filled with dolls and stuffed animals. The room shocked her. It was as if Morgan had never left. Transfixed, she stopped and just stood there while Helen opened the door on the right and Morgan rushed into her grandmother's room. There were loud exclamations of joy.

Feeling awkward about intruding on their reunion, Jasmine entered Morgan's room and picked up a stuffed elephant from the bed. The furniture in the room was white—a little desk, chest of drawers, a dressing table. She gazed at a bookcase that contained a colorful children's book of Bible verses, juvenile history books and lots of stories, from Mary Poppins to Grimm's fairytales. It was the perfect little girl's room. The kind of room she would have liked to have had when she was a child. It was the kind of room she had envisioned for Dawn.

"Jasmine, Grandma wants to see you."

She turned with a start to see Morgan behind her. "Morgan . . . yes, of course."

She realized that she must have been wandering around the room hugging the stuffed animal for at least fifteen minutes. Annoyed at herself, she tossed it back on the bed.

Mrs. Garcia did not look like a dying woman. It was true that she was confined to her bed, but she didn't have that gaunt, shadowy pallor about her. Her salt and pepper black hair was long and neatly contained in a braid bunched at the back of her head. Her dark eyes were sharp. She had an electric hospital-type bed, which was elevated to a sitting position. A wheelchair was near the bed.

"Jasmine, I am so glad . . . so thankful that you have been taking care of my Morgan. She has told me so much about you."

Jasmine looked surprised. "Morgan has told you a lot about me? You mean just now?"

"Oh, no. Not just now . . . months ago."

"I thought . . . I guess I was wrong . . . that Morgan hasn't had any contact with you until now."

"Oh, I haven't been able to *see* her because of that Rachel, but Morgan has written me letters."

Jasmine smiled. "I guess I shouldn't be surprised that she would find a way to reach you. I've noticed that Morgan loves to write. She's a very special little girl."

"Yes, she is. As a matter of fact, she's been reading since she was three. Come . . . move that wheelchair out of the way and sit down." She indicated a chair near the bed. "Do you think you could let Morgan stay with me over the weekend? I know I can't look out for her, but Helen has said she would."

Jasmine blinked. "Well, I don't know. I mean, I'd love to, but it's really not my decision to make." It had never occurred to her that she would be leaving Morgan over the weekend. She wasn't sure how to respond.

"You made the right decision to bring her here to see me, and I am very grateful. I think you're capable of making good decisions."

"But I'm only a friend," she protested weakly. "This should be up to her mother."

"Rachel is a devil and she has no sense," Mrs. Garcia said bitterly. "Please. I'm sure you've heard about my condition. Morgan needs me now, and I need her."

Jasmine folded and unfolded her hands. Why was she even considering Rachel in the first place? The woman was an irresponsible, drug-using moron who had dumped her precious child like a bundle of rags at her doorstep with no regard for anyone but herself.

"Yes," she said defiantly. "You can have Morgan for the weekend if Helen looks out for her." She stood up.

Mrs. Garcia smiled. "Your kindness will be rewarded, I'm sure." She took a deep breath. "But there is more I have to say. Perhaps you can ask your husband to come inside, too."

"My husband?" Jasmine echoed with a start.

"Yes. His name is Noah, isn't it?"

Jasmine laughed. "Mrs. Garcia, Noah is *not* my husband."

Unfazed, Mrs. Garcia did not even blink. "Please tell him to come in."

"I'll get him, Grandma," Morgan shouted from out-side the door.

"Young lady, open that door."

The door opened a crack and Morgan peeked in.

"How many times have I told you about eaves-dropping?"

"I'm sorry, Grandma. I was just getting ready to come back in and I heard you ask for Mr. Noah."

Mrs. Garcia laughed. "Go get him, honey."

Disturbed, Jasmine started to protest, but the next second Noah was in the room standing beside her. His presence seemed even more dominating in the small room.

"You have the most beautiful eyes," Mrs. Garcia said, assessing him intently. "But there is something about them—something that tells me you've been in a lot of places and seen many things, perhaps some things you shouldn't have seen."

"You may be right, Mrs. Garcia," Noah said quietly.

"My oldest son, Morgan's father, used to love poetry. I can't quite remember how it all goes, but there is a poem that describes a man stopping to admire some woods filling up with snow but then moving on because of a promise he needed to keep."

Noah nodded, smiling as he quoted word-for-word the ending of the Robert Frost poem. "That's a popular one," he said. "It's one of my favorites too."

"Of course," Mrs. Garcia said. "I think you're like that man."

Jasmine was mesmerized into silence by the eerie vibe that was transpiring between Noah and the older woman—a connection or something. Why did they both have that strange distant look? And why was he suddenly remembering that Robert Frost was one of his favorite poets?

Trembling slightly, Mrs. Garcia suddenly reached for Jasmine's hand.

"I need to know," she whispered urgently, "that you and Noah will look out for Morgan when I'm gone."

Jasmine's heart caught in her throat. What did looking out for Morgan entail? How could she make such a commitment long term? "But . . ." she began.

"I need you to promise."

"Mrs. Garcia, I'd really love to, but I'm not family I . . ."

"We will," Noah said.

We? Seized by anger and panic, Jasmine jabbed him in the ribs with her elbow. Noah didn't even flinch, and Mrs. Garcia showed no sign of awareness.

"Oh, thank you, thank you," she said, tears filling her eyes.

"I . . . I'll do what I can," Jasmine answered weakly, resigned.

"You won't regret it. God will reward you."

❧

Back outside in the SUV, Jasmine glared venomously at Noah. "How could you?" she seethed. "How could you make a promise like that to a dying woman?"

"I did it because she is dying," he replied calmly.

"Are you *completely* nuts? Do you know what a promise like that means?"

Noah started to put the key in the ignition, but she grabbed his hand and the key dropped to the floor.

"Don't tune me out!" she practically screamed. "I'm not qualified to be a good mother and you . . . you don't have anything to do with this. You're just some delusional stranger with amnesia. When you finally remember who you really are, you won't even want to recall Morgan, me, or your stupid promise."

Noah regarded her in silence, his eyes reflecting shafts of light into hers. She was immediately compelled to observe the sensuous curve of his mouth, the enigmatic depths of his eyes, and slowly she felt her anger dissipating. It disturbed her that he possessed the power to overwhelm her with just a simple look. She tried not to wilt under his silent scrutiny.

"Well," she muttered, "don't just look at me like that. Say something."

He rubbed the side of his face ruefully. "I'm trying to understand why you are so angry. I don't recall Mrs. Garcia asking you to be Morgan's mother. She asked us to look out for her. Why is that so traumatic? You're already doing it, have been doing it for a couple of months now."

Suddenly she felt the awful urge to laugh. How typical of a man to focus on mere words and not the impetus behind them.

"Noah, whatever Mrs. Garcia may have said, she meant that to be long term. I don't know where I'll be in the future, or even where Morgan will be. Rachel might just decide to move out of the building, and that will be it. I can't follow them around, and I have no right to."

"You don't have to try to predict the future," Noah said. "I think the whole point of living is taking one day at a time. If you always look at the big picture you miss the little things that make it up and you get overwhelmed and stressed out."

"That might be true, but it's easy for you to say. You've never been responsible for the death of a child."

"You don't know what I might have been responsible for." He spoke slowly, deliberately.

"That's right, I don't know, and neither do you . . . as long as you have amnesia . . . or do you really? For all I know, maybe you're just pretending, and if you are, I'd sure like to know why."

"I'm not pretending. If you're referring to the Robert Frost incident, that's not unusual because that's how its been for me so far. Somebody will say something, and suddenly out of the blue there will be a memory, but it stops right there."

She folded her arms and leaned back in the seat, looking directly ahead. "How convenient for you."

"It's not convenient. It's maddening. But what really hurts is knowing that you think so little of me as a person."

Jasmine sighed, clenching her hands together. "What do you mean?"

"You believe that once I get my memory back, I'll forget all about you and my promise to Morgan's grandmother."

"I'm sorry if what I said sounded cruel, but this is frustrating, Noah. I can only be honest . . . I don't know what to believe. I mean, I still don't know you all that well." She gestured emphatically. "I just don't know."

He took a deep breath. "It's all right. I understand what you're saying. Actually, your honesty is something I've always liked about you . . . from back when you used to talk to me at the hospice. I guess I have a lot to prove. I hope you'll be patient." He picked up the key and slid it back into the ignition.

Jasmine was silent because she really didn't know what to say. She was still disturbed over the promise to Morgan's grandmother, but in her heart she knew she would be patient because she definitely did not want to lose him. He was intriguing, accommodating and handsome as the devil. Ever since he had first spoken to her at the hospice, she had started to see herself as a person again, a person who could be kind, caring and productive . . . maybe.

"I apologize for putting you on the spot with Mrs. Garcia," Noah said, starting the car. "The truth is, something just compelled me to make that promise. It's like a lot of things that have been happening to me lately. The words just came out automatically."

Jasmine stared out the side window as the car pulled onto the road.

"Noah."

"Yes?"

"You do remember from Glendale that I always like to have the final word."

He smiled sardonically. "Of course."

"Okay, now that we've got that straight, I want you to always remember that *I'm* the one who told Mrs. Garcia that I would do the best I could, but *you* were the one who made the promise."

CHAPTER 9

The house rose from the earth like the mighty oaks and pine trees of the forest. It was constructed of carefully primed mahogany-colored logs, but it was no log cabin. Instead, it was more like a sprawling chateau with sloping dormers and magnificent sun-spangled cathedral windows.

Jasmine gaped in awe at the sight. "This is it? This is where you used to live?"

"That's what they tell me," Noah said, slightly puzzled by her reaction.

"It's perfect. It's Alex Leiber, isn't it?"

"What? Who?"

She didn't even hear his response. She had already opened the car door and was getting out. Noah watched her as she approached the house, moving as though she were mesmerized. He shook his head. It was a beautiful house, but what on earth was she talking about? He got out of the car and joined her.

"I guess you like it," he said.

"It's magnificent." She noticed Noah's bewilderment and laughed. "You must think I've lost it. It's just that Alex Leiber is one of my favorite contemporary architects. I'd know one of his houses anywhere because they always blend so perfectly with the environment. Did you know that I once wanted to join the Leiber firm?"

Noah was captivated by her enthused transformation. Even though she still sported the tacky, dried up dreadlocks, her face glowed with excitement and her eyes sparkled like the light filtering through the Ramapo mountain trees. He reached for her hand.

"Why didn't you join the Leiber firm?"

"Because their base was in Colorado. I couldn't see myself moving there at the time . . . not to mention they probably wouldn't have let a skinny black woman infiltrate their all-male network anyway." She tugged urgently, childishly, at his hand. "Is anyone living here now? Can we go inside?"

"Hold on, Jasmine" he said, laughing. "I'm trying to find my key." He fumbled in his pocket. "The people who were renting it just moved out. The place is officially for sale now."

"Since your family's in South Carolina, who's been acting as landlord?" she asked.

"Aaron was. He lives in this area to be near the airport. His company, Avian International, has a major hub at Newark Liberty."

"You mean *your* company and Aaron's," she corrected.

"If you say so."

He watched her gently running her hand over the logs as though she were stroking something priceless, revered. Impulsively he wished he were one of the logs. The thought almost made him laugh.

Inside, he allowed her to walk ahead of him. With no furniture or any signs of habitation, the house seemed huge and cavernous. He could see how its wood-beamed, rustic beauty must have once appealed to him, but now it seemed cold, and strangely enough, a bit hostile. He had been trying to deny it, but maybe the alienation was increasing because a familiar headache was starting.

"Alex Leiber. Alex Leiber," he muttered to himself. There was definitely something about that name. He stood near one of the towering windows and looked out at the pristine woodland. The ash and maple trees were just beginning to change color. He faintly remembered looking over blueprints, talking to a man, an architect, discussing how the house should be built. He remembered the varied stages of construction and he heard a distinct voice. It was getting louder. He stared at the forest again.

"It's beautiful, Noah, the forest, I mean. Is there a lake?"

"No, but there is a pond on the property."

The voice in his head was not coming from Jasmine. She was a few feet away from him, inspecting the staircase. Whose voice was it? His heart beat faster and his head pounded. The voice was Isabella's. The past was calling him.

"It really is beautiful, and I know it's a gift and all, but I'm not sure it's right for us. It's so isolated out here."

"Isolated? We're only about forty minutes away from Manhattan. I don't call that isolated."

"Of course you don't. You spend most of your time flying around the world anyway. I'm the one who has to be here!"

"Who said you have to constantly be here? How about a job . . . a hobby . . . something?"

"Great! Now you're trying to keep me occupied, instead of doing what you should be doing. What about our home?"

"This is home."

"It is not! Home is Cielo Vista. I'm sick of this, Noah, sick of it. The things everyone said about you are all lies. You're nothing but a coward."

His headache increased and he remembered another time coming home from somewhere, pulling into the driveway—this same driveway. He remembered walking up the stairs, hearing something he should not have heard. He remembered opening a door to a bedroom—his bedroom—and seeing two pairs of shocked, guilty eyes staring back at him.

"Western red cedar," Jasmine was saying.

"Western what?" Noah echoed, jolted back into the present.

She joined him near the window. "I was talking about the type of logs that were used to construct the house. They're very expensive. Leiber must have imported them from Canada. They . . ." She stopped. "Noah, are you okay?"

"Just a headache. It'll pass."

"My God, you look like you're about to pass out. You're turning gray." Worriedly, she fished around in her bag. "I have a bottle of water with me. Did you bring anything . . . medication?"

"Yeah, I did." He stepped away from the window, leaned back against the wall and slowly sank to a sitting position on the hardwood floor, burying his face in his arms. "It's bad right now," he admitted, "but don't worry, it'll go away. It always does. Just give me a couple of minutes."

She crouched on the floor beside him, offering him the water. He lifted his head and took a long swig from the bottle. Instinctively, she laid her hand lightly on the back of his neck. He liked her gentle, reassuring caress, and gradually he felt the throbbing subside somewhat.

"Noah?" she quizzed.

"I think we need to get out of here," he said, rising slowly, taking her hand and lightly pulling her up with him.

She didn't object. They stepped back outside and he locked the door. He wasn't quite sure what it was, but he knew he had to get far away from the house—far away from those voices. Even the thought of hearing more was making him nauseated. He hesitated near the SUV.

"I hate to do this to you, but I'm not sure I should be driving right now. You might have to."

He was right, but she felt panic creep over her. The car was a SUV, similar to the one she used to own—similar to the one that had killed Dawn. Could she do it? Could she actually drive that thing?

"You can do it," he said. "I know you can."

There was no other alternative. Taking the keys from him, she murmured a silent prayer and climbed into the driver's seat. Noah got in on the passenger side. When she turned the key in the ignition, the engine roared to life like a demonic beast and she imagined it bucked forward as she slid the gear into drive. Her hands shook uncontrollably. "Calm down. Calm down," she murmured. Her fears were irrational; there were no children in the area.

"Just relax and take it slow," Noah said, his voice steady, reassuring.

She bit down on her lip. Didn't it bother him that her hands were shaking? Didn't it make him nervous?

She clenched her teeth and the car began to move, leaving the circular driveway behind, cruising out onto the narrow, two-lane road. It was okay. She felt fine. The shaking subsided.

The road wound downward through the mountains and she sensed the high elevation more than saw it. They were surrounded on both sides by trees that were starting to display their autumn finery. In about two weeks, the woods would be in glorious Technicolor. She thought about how she'd like to come back and see it all. She relaxed further, steering with the rhythm of the road, liking the feeling, and liking that he was right beside her.

"Slow down," Noah said suddenly.

"I'm riding the brake as it is," she said. "We're only going about 25 mph."

"I don't mean that you're speeding." His head was turned as he looked intently out the window. "There's just something about this spot. Stop the car."

"But it's a two-lane road and there's no shoulder," she objected. "What if someone comes behind us?"

"No one's coming. Put your blinkers on and pull off to the side as much as possible."

She had to oblige because he had the door open already. Nervously, she scanned the rearview mirror as he got out and stood near the guardrail. He looked down into a steep ravine.

"What is it?" she shouted from the car. "What are you seeing?"

"This is it," he said. "This is where I had the accident." He stood there, transfixed.

"Please get back in the car. You're making me very nervous," she pleaded.

He closed his eyes and recalled the eerie sensation of his accident as though a bad dream. He heard the screeching sound of splitting metal, felt the bizarre sensation of flying through the air and then an intense, all-encompassing darkness.

"Noah, please." Jasmine hurried out of the car and grabbed him by the arm. She looked beyond the guardrail into a jagged, rocky abyss that seemed to plummet endlessly. Her heart leaped into her throat. How could anyone have survived that fall? "Let's go. Now!"

He obeyed, and once they were back in the car she quickly checked the mirror and pulled back onto the road. Relief and anger washed over her. "Don't you ever do that again!" she shouted.

"I'm sorry. I didn't mean to make you nervous. It's just that . . . that I was kind of having a flashback and I remembered."

With her eyes on the road, she breathed in and out to calm herself. "Do you remember anything that happened right before the accident?"

He tilted his head back and closed his eyes. "Nothing."

She felt bad for him. It was quite obvious that he still had the headache, and now all she wanted was to get them both safely back home. Right then she decided exactly where he was going to be staying that night. She was not going to take no for an answer.

"My bedroom's all yours. You can sleep as long as you like," she announced, ushering him in. "The apartment may be hideous, but I do have a decent bed."

She was grateful that she had changed the linen that morning. Noah had taken his medication a half hour before they arrived back at her place, and he didn't seem to care one way or the other. His attention seemed to be focused only on sleep. She managed to wrestle him out of his dark suede jacket before he collapsed face down on the bed.

Jasmine found herself paying more than usual attention to his physique. Under the jacket he had on a charcoal-gray V-necked sweater that was well suited to his sleek, sinewy body, which was partially defined by his black jeans. What a marvelously sculpted body it was. She had to clench her hands together just to keep from touching him. Maybe she could, though. After all, he was so zoned out from the medication that he probably wouldn't notice. She reached out and—stopped. "None of that stuff," she muttered aloud. The man was infamous for his subconscious memory. She didn't want to add more fuel to the fire.

Sighing, she tugged off his shoes, noting that his socks were also black. *He sure likes dark colors,* she thought idly, and forced herself out of the room, leaving the door ajar.

It was only 5:00 P.M. She thought about supper and realized there was nothing in the house that a man would find appealing. She was not the least bit hungry herself, but Noah might be later. Neither of them had eaten since morning.

She scribbled a quick note in case he woke up, and left it on the kitchen table. As she started to leave, she noticed that his car keys were on the table. Why walk when she could just borrow his car? It certainly beat walking loaded down with packages. She hesitated. Was the fear still there? She had just driven home on a narrow, winding two-lane road. But there was a difference. That road had been isolated. This was Brooklyn. There would be people everywhere, including children. No. Her unstylish, old lady shopping cart would have to suffice.

Jasmine shopped as she hadn't done in a long time. She even enjoyed it. Beer? Maybe he liked that. Salmon, steak, ground beef, frozen vegetables, salad fixings and a bottle of white wine.

"Girl, you're nuts," she told herself, but she couldn't control the impulse—didn't want to control it. She didn't want to think, period.

When she got back home, Noah was still asleep. She checked on him to make sure he was okay, and once assured that he was, she stashed the food in the refrigerator and considered the possibility that he might not even wake up until late at night. He probably wouldn't want anything at midnight—nothing heavy, anyway. The great dinner would have to wait for Sunday. She cooked hamburgers that could be re-heated in the microwave for later if he wanted any, and she made a fresh salad, which she nibbled at.

Now what was she going to do? She retired to the living room and flopped on the couch. Her thoughts returned to Morgan. She was tempted to call and find out how she and her grandmother were doing, but she resisted the urge. Everything was going fine, she was sure, and her call would only be an intrusion that they did not need.

On any other given Saturday evening, she would be sleeping, watching TV or listening to Morgan chatter, but on this Saturday she felt absolutely energized and stir-crazy. She was both relieved and anxious that Noah was still asleep. She wanted to talk to him, but she was afraid of what he was going to say—of what he might be remembering. She wanted to talk, had to talk, to somebody.

She reached for the telephone and, before she could even think or stop herself, she had dialed Valerie's number.

"Val," she began tentatively, when she heard the familiar voice on the other end.

"Jasmine?" Val questioned as though hearing a ghost.

"Yes, it's me."

"Oh, my God. It really is you!" she erupted. "Where on earth are you?"

"Well, I'm living in Brooklyn."

"Why haven't you called me in all this time?"

"I wanted to. Believe me, I did. But the time just wasn't right."

"Oh, never mind all that. I'm so glad to hear from you! Talk to me!"

"Well, there really isn't that much to say."

"It's been what, two years? How could you not have anything to say?"

Jasmine laughed in spite of herself. "I've been in hibernation. That's not very exciting. What about you? It has been two years, as you just said."

It was Valerie's turn to laugh now. "You know what, you're right. Nothing much has changed. I'm still playing nurse at Englewood and I'm still single. It's been terrible without my best friend. I miss going to dinner with you. The laughs, the movies, the guys we hung with and your crazy sister's kids . . ." She stopped.

Jasmine took a deep breath. "It's okay. Do you ever hear from Natalie?"

"Jasmine, listen to me. I hear from Natalie, and she's worried to death about you. She bugs me all the time, asking if I know anything."

Unable to believe what she was hearing, Jasmine was speechless. She listened to Val babble on.

"You have to call her," Val said.

She finally found her voice. "Am I hearing you correctly? You remember what Natalie said at Dawn's funeral. She screamed at me in front of all those people. She said she hated me and that she never wanted to see me again. She called me a murd—"

"I know," Valerie interrupted. "I remember it well. That was awful, wasn't it?" She hesitated for a long moment. "But, Jas, she's your sister. You know how she is. I guess you don't know anything about what's been going on with Natalie, do you?"

"No, I don't. I'm not sure I want to."

"Well, you listen to this," Val interrupted. "Natalie is married and she's expecting another baby."

"What!"

"That's right. She married Michael Brooks, that young minister who preached at Dawn's funeral. Your nephew is now two, and like I was saying, Nat's expecting another baby. She wants to see you, Jas. Life goes on."

Natalie had forgiven her and Natalie was married to a minister—Natalie who'd always scoffed at going to church and believed that all religious people were hypocrites. Jasmine could not begin to explain the feeling that came over her.

"Val. Please don't worry about me. I will call you back again, and it's not going to take another two years. But right now I just can't talk anymore." She hung up the phone and sat still in shocked silence.

CHAPTER 10

Jasmine felt dizzy as the tiny living room seemed to close up around her and anguished screams from the past reverberated in her head. She sat still and squeezed her eyes shut as blackness enveloped her and time rolled back, back to the awful day of Dawn's funeral.

The raindrops beat a mournful rhythm on the windshield and the wipers increased their tempo in an effort to keep up as Valerie piloted the car to its sad destination, Hendricks Funeral Home.

"I don't think I can do this," Jasmine murmured.

"Yes, you can. There's no way you can avoid the funeral. It's closure . . . a way to say goodbye."

"I don't want to say goodbye."

"Nobody does, but you can't pretend it didn't happen. Besides, Natalie needs you."

Natalie. Jasmine barely felt her feet touch the ground as she and Valerie got out of the car. The rain had subsided a bit, but the air hung thick and heavy, its dampness and weight seeping into her very bones. As though controlled by an invisible force, her legs propelled her forward through the open doors of the somber white building.

Numerous people, dressed in black, were gathered in the dimly lit parlor. Jasmine recognized only Natalie's adoptive parents, Natalie, and the boyish-looking minister who was to preside over the service. She cast her eyes upon the tiny white coffin set amidst sprays of pink and white floral arrangements. The coffin was open.

Jasmine quickly moved to the rear of the room and sat down heavily on one of the folding chairs, ignoring Valerie, who had stopped to talk to someone. Warily, she looked at the coffin again from a safe distance. Dawn's small head and shoulders were propped up by satin pillows, and she appeared to be asleep. Her luxurious rippled tresses crowned her head like a wreath. Suddenly her head turned and her large, shimmering eyes looked directly at Jasmine. Jasmine gasped and clapped her hand over her mouth.

"Jas, what are you doing way back here? You're supposed to be in the front with the family."

Jasmine didn't hear Valerie. She looked at the coffin again and realized that Dawn's head had not moved at all. The body was as motionless as before. She was having delusions.

"Jasmine, are you okay?" Valerie was looking at her anxiously.

"I . . . I'm fine." Jasmine stood up abruptly and immediately her eyes connected with those of Natalie, who was in the front of the room.

Natalie's mouth opened and closed silently. Shakily, Jasmine moved toward her, wanting to embrace her, to share their grief.

"Get out!" Natalie hissed. " I never want to see you again."

Jasmine stopped in her tracks.

"I hate you! Murderer! You killed her! You killed my baby!"

For a second, the only sound that could be heard was the ticking of the giant grandfather's clock in the hallway as all heads in the room turned to stare accusingly at Jasmine. The next second, Natalie lunged toward her, raking the air with her long fingernails. Her hysterical assault was quickly halted by the minister, who embraced her and spoke softly, consolingly, to her. Natalie would have fallen flat on the floor if he had not been holding her up.

The room swam madly before Jasmine's stricken eyes and she bolted from the room into the reception area. She kept running until she was outside in the pouring rain, and even then she didn't stop. She heard Valerie shouting her name, but she continued to run until the heel on her left shoe suddenly snapped and she pitched forward onto the hood of a parked car. Temporarily stunned, she slid helplessly off the hood and crumpled to the wet ground.

"Jasmine! Jasmine! Are you okay?" She felt Valerie's hand on her. "Please get up. I'm so sorry . . . please get up. We're going back home . . . to my house. Please get up."

The rain continued to pour down relentlessly.

As the nightmarish flashback slowly faded from her mind, Jasmine opened her eyes and remembered to exhale.

Now she knew that Natalie had quickly moved on— married the minister, no less. How she must have played on his sympathy. Why was she shocked? Finding another man was typical of Natalie, very typical. But it was actually a good thing—wasn't it? Jasmine buried her face in her hands and alternated between laughter and tears. Whatever went down, it still didn't change the fact that little Dawn was dead and that she had so far lost two years of her own life.

Rising, Jasmine went quietly to the bedroom. It was now 9:00 P.M. and Noah was still out. It was pretty clear who'd be sleeping on the couch. She leaned over him and gently smoothed down his rumpled black hair. Afterward, she went to her dresser and removed a long jungle print T-shirt from the drawer. Glancing back at Noah's sleeping form, she defiantly stripped down to her underwear and pulled the dress length T-shirt on over her head.

She hesitated for a brief second and entertained the deliciously wicked thought of lying down next to him. It was a queen-sized bed, big enough for both. It was her room and her bed. What was stopping her? *Don't go there,* she silently reprimanded herself. *You're not even thinking straight. Just because you're going through an emotional dilemma doesn't mean you have the right to use someone else as an outlet for your frustrations. Use?* She looked at Noah again; even without total control of his memory, he didn't strike her as the type of man who was easily used.

Stop looking at him like that.

Why?

God doesn't like it.

But if there really is a God, he doesn't care about me anyway.

She left the bedroom quickly and stormed into the bathroom, silencing the voices. What a deranged idiot she was. She had stopped listening to God's voice long ago, and had lived through two disastrous affairs to prove it. Why should this situation be any different? Why did she want it to be different?

She switched on the light and glared at herself in the cracked mirror. The crack ran horizontally across her face, giving her a twisted Jekyll and Hyde appearance. Maybe that's what she was, a woman split into two unequal parts. She released the thick braids and watched the matted snakes tumble below her shoulders. Slowly, resolutely, she reached for one braid and began undoing it. She undid another and another. She couldn't stop. Her fingers were literally tearing, ripping, at the thick hair, pulling it loose, setting it free. Next, she flung open the cabinet and removed a bottle of shampoo. She turned the warm water on full force and watched it fill the porcelain bowl. Then she plunged her head into the water.

"Mind if I . . . ?"

She stiffened slightly as she became aware that she had not closed the door and Noah had entered the room. He leaned over her without waiting for a response or permission and she felt his hands lightly on her shoulders, steadying her. It should have felt awkward to be bent over a sink, dressed in a flimsy T-shirt, with his lean, muscled body pressed against her, but it felt natural. She relaxed.

His hands moved magically up and down her neck; his fingers swirled through her billowing wet mane, massaging her scalp, her hair, and her pain. The pungent, citrus scent of the shampoo and his warm breath on the back of her neck took her away. Far, far away. To some exotic island someplace. Alone. Just the two of them.

"How like the devil," she murmured.

"What?"

"Nothing. Nothing at all." She wished he would never stop what he was doing, that they could remain mindlessly locked this way forever.

Noah didn't want to think either. He knew he was being overly forward as he gently kissed the back of her neck, but she definitely had not said no. He loved the lemony scent of her mingled with the steam in the tiny bathroom. And she was beautiful, as beautiful as he'd imagined she was, with soft tawny skin and subtle curves in all the right places. Despite her occasionally volatile, stubborn attitude and her bouts of negativity, she was as vulnerable as a child.

He rinsed her hair slowly, savoring the feel of the thick-textured ripples, and then he reached for a towel on the nearby rack and gently urged her to stand up straight.

"Your hair is absolutely amazing," he said. "I didn't realize it was so long."

"This mess," Jasmine said, laughing as she accepted the towel and swathed it around her head. "I must look like the wild queen of Borneo."

"I'll have to visit Borneo, if all the women look like you."

She started to say something else, but Noah did not want to talk. He swooped her up in his arms, wet hair, towel and all and carried her back to the bedroom. He lowered her gently down on the bed. The next minute they were lying there locked in each other's embrace, kissing desperately, as though it were their last moment on earth, murmuring impassioned nothings, restrained only by their clothing, which at any second she was expecting to disintegrate. And even though she loved it, common sense was telling her to stop, that the time wasn't right, but she couldn't until . . .

"Isabella," he murmured.

"Isabella?" she repeated. Immediately the spell was broken. She stiffened and pulled away.

"I'm an insensitive idiot," Noah said, standing awkwardly a few feet away from her. "I'm sorry."

"It's all right," Jasmine replied mechanically. She was huddled on the living room couch, wrapped tightly from neck to ankles in a thick lavender-colored robe.

He moved closer. "No. It's not all right. I'm obviously still not quite there in the brain department. No way did I mean to call you by that name."

He looked so handsome, even with tousled hair and disheveled clothes. She refused to meet his eyes. "I told you it doesn't matter."

"It does matter." He shook his head in frustration. "I have to tell you why it happened."

"You don't have to tell me anything."

"Isabella used to be my wife," he insisted. "I started to remember that part when we were back at my house. I could almost see her."

"That's nice. She must've been beautiful." Jasmine clicked the TV on with the remote. She was amazed that she was able to maintain such a detached attitude while experiencing a whole range of conflicting emotions—relief that the moment hadn't been consummated, ridiculous jealousy and complete confusion.

"It's *not* nice," he interjected. "She was physically beautiful, yes, but that's beside the point. There was something very wrong about her . . . something very cold. My family told me they never trusted her and that we were in the process of getting a divorce. Anyway, she's not my wife anymore. She returned to Cielo Vista almost immediately after I had the accident."

Why did the idiot go back to Cielo Vista? Jasmine wondered. Hadn't her family been assassinated there too? She didn't ask the question; instead, she clenched the remote tighter. "I'm not surprised to find out she was your wife. You always seemed to have some kind of reaction every time you mentioned her name. Do you remember why you were getting a divorce?"

"No, but when I was in the house, right when I started getting the headache, I remembered that she hated the place. She accused me of trying to isolate her."

"Most couples argue at times. Surely you wouldn't want a divorce just because of that."

"I know there *had* to be much more but—"

"You don't remember," she interrupted sarcastically. "Do you have a picture of her?"

The question must have caught him off guard because he hesitated longer than usual before speaking. "Yes."

"Can I see it?"

"Do you really want to?"

"Yes."

"It's in my jacket pocket. I don't know where you put it."

She indicated the closet where she'd hung his jacket and he retrieved the photo from his wallet. He extracted the picture and handed it to her.

Jasmine gazed at the woman. She was perfect looking, almost unreal—doll-like, and like a doll, emptiness radiated from her glassy blue eyes.

"You weren't kidding when you said she was beautiful." She handed the photo back.

Noah frowned. "At this moment, I'm not finding her very attractive at all. She doesn't compare to you."

"Oh, *please*, spare me." Jasmine felt her eyes glaze over.

"Yeah, I know. I'm not very convincing. But for what it's worth, I *really* do mean it." He held the photo between thumbs and forefingers and ripped it in half.

The action surprised her a little. Her eyebrows lifted as she watched him continue to tear it, sending bits and pieces showering into the wastebasket. *Of course that's probably not the only picture you have of her,* she thought.

"This is the only picture of her I have with me," he said, searching her eyes. "There are more back at the family home in South Carolina, but I will be getting rid of them when I return."

He sat on the couch near her and reached up to lightly touch her rippling coils of damp hair. She moved her head ever so slightly in the opposite direction.

"Please don't," she said. "It's nothing against you personally at all. I'm sure the fact that I'm like putty in your hands shows how I feel. But the real truth is, I'm glad you did call me Isabella because it made us stop."

Noah rubbed his eyes. "As far as I'm concerned, we're two consenting adults. What's wrong with what we almost . . ."

"Plenty," she interrupted. "I don't want to have another pointless relationship with someone. I've been there, done that. I think people should learn from their mistakes."

"I'm not like Drew and Steven," he said.

She flinched. He even remembered their names. She closed her eyes, realizing that she was the one who was starting to get a headache now as she recalled her painful relationship with Drew Larsen. She had been twenty years old, fresh out of college and working as an apprentice at Horizon Architecture in Indiana. Drew, a twice-divorced, Swedish-born man in his late thirties, had been one of the partners and her mentor. She'd naively allowed herself to fall prey to his relentless seduction and they'd inevitably become lovers—until Drew decided to move on and married an heiress from Palm Beach.

But the worst part had been his ultimate betrayal. They had been working as a team on the construction of a high-rise office complex and she had shared with him her design for incorporating improved safety features in the building's elevator shaft, and he'd told her the idea was brilliant, but the cost would be astronomical and therefore not feasible. After they'd parted, he went on to use her design, labeled it as his own and made millions.

Pharmaceutical rep Steven Turner had been no better. Five years after Drew, she'd met Steven on a plane bound for England. He had seemed different. Their ages were comparable and they had come from similar lifestyles and ethnic backgrounds. Steven had been kind, generous and fun to be around—until she received a phone call from a woman claiming to be his wife, who'd called her every name under the sun and informed her that Steven was not only married, but he had three young children, a dog, and a goldfish.

"Earth to Jasmine, are you listening?" Noah asked.

"I heard you," she said, unconsciously twisting strands of hair around her finger. "Maybe you really aren't like Drew and Steven, but I can't read hearts and motivations like God can, so I guess I'll never really know."

"Part of being human involves trusting and taking risks. If you never risk anything, you stop growing and learning," he said.

"That's probably true for most people." She stared at the TV screen. A woman was screaming as an assailant was about to attack her with a knife. She switched the channel. "Anyway, this whole thing with us is just too complicated. And don't you *dare* laugh at this: I've been having some odd spiritual urges lately, and that's another reason why we shouldn't get involved physically. According to the Bible, God says that people should be married."

His eyebrows rose. "Where is this coming from? Back at the hospice, you told me you didn't believe in God."

"Gotcha! You can't always read me correctly. I was angry, bitter, and I'm sure I said a lot of things I didn't really mean. The honest truth is I'm not sure what I believe, but the feeling is there and I can't explain it."

Noah was silent for a few moments, and then spoke. "When I was in South Carolina, I got a full dose of spirituality from Mariel."

"Mariel?"

"My mother. She's very much a believer."

"Do you think you were a believer before you lost your memory?"

"Good question. I know for sure I've never had the kind of faith she has, but maybe there was a slight pull in that direction."

Jasmine was exhausted and it was getting late, yet, because of her past relationship with him, she could not seem to keep her mouth shut. "While you were sleeping, I called an old friend."

"Valerie?"

"Yes, Valerie. She told me what's been going on and the things I heard kind of shocked me."

Noah leaned closer. Their shoulders were touching. Jasmine chewed on the edge of her lip. She wanted to stop talking but couldn't. Their relationship since the days of the hospice had definitely evolved. It still felt comfortable talking to him, but now he could respond, and his response obviously wasn't always going to be what she wanted to hear.

"What did Valerie say?"

"She told me that my sister married the minister who preached at Dawn's funeral and she's now expecting another baby."

"Little sister sure works fast," he said.

She looked at the twinkle in his eyes. "It's not funny, Noah."

"Am I laughing?"

"No, but your eyes are."

He slid his arm around her. His embrace was warm, but this time it felt more paternal than amorous. She relaxed.

"Don't you think it's a good thing that Natalie has moved on?" he ventured.

"I suppose. She also wants to see me again."

"Are you going to see her?"

"I don't know."

"I think you should."

She rolled her eyes and focused back on the television.

"You're probably a little taken aback by how quickly she's recovered in contrast with . . ."

"Please . . . let's not talk about that," she interrupted. "I'm sorry for bringing it up. It's just something I have to sort out for myself."

Noah took a deep breath. "Okay. We won't talk about it. But in between making your decision, could you do me a favor?"

"It depends. What?"

"I'm going to have to return to South Carolina soon . . . for a few days. Would you come back with me?"

She laughed. "Are you serious? I'm sure your mother, who you hardly even remember, isn't interested in meeting the likes of me."

"Actually, you're wrong. I've told her a few things about you and she said she wants to meet you."

"Did you tell her that I'm not only a nut case, but I'm also black?"

It was Noah's turn to laugh. "Mariel's second husband was Nigerian. My little sister Gianna is their child, so you tell me if you think race matters."

She wanted to go. She wanted to learn everything she could about the people behind the mysterious man who was capturing her heart.

"I'll have to think about it," she replied.

Noah insisted that he no longer had a headache, and he left before daybreak. Jasmine was slightly relieved because it gave her time to collect her thoughts and come to grips with everything that was happening. She didn't have too long to think, however, because he returned promptly the next day, and on Sunday afternoon they drove back to Queens to get Morgan.

Jasmine did end up cooking a big dinner, but the whole romantic aspect of the event was lost now that they were a threesome. Ironically, it didn't disappoint her all that much and it didn't seem to bother Noah in the least. As they sat around the table, she became aware of a brand new feeling, a very different one. They felt like family.

Morgan seemed slightly subdued at first. Perhaps the enormity of the whole situation with her grandmother was sinking in and she was realizing and possibly accepting that she would never be able to go back there to live.

"Do I have to go back with Rachel?" Morgan asked abruptly.

"Well, yes. Didn't your grandmother talk to you about that?"

She toyed with her glass of milk. "Yes."

"It won't be so bad. I'm still here most of the time, and you can visit and spend the night like you've been doing."

"I'm not gonna tell Rachel that I stayed with Grandma."

Jasmine breathed a sigh of relief. "That's probably a good idea, but it really is up to you."

"I can't tell her. She'll be mad and she'll get mad at you, too."

Noah listened to their conversation in silence. It was unjust that Morgan had to go back to her negligent mother. Even a good foster parent seemed better than the current arrangement. He wished there were something he could do, but at the moment there was nothing. His own life was still on hold, even though he did feel as though he were on the brink of awakening.

He gazed around the tiny, narrow kitchen and then back at the two faces near him—Jasmine, who literally glowed with vibrant, awakening beauty, despite having temporarily restyled her hair into bizarre twists, and the little girl with her angelic princess smile and large, brown eyes that were so eager and yearning for love and a sense of security. The two of them looked alike. Any stranger would assume that they were mother and daughter. It was almost eerie.

"Mr. Noah, are you from Puerto Rico like my daddy was?"

"No, but when I was your age I used to live in a small country that's almost like Puerto Rico. It's called Cielo Vista, and it's in Africa."

"Africa?" Her eyes shimmered with excitement. "Did you play with elephants and zebras?"

He smiled. "No, I didn't exactly play with them. Wild animals are very dangerous, but yes, in the mountains of Cielo Vista there are elephants and zebras."

"Are the mountains pretty?"

"Very pretty."

"Why did you leave?"

Jasmine glanced at Noah. His expression was slightly reflective, yet distant and disturbing.

"I had to go. Bad people took over the country and they destroyed everything that was good."

"Why did the good people let them?" Morgan asked, swinging her legs back and forth under the table. "I think . . ."

"Morgan, how about some chocolate chip ice cream for desert?" Jasmine interrupted, distracting her on Noah's behalf. It was as if she wanted him to remember his past, and then selfishly hoped he wouldn't at the same time. Hints of intrigue and extreme danger flashed through her head. She did not want to be reminded of political turmoil and bloodshed in a foreign country or his possible role in it because she was enjoying the simplicity of the moment they were having right now. She also did not want the reminiscing to trigger another headache. The signs were all there.

Her diversion tactic worked. Morgan launched into a new discussion about what her favorite ice cream was. Noah smiled in amusement now, but his gray eyes studied Jasmine knowingly. "I'm going to ask you again," he said.

"What?"

"Will you come back with me to South Carolina?"

"Yes," she said, helping Morgan spoon out the ice cream.

CHAPTER 11

The scent of salt marshes mingled with the perfume of flowers and the breeze off the not-too-distant ocean to create a distinct, unforgettable aroma. Jasmine inhaled deeply as Noah opened the passenger door of the rental car and she stepped out.

Before them stood a modest-sized white plantation-style house, well landscaped with beautiful, multi-colored flowers beds surrounding it. The place said wealth, but in a toned-down, non-ostentatious way.

"Home sweet home," Noah announced a bit sarcastically.

"It looks very peaceful," Jasmine said, admiring the garden.

"I guess it probably wasn't such a bad place to grow up," Noah admitted. They ascended the steps to the porch, and before he even knocked, the door opened and they were face to face with a regally attractive dark-haired woman. She had to be in her sixties, Jasmine thought, but she definitely looked a lot younger.

"Welcome," she exclaimed. "Noah, I'm so glad you're back. I was really worried." She hugged him.

Noah returned the hug, albeit somewhat stiffly. "You had no need to worry," he said, and then turned to Jasmine. "This is Mariel."

Sensing Mariel's disappointment that her son didn't address her as Mother, Jasmine extended her hand. The older woman took it.

"So we finally meet. I've heard so much about you," Mariel said, her eyes gleaming with sincerity. "I must say my son's eye for beauty has not changed. It's a wonderful thing when beauty is combined with insight as well." She smiled at Noah, who didn't return it.

"Thank you," Jasmine said a bit uncertainly, glancing at the stoic Noah, not quite sure how the comment was to be taken. She had returned to her customary braided hairstyle, but the braids had been done by an accomplished beautician at an over-priced salon, and she knew she looked more than halfway decent.

She smiled at Mariel. "I don't really know what you've been told about me, but you may have heard that I've been through a lot. It's a relief to know that my angst isn't showing." She nudged Noah lightly in the ribs. *Lighten up,* she mouthed silently.

His expression remained impassive. "I'll go get the bags," he said.

"Come, I'll show you to the guest room," Mariel said. "You must want to settle in a bit. We can talk later."

Jasmine glanced at Noah again but he was already moving out the door, as if he couldn't wait to get back out in the air.

"Don't worry about him," Mariel said after he'd disappeared. "I'm not upset by his aloofness. Of course, I wish he had returned from New York with his memory intact, but I don't doubt for a minute that it will return very soon."

"You seem to have a lot of faith," Jasmine said, following her down the hall.

"Of course. We are all created with spiritual needs. We need to rely on a higher source."

"You're probably right." Jasmine did not want to linger on that subject. "Doesn't Noah have a brother and a younger sister?"

"Yes. Noah's brother is not close to the family. No one hears from him. But he has a sister, Gianna, my late-in-life child. She's still in high school. She'll be home soon." She opened the door to a bedroom. "I also have a good friend and her husband living here. They have an apartment on the lower level of the house."

The guest room was large and comfortable, with cream-colored walls and reproductions of peaceful Monet paintings on the walls. A large four-poster bed with a patchwork quilt dominated the room. Her eyes lifted to inspect the ceiling fan, which reminded her of a trip to New Orleans years ago.

"This is a pretty room," Jasmine said, smiling.

"Thank you. It doesn't get much use now that my husband is gone. He came from a rather large family, and he used to enjoy having them stay over."

"You're divorced?"

"I'm a widow," Mariel said. "I'm surprised Noah didn't tell you that."

"I'm sorry. He did say that you married again after his father, but he didn't mention that your second husband had . . ." She hesitated.

"Amadi died nearly a decade ago. He was a good man. But two marriages are quite enough for anyone. I never felt the desire to marry again. Now I'm content with my family, my friends and my business."

"What sort of business are you in?"

"I own a bookstore in town. Our books deal primarily with spirituality and holistic healing."

"That's interesting. Noah didn't tell me that either."

Noah entered the room carrying her suitcase. His hair was so black it gleamed, the color set off by the contrasting white of his T-shirt. Jasmine couldn't resist giving him a lingering gaze.

"Everything okay in here?" he asked.

"Fine. It's perfect," Jasmine replied, sitting on the bed.

"Jasmine, do you mind if we leave you for a few minutes?" Mariel asked. "Noah and I really must talk."

"Of course I don't mind. I'll just unpack some of my things."

"Good. The bathroom connects to this room and the kitchen is downstairs to the right if you need . . ."

Jasmine laughed. "I'll be okay. I'm fine. Go have your talk."

Mariel exited, urging Noah out with her. She *had* to be his mother, Jasmine thought. She could detect a slight resemblance, even though she was sure he probably looked more like his father.

Noah sat on the sofa in the huge living room, his eyes focused on the restored antique fireplace instead of on

Mariel, who sat in a wing-backed chair facing him. "Do you think going back to New York helped you any?" she asked.

"Yes."

"Would you like to tell me what you remember? I mean, aside from your moments at the hospital with Jasmine."

Noah shifted impatiently on the sofa. "I went back to visit the house in New Jersey and I started remembering some things about Isabella—not a lot, but some things. I want you to tell me everything you know about her."

Mariel folded her arms. "Before I do that, I need to know first where your memory ends."

"I remember arguing with her and I remember having the accident. How does this connect?"

"Noah, are you sure you're ready for this?"

"Yes," he said impatiently. "If you're worried that I'm still in love with Isabella, forget it. I'm not."

Mariel sighed. "Even after everything that happened when she was a child, Isabella never wanted to leave Cielo Vista. She was a princess with no true loyalties. She married you with the hope that you would return to claim your right as heir. She wanted the kind of lifestyle that comes only from being married to some powerful person, presumably in government. When things didn't happen according to her time frame, she wanted out."

Noah stood up, his eyes narrowed. "I realize that we were getting a divorce, or on the brink of it. Did she find someone else to go back to Cielo Vista with?"

"Apparently."

"Do you know this person?"

"I can't answer that because I'm not sure."

Noah clenched his fists, both hands jammed in his pockets. "I knew there was someone else involved. I knew. But I just can't see him. I can't remember his face."

"You don't have to," Mariel said, standing up. She reached out and placed her hand on his shoulder. "I want you to think hard about what you're going to do next. It's not about anger or revenge. It's not about a deceitful wife. It's about what a greater force has willed for Cielo Vista, its future, its people."

"What *are* you talking about?"

"You know exactly what I'm talking about because you are the instrument the force is using. Do you remember Simon? Think. Think hard."

"Enough!" Noah's frustration turned to anger. "I don't want to talk about this anymore. I'm sorry I even mentioned remembering anything. What do I owe Cielo Vista? Nothing. It killed my father, my friends. It made me an exile. Why do you expect me to be instrumental in its future?"

"The expectations are not mine. They are coming from a higher source," Mariel said urgently. "Noah, please, I—"

"Well, I hate to disappoint whatever this higher source is," Noah snapped, "but I have no intention of even going back to that place, let alone ruling it. I feel no connection to it at all."

"Are you sure? Look at you. You're getting all worked up, angry. Does that sound like someone with no emotional connection? Before you left, I knew what you were telling me was true because your voice was cold and flat. Now it has fire and passion. You're starting to remember."

"I don't want to remember!" he shouted.

Startled by the loud voices, Jasmine entered the living room "Excuse me for interrupting, but what's going on? Noah, why are you yelling?

"It's okay. It's okay," Noah said, coming to her. "I apologize to both of you. I guess I was just trying so hard to remember, or not remember, that it got out of control."

Refusing to back down, Mariel did not acknowledge Jasmine's presence in the room. "I'm not taking your reaction personally," she said. "I only want you to remember, and it seems to me that you really were on the brink of doing it. You have to remember, Noah. You must. There isn't much time."

Jasmine watched a flame ignite in Noah's eyes. It was compelling, fierce, almost frightening, and then it quickly vanished. "I refuse to talk about this anymore," he said to Mariel. "Jasmine, come outside with me." He took her hand. "We have to talk."

"My mother is insane," Noah said flatly. "It would probably be best if you don't take anything she says too seriously."

They were in the backyard, standing inside an elegant, lattice-trimmed gazebo. From it, Jasmine could see towering oak trees draped with Spanish moss, rolling acres of green grass and a sliver of blue that was the Atlantic Ocean in the distance, a scene that was way too romantic to fit the mood and the conversation.

"I certainly don't mean to dispute you, because obviously you know more about her than I do, but she doesn't seem insane to me. Just very driven," Jasmine said.

"She doesn't care about me as a person," Noah insisted. "The most important thing in the world to her is that I remember things about Cielo Vista. Did you hear what she said? She said there isn't much time. Time for what? I don't see sand running down an hourglass, do you?"

"No."

Jasmine took a deep breath and studied Noah as he leaned against the post at the gazebo's entrance, his arms folded across his chest, his face ruggedly handsome, his expression grim and determined. There was nothing at all about him that suggested a genteel Southern boy. And here she was in her puffy beige silk blouse and flowing white skirt like some mocha version of Scarlett O'Hara. She almost expected the floor of the gazebo to dissolve under his feet and the elegant white posts and railings to wither and shrink to ashes.

She squeezed her eyes shut and then opened them, trying to clear the bizarre image. "What can I say?" she said. "I don't understand enough of what's going on. But I do know one thing . . . you need to relax, because you're going to make yourself sick."

Noah stood straight, hands jammed in the pockets of his jeans. He looked directly into her eyes and then down at his feet.

"Noah, please." She placed her hand on the side of his face. His prism-like eyes glittered and connected with hers again. "Relax." She let her hand slide down until it rested on his chest. She could feel his heart beating.

He caught her hand and held it, bringing it slowly toward his lips. He kissed her hand, a whisper of a kiss. "You're right," he admitted. We're only here for three days. You can reach your own conclusion about Mariel. She is right about one thing, though."

"What is that?"

"Two things actually. The first is that you are beautiful, and you definitely have insight. The other thing is . . ." He hesitated. "The other thing is, I probably am getting very close to remembering, but there is a barrier like a brick wall in my head that I just can't seem to break through. It's strange."

"That's not strange at all," Jasmine whispered. "From what I know and feel about you, I doubt if you're blocking whatever it is out of fear of some outside thing. I think you're afraid of your own anger—afraid of what you may be capable of doing."

"What am I capable of doing?"

The question struck her. She looked up at him. He was a tall man, and now he seemed larger than ever. He was only one person, but there was a determination, a strength that emanated from his very being. She shuddered. This was a man who was definitely meant to fulfill some grander purpose than just going about an ordinary life, working, maybe raising a family and quietly retiring to play with his grandchildren.

"I see many things, but I can't answer that in detail. Only you can."

Noah studied Jasmine's eyes, which gleamed like molten gold. Her head was tilted slightly as she looked up at him. Her eyebrows had a natural slant to them and her lips were pink and gently curved like lotus blossoms. The once uncomely braids were now long, thin and cascading down her back with tiny beads on the ends. She resembled a queen from ancient Egypt. He thought about the night back at her apartment when they had almost become one.

"Why didn't I meet you first?" he whispered, drawing her close to him. "Things could have been so different."

That afternoon Noah insisted that they go out for dinner, and Jasmine wound up apologizing to Mariel for not staying. They dined at a small restaurant in Charleston. He didn't offer to show her around the historic town because he didn't remember much about it himself. She thought it would have been nice to stroll around, but at the same time it was probably just as well they didn't since she wasn't particularly in the mood for being observed by people who felt there was nothing wrong with gawking at interracial couples.

Late in the evening, she sat alone on the porch steps of the house, watching fireflies flicker and listening to the choir of night birds and insects. Mariel was working late at her bookstore and Noah had told her that Aaron was in town and he had to meet with him at the airport. She had no idea why. He had simply told her that it was concerning business. She had been hoping that she would finally get to meet the mysterious Aaron, but he seemed adamant about lurking in the shadows.

What was she doing here? Just last month she'd been hibernating in a city of millions, a woman scorned, faceless, a blob among multitudes, a grieving, bitter woman who was only one step away from becoming a homeless person wandering the streets, dragging around a shopping cart and eating out of dumpsters. Now she was sitting on the spotless porch steps of a complete stranger's home, infatuated with a man who didn't even know who he was, and possibly on the brink of an adventure that could consume both of them.

"Do you like living in the city?"

Her thoughts were interrupted by the sudden appearance of the only other person in the house, Noah's sister. They had met briefly but had not had any conversation. Petite and mocha-complexioned with long, shiny, brown hair and dreamy eyes, Gianna was definitely pretty. She was attired in typical teenage garb: flip-flops, a pair of body-hugging jeans and a pink T-shirt that looked Morgan's size.

"Actually I prefer the country," Jasmine said. "The sounds are so relaxing."

"You mean the insects?"

"Yes."

Gianna sat down on the steps near her. "I used to catch the fireflies when I was little. I would keep them in my room so I could watch them light up, but I'd let them go the next day. Noah always told me it was cruel to keep them."

"That sounds like him. Did you and Noah do many things together?"

"A lot. My father died when I was five. I remember him a little, but he was always away on business. Noah's my brother, but sometimes he was more like my dad. He always talked to me and took me to movies and stuff. He taught me how to drive and he paid for my art classes and a lot of other things."

"It's good to have someone like that," Jasmine said.

"I feel really bad that he doesn't even remember me now."

Instinctively, Jasmine slipped her arm around the girl's slim shoulders. "I hear you. I can imagine how awful that feeling must be . . . but do you know what? He's getting better every day, slowly but surely. I'll bet you'll be the first person he remembers."

Gianna looked misty-eyed. "I wish things hadn't happened the way they did. I don't understand anything about why Noah and Isabella broke up." She hesitated. "It's so weird . . . I mean, people get divorced all the time, but it shouldn't have happened to them. They were like that one love thing . . . you know, two people meant to be together. If I were her, I wouldn't have left him even if I thought he was going to die."

"Some people just don't know how to handle traumatic situations," Jasmine said slowly. "The thought of losing someone you love is just so unbearable that you run away and try to bury the past, thinking that if you shut it out it never happened." She flinched as the words came out to mock her. She didn't know why she had responded in that way. It certainly wasn't an attempt to defend Isabella.

"That's so stupid," Gianna said. "If she had waited, they would still be together."

"Did you like her?" Jasmine asked.

Gianna shrugged. "Noah did. If she were still here, he'd probably remember everything."

Jasmine waited, hoping Gianna would say more about the mysterious Isabella, but the girl seemed far away, almost oblivious to her presence.

"I guess it's a good thing Noah has you for a friend. He can't trust everybody, not even in this family—" Gianna stopped.

"Could you tell me what you mean by that? Do you think someone here is trying to harm him?"

Gianna shifted restlessly. "Well, no. Not here . . . not anymore." She rose abruptly. "I'm sorry, but I really can't keep talking. I have an awful lot of homework to do."

Jasmine expelled her breath slowly as she turned to watch Gianna vanish back into the house, taking the illusion of a typical teenager with her. The girl looked the part, but she was far from outgoing and bubbly. Instead, she seemed nervous, frightened even.

The night sounds no longer soothed her. Jasmine stood up and scanned the starry heaven. Time was moving on. She was getting tired of being left in the dark. The whole truth about Noah's life and what or who could possibly be threatening him was out there; it no longer made any sense to try to convince herself that she was not involved because that involvement was growing every second. She had to know.

CHAPTER 12

Early the next morning, over breakfast in the large kitchen, Noah informed her that he had another business meeting with Aaron at the airport. He seemed restless, agitated, and distracted. She asked if it would be okay if she came along.

"I don't think that would be a good idea. I should be back in a few hours. Maybe we can do something together then. We only have one more day anyway." Jasmine toyed with her spoon, making tinkling noises against the coffee cup. "I realize you have things to catch up on, but why did you ask me to come here if all I'm going to be doing is sitting around the house?"

He looked into her eyes. "You're right. I am being rather selfish and inconsiderate. It's just that to me you are doing a lot more than just sitting around the house. Just knowing you're with me is giving me a kind of focus that I didn't have before. You're the only person I can talk to who isn't making some kind of unrealistic demand."

"I'm glad you feel that way about me, but Noah, we're not even talking anymore. You aren't telling me anything about what's going on with you."

His cell phone buzzed impatiently, but he leaned back in the chair and ignored it. "What do you want to know?"

The question confused her because there were so many things to ask, she didn't know where to start. "Will I ever get to meet Aaron?"

"You'll see him on the way back to New York. He has a freight delivery out of Stewart tomorrow so he has to be back there. We'll fly back on one of our cargo jets."

"Isn't Stewart mainly a military airport?

"Not as much as in the past. A lot of civilian flights leave from there now."

She hoped she didn't sound as uninformed or idiotic as she felt at the moment, but she had to ask. "I know nothing about running a cargo jet company, but it just seems unusual that Aaron is co-owner of the company and he makes the deliveries, too. Don't most owners just handle the business end and delegate the flying to their employees?"

Noah smiled somewhat grimly. "Avian International is not your typical company, but yes, we do employ a lot of pilots and most of the of the delivery runs are delegated, but this company goes to places where UPS and FEDEX do not. There are some assignments we handle personally."

"Such as?" she asked, honing in on the fact that he was using the word *we* quite liberally.

"I was afraid you were going to ask that, and I'd love to answer you, but I can't."

Her eyes gleamed in the morning light. "You don't trust me?"

"I'd trust you with my life at this moment, but we're not just talking about my life here. The business involves

other people. You do remember I told you that Aaron has
friends in high places. Well, Aaron trusts me to keep
things confidential, and that's saying a lot because he's
about as cynical as a human can get."

Jasmine lowered her head in silence. She exhaled
slowly. "It's all right. I'm not going to have a fit over not
knowing. I just hope . . . please tell me that you're not
involved in something illegal."

His eyes glittered strangely. "In the paths we walk,
there is often a very thin line dividing what is legal and
what is not . . . what is just and what is cruel. Sometimes
it depends on who or what is making the rules."

"Noah, you're scaring me."

His eyes lost their harsh glitter. "Am I going off again?
I'm sorry about that. I assure you that whatever we do is
not unjust before God or man."

On the last morning, Jasmine knocked on the door of
Mariel's study and was invited in. Mariel was sitting at
the desk poring over some papers, preparing for a seminar she was giving at the local college.

"I'll be leaving in a few hours and I'm sorry that we
haven't had much time to talk," Jasmine said.

Mariel looked up. "I'm sorry about that, too. I wish
Noah weren't so insistent on leaving, but I've never had
any control over what he does. Not before the accident
and not now."

Jasmine helped herself to a chair nearby. "I do think you're getting your wish, though. It seems to me that he really is remembering, even though he doesn't openly admit it."

"Perhaps, but he's fighting it every step of the way. He's barely spoken to me since he accused me of pushing him to the brink on your first day here."

Jasmine felt frustrated. There were so many things she wanted to ask, but she wasn't quite sure just how to go about it. Instead, she found herself staring at a picture on a bookshelf behind Mariel's desk. The picture was of two very handsome boys standing together—one black, one white. They were dressed conservatively, both wearing dark blazers, white shirts and ties, possibly some kind of school uniform. They looked to be about ten or eleven years old. She knew instinctively that the white one was Noah.

She rose abruptly, went to the shelf, and picked up the picture. "Noah and a friend?" she asked.

"Yes. The other boy is Simon Baraka. His father was one of the highest-ranking officials in Cielo Vista when Noah's father ruled. Those two were inseparable; they were schoolmates. Simon lost his parents during the coup also."

"I've heard of Simon Baraka from the news. I don't recall much, but wasn't he an activist, a spokesman for minority rights in Europe and Africa?"

"One and the same."

"Where is Simon now? I haven't heard anything about him for years."

"He was sentenced to life in prison in Cielo Vista for trying to overthrow the government. It's been quite a few years. No one knows if he's still alive. Good people tend to disappear in that country."

Feeling her inner tension rise, Jasmine put the picture down. "Please forgive me if I'm being nosy or rude," she hesitated, "but there are things I don't understand about any of this . . . to begin with, your relationship with Noah. I'm hearing about people being assassinated, people in prison. I don't understand why a mother would encourage her son to get involved in something that could be dangerous. Noah told me that you don't care about him as a person, and you know what?"

Mariel adjusted her glasses and leaned forward, giving Jasmine her fullest attention.

"It seems to me that he's telling the truth," she concluded, returning to her seat.

"Why do you think that?" Mariel asked.

Without warning, anger crept into her voice. "What kind of mother abandons her child in some depressing nursing home, miles and miles away from home? I worked there at Glendale for almost a year. The nurses told me that no one ever visited him. It was a cold, ugly place. You left him to die."

Mariel's expression was tight-lipped as she rose to shut the study door. She returned silently to the desk and sat down again.

"How could you?" Emotion choked Jasmine's voice.

"You have very strong feelings about this because you are a good person," Mariel said slowly. "I know there are things that happened to you when you were a child, but I am not going to dwell on that now. First, we will talk about Noah."

Jasmine was furious with herself. She was normally not the type of person who became overwrought in the presence of another. She was also struck by the fact that Mariel was homing in on her childhood insecurities related to abandonment. Had Noah told her everything about her personal life?

"I did not want Noah to be in a nursing home in New York. The first two weeks after the accident, he was sent to a hospital here in South Carolina. The family and I were at his side night and day, praying for his recovery."

"Isabella too?"

"She was present, yes. The doctors told me that it was unlikely he would ever recover. They advised us to shut down the life support system. Isabella agreed to do it right away, and that is what happened. I prayed that he would continue to live, and he did."

"So it was Isabella who had him sent to Glendale?"

"No. Aaron did."

"Aaron? But Aaron isn't even family. Where does he get off making a decision like that?"

Mariel took a deep breath. "Has Noah told you anything about him?"

"A little. My conclusion is that he and maybe even Noah were involved in some kind of undercover work, possibly for the government."

"I am not going to tell you that that is so, but it is a reasonable conclusion. Anyway, Aaron strongly believes that someone deliberately caused Noah's accident . . . someone we know, and he felt that he could protect him better in New York, since he is based there."

Jasmine swallowed hard. "Is Isabella a suspect?"

"Maybe."

"How was he better protected at Glendale?"

"You're going to find this disturbing, but there was surveillance in that room 24 hours a day. Security could reach him in seconds if they felt he was being threatened."

Jasmine's head swam. Her mouth went dry. "In other words . . . in other words, Aaron watched me every night and listened to everything I said to Noah?"

Mariel closed her eyes and opened them again. "He or his allies always watched, but they only listened for the first two weeks before we both reached the conclusion that you were harmless. I sensed that your visits were a good thing, and I wanted them to continue. I knew you would be the key to bringing Noah back."

"How? How could you know that?"

"Faith. I couldn't be there because I was forced to play a role. I had to convince Isabella and others that I no longer believed Noah would recover, even though I felt he would. When he did recover, Aaron arranged it so that any potential enemies would believe he had died."

"And now Isabella's back in Cielo Vista with the belief that Noah is dead and therefore no longer a threat to possibly take over the country. Did she remarry?"

"Yes."

"Who?"

"A government official."

Jasmine was speechless. Mariel continued to talk. "You have no idea what it was like for me. For the past two years, I could only put my faith in God that things would work out. I had to go on with my own life as if my son no longer existed. You came into Noah's life for a reason, Jasmine. You were there when I couldn't be."

"But why is this country, Cielo Vista, so important to you?" Jasmine asked.

"Because I loved Noah's father. Diego was the only man I ever loved in a purely romantic way. When he was president, he allowed religious freedom in the country, even though he was not completely a believer himself. There is no such freedom there now."

"Why did you divorce him if he was the love of your life?"

Mariel stared at the ceiling and, for a brief moment, Jasmine saw her eyes grow misty. "I first came to Cielo Vista as a teenager. My parents were Christian missionaries there. I met Diego and, being young and foolish, fell in love. Against my parents' wishes, we got married. To sum things up, I soon learned that he had no faith in God. He trusted only in his own power and he broke God's commandments. He had many wives. I was number three."

She glanced down at the papers on her desk and shuffled them. Jasmine waited for her to continue. There was a long silence before she spoke again.

"Noah was born, and for his sake, I continued to live with Diego and his harem until I couldn't take it anymore. When I threatened to leave him, he told me his feelings about polygamy had changed and that he would rid himself of the other wives and stay with me. I told him no. I told him that it wasn't fair and that he had to choose the first wife."

"That must have been really difficult," Jasmine said, sympathizing.

"It was. Anyway, Diego remained with his first wife and I returned home to the United States, but I didn't have the heart to take our son away from him. He was closer to Noah than he was to any of his older children by the other wives."

The enormity of the situation settled in as Jasmine realized that if Mariel had not left Diego she would have been assassinated, along with the other wife and family.

"God looked out for me back then," Mariel said softly. "And he looked out for my son, too."

Jasmine stood up. She paced, driven by nervous energy and apprehension.

Negative feelings about her own invasion of privacy lingered, but personal insults somehow paled after what she had just heard. It had to be true. Noah had been planning some sort of military coup to take Cielo Vista back. But why had his own wife betrayed him? No wonder his brain had erected a mental block. The things that were possibly expected of him were enormous. Could he still do it? Would he? Did she want him to do it? And just where did she fit into this larger-than-life picture anyway?

"I had so much to say," she murmured aloud. "But what you've told me has kind of . . . well, left me speechless. What am I supposed to do?"

"Just continue doing what you are doing. However, I must warn you that Aaron doesn't think your relationship with my son is a good idea. He thought it would be over the minute Noah left the hospital and that he would stay here with me until his memory returned. He wasn't anticipating that he would return to you."

"I guess that explains why Aaron hasn't gone out of his way to meet me," Jasmine said.

"Aaron is intensely military minded and brilliant, but he is clueless when it comes to matters of the heart."

"Maybe we're all clueless. Everyone, that is, except you." Jasmine sat back down abruptly. "How do you do it? I mean, how do you have such strong faith and conviction? I used to believe in God once, but I don't think he ever really cared about me as an individual. Terrible things always happened. I know I'm not the only one who has lived through terrible things, but I accidentally killed my sister's baby. Dawn was only two years old. I loved her. She was so alive and cute and . . ."

"And you're angry at yourself and at God for allowing it to happen?"

"I *was* angry at myself. I still am, but I'm starting to accept what I can't change. As far as God is concerned, I just don't know. I probably shouldn't blame him, but then the question that must run through the minds of a lot of people stays there. If God created people in his image, why is there so much sadness, cruelty and violence in the world?"

"I can go into a lot of theological reasoning beginning with Adam and Eve as to why that is so, but I suspect you don't want to hear that at this time," Mariel said. She continued, "Noah told me that you are an architect."

"I was," Jasmine said, wondering what that had to do with the conversation.

"As an architect, don't you give your clients instructions on how to maintain any building you might design?"

"Yes."

"Well, suppose the client ignored all your knowledgeable instructions and just went about doing everything the way they wanted to because it seemed right and felt right to them. When the building collapsed and fell apart, would it be fair for the client to blame you, the architect?"

Jasmine had to laugh. "You're very good. I see where you're going with this, and you definitely make a valid point." She glanced at the clock and noticed there were only two hours before she and Noah would be leaving. "I'm really glad we had this talk. Thank you for not keeping me completely in the dark about Noah's situation and for the other encouraging things you've said. You've given me a lot to think about."

Mariel slowly came from behind the desk and the two women embraced. "Things may be tough, but God has made you a lot stronger than you think you are. Please don't give up on Him or on Noah."

CHAPTER 13

From the window of the Jeep, Jasmine could see that the plane waiting on the tarmac was a large, stripped-down Douglas DC-10, silver, with three red stripes on its massive sides and the Avian International logo prominently displayed. Noah parked the Jeep in front of a warehouse adjacent to the airfield. He got out and came around to her side to open the door.

She stepped out into blinding sunlight and heat so fierce and penetrating that she instantly felt like a wilted flower. The warehouse door swung open, and a man of large stature, dressed in khakis, came out and approached them. Jasmine blinked. He was slightly taller than Noah and more solidly built.

"Jasmine, this is Aaron Weiss, my friend and business partner," Noah announced.

Aaron extended a hand and Jasmine took it, immediately imagining how it must feel to be a Chihuahua suddenly confronted by a Great Dane. His grip was solid, firm and a bit unnerving. His eyes, as dark and infinite as the midnight sky, were set in a swarthy complexion that also showcased harshly chiseled features. His black hair was tightly curled, with streaks of silver running through it. He was not smiling.

Having been forewarned, she was not overly intimidated by his presence, but she was surprised to note that he was biracial, a combination of Jewish and African blood.

"Ahh, a beautiful woman. I should have anticipated no less," he said, assessing her.

"If that's a compliment, thank you," she said with a clipped smile, releasing his hand. The way he looked at her was humiliating, not because it was sexually insinuating, but because it was judgmental.

Noah placed a hand lightly on her shoulder. "It's getting late," he said to Aaron. "Let's go."

Aaron nodded in agreement, and they strode across the field to the waiting aircraft. Its powerful engines were already running, and they climbed up the boarding stairs. The forward interior space consisted of the flight crew cabin, where Aaron as pilot entered, and a small two-seat area for any additional passengers, along with a bathroom and a narrow galley. The rest of the space was devoted to the top priority, cargo.

The flight back to New York took less than two hours. At Stewart airport in Newburgh a rented limo was waiting and took them back to Brooklyn, where Noah reclaimed his SUV from a parking garage. He drove her to her apartment building.

Jasmine felt totally disoriented to be right back in front of the ugly urban building she had called home for the last two years. The stark surroundings disturbed her, and she felt trapped and vulnerable.

"You're very quiet," Noah said as they sat in the car.

"Are you coming in with me?" she asked.

"I'll walk you to the door but I can't stay. I have some . . ."

"Business to take care of," she finished for him.

They got out of the car and walked up the chipped concrete steps, past a bunch of laughing, loitering teens who should have been in school. One of them ogled her. She ignored it. Once inside, Noah pushed the button for the elevator.

"Why does Aaron find me so offensive?" she asked abruptly.

Noah didn't even blink. "I told you it's not totally about you. He's like that with most people."

"By people, you mean women. Is it that he's chauvinistic and believes that females shouldn't be privy to any kind of important information?"

"Maybe. Is this elevator always so slow?"

"Sometimes it doesn't come at all. Noah, you never mentioned that Aaron was biracial."

Noah looked slightly amused. "Should I have? I didn't realize it was important."

Jasmine laughed in spite of herself. "You're right. It's not important. I don't even know why I said that. Maybe it's jet lag and the contrast between here and South Carolina."

The elevator door groaned open and they stepped in. It began its maddeningly slow ascent. "Aaron's mother was African, from Cielo Vista," Noah said. "She died a long time ago, soon after he was born. His father took him back to Israel, where he grew up."

She made no further comment, but silently thanked him for continuing the conversation. Aaron's background explained why he had ties to Cielo Vista.

The elevator finally reached her floor, and she nearly gagged on the lingering odor of cigarettes and burnt food in the hallway. A naked light bulb overhead flickered, about to go out.

"I hope you're thinking seriously about finding a better, safer place to live," Noah said as he took both of her hands in his while they stood near her door.

"I'm thinking about a lot of things," she murmured.

He kissed her, a promising kiss—not brotherly—yet not overly passionate either. She wanted to return it. Boy, did she want to return it, with no holds barred. But instead she gave him a peck on the cheek.

"I'll be calling you," he said. "Take care of Morgan."

She watched him walk away. His walk was brisk, purposeful, the stride of a man who knew exactly where he was going and what he was going to do.

She entered her apartment and shook her head. Where was all of this going to lead? She didn't mind being helpful to his recovery, but the possibility of being used and discarded like an old garment when he actually did recover still bothered her. "I'm a person, too," she murmured aloud to herself. "A person who used to have hopes and dreams. Maybe I still do."

She wished Noah had stayed, but she couldn't blame him for preferring a hotel room. Coming from an upper middle class family, after all, it must have been terribly uncomfortable for him to stay in this squalor. The guest room alone in Mariel's South Carolina home was as big as most of her cubicle of an apartment.

Time was moving on. It was already a little past noon. Morgan would probably stop by after school and stay for supper. What was she going to have? She went to the kitchen and opened the refrigerator. Thanks to Noah's visits, it was well stocked. She took out a package of frozen ground beef and left it on the counter to thaw out. From the cabinet she removed a jar of tomato sauce and a box of pasta. Spaghetti sounded like a good idea.

As she left the kitchen, she noticed for the first time a purple-crayoned note that had been shoved under the door. She picked it up and read it. It was from Morgan. The child had written that she was being good and going to school. She also mentioned that she couldn't wait for her to come back because she had a lot of stuff to tell her. Jasmine smiled at the way it was phrased, but then she stopped to read over and over again the last lines: "I wish you were my mommy. Tell Mr. Noah I like him, too."

She put the note down. *I wish you were my mommy.* The words lingered. A flashback of Dawn played in her head. *Stop it,* she told herself. *Don't go there again.* There was nothing *that* profound about what Morgan had written. With a mother like Rachel, anybody would seem great in comparison. Even her.

"Jasmine!"

"Morgan!"

She wrapped her arms around the little girl, lifting her off the floor. They both laughed. Morgan was wearing a boyish baseball cap and raggedy jeans with a blue sweater that probably belonged to one of the other kids because it was way too big.

"You look really pretty," Morgan exclaimed in awe, touching the thin braids, "like Alicia Keys."

"Thanks, sweetie. I had this done at the hair salon."

"Could you come to my school on Friday night? It's Parents' Night. All the mommies and daddies come to see what the kids do."

"I'd . . ." Jasmine stopped herself. "Did you ask Rachel?"

Morgan frowned. "I don't want Rachel to go."

Jasmine hated herself for having to say it, but she felt compelled to. "But don't you think it would be kind of nice to ask her anyway?"

"My teacher sent her a inva . . . inva . . ."

"Invitation?"

"Yeah. And she threw it out. She didn't even read it."

Jasmine grimaced in contempt. "Well, I guess I'll see what I can do, but I can't promise you because I might have to work that night."

Morgan looked disappointed. Jasmine did not want to dwell on the inevitable at the moment. "Guess what we're having for supper tonight?"

"Pizza?" Morgan asked hopefully.

Jasmine laughed. "No, silly. We can't have pizza all the time. We're having spaghetti."

Morgan beamed. "I like spaghetti when you make it."

"Good. Take off that hat and let's . . ." She reached for the hat, and Morgan's hands instinctively flew up to hold it there.

Jasmine looked at her in puzzlement. "What? Why don't you want to take off the hat?"

Morgan stared down at her feet. "You're not gonna like it," she said. "It looks bad."

"Is it because you didn't comb your hair? That's not a problem. I'll fix it."

Morgan slowly removed the cap and a short, unruly tumble of curls sprang out. Her once-beautiful long hair had been cut into a curly mop like Orphan Annie's.

Jasmine's heart sank. "Morgan, why did you cut your hair like that?"

"I didn't," Morgan said, her lips trembling, tears forming in her eyes as Jasmine inspected it. "Rachel did. She said it was 'cause she was tired of fixing it. Now I look like a boy."

Jasmine bit her lip. It was difficult to control her angry reaction. She wanted to strangle Rachel. She had been totally responsible for the child for only three days, and she couldn't even deal with something as simple as hair. All she had to do was braid it.

"I'm sorry she did that to you," Jasmine said. "But it's not true. You're way too pretty to look like a boy. We'll just see what can be done with this." She ran her fingers through the uneven, tousled curls. "I might have to cut it a little more to make it even, but I promise you'll still be pretty and it will grow back."

Morgan sulked. "You look like a princess, and I look ugly. I want my hair to be long again, like yours."

"It will grow back," Jasmine said with a sigh. "But you'll have to be patient. It takes a while."

Morgan tugged on a straggling curl. "You mean like my tooth? Mr. Noah told me my tooth would grow back and it did. Look." She opened her mouth so that Jasmine could see the brand new tooth emerging.

"Yes, just like your tooth. In the meantime, come with me to the kitchen. You can help me cook."

Morgan followed eagerly.

When Morgan was asleep on the cot next to her bed, Jasmine went to the living room and dialed Valerie's number. "Val, I told you it wouldn't be another year."

"Jasmine, I'm going to strangle you. Why did you hang up on me last time? I want to know your address in Brooklyn and your phone number."

"I'm sorry about last time, but I was kind of in shock. I'll give you my number if you promise not to give it to Natalie."

"Still not ready to deal with her?"

"No. Not yet."

"If it means anything, Natalie told me to tell you again that she's really sorry about what she said to you and that the whole nightmare was just a terrible, terrible accident. She also said *she's* responsible for what happened to Dawn."

"*She's* responsible?" Jasmine echoed. "She wasn't driving that car. I was."

"She said she was responsible, too, because Dawn was her baby and she should have been watching her."

Jasmine swallowed hard. For a moment, she wondered if Valerie had just made that up as a ploy to get the two sisters back together. The Natalie she knew thought the whole world owed her a living and she never took responsibility, even partially, for anything that went wrong. On the other hand, it was not typical of Valerie to be untruthful.

"Tell you what." Jasmine hesitated. "How about you giving me Natalie's number so I can call her when I'm ready."

"Good idea," Valerie agreed, reciting the number while Jasmine wrote it down. "So, tell me. What's going on? When am I going to see you?"

"Well, I'm not sure when we can meet just yet. As for the what's going on part, you wouldn't believe me if I told you."

"Girl, are you holding out on me? Does this have something to do with a man?"

"Kind of."

"Stop messing with me. There's either a man or there isn't."

Jasmine laughed. "I'm not messing with you. The situation is very complicated. If it ever straightens out, then I'll be able to talk about it."

"You always did know how to drive me crazy."

They both laughed. The conversation, mostly about the past, lasted for nearly an hour, until Jasmine finally ended it on a positive note. She said she had a few more things to work out, but she would reconnect again. She gave Valerie her phone number.

CHAPTER 14

Noah stood in a blinding shaft of light piercing the arched cathedral window. He felt the sunlight on his face as he stood still and listened, but there was nothing to hear other than the sounds of birds and the rustling of leaves. He frowned. It had probably been a bad idea to come back here alone.

He moved away from the window, his footsteps abnormally loud on the hardwood floor. He stopped in a room that looked to have been an office, then turned and walked toward the stairs. He ascended them slowly and hesitated at the second floor landing. A familiar throb had started right between his eyes. He raised his hand to his forehead and stood still with his eyes shut. The pain dulled. He remained rooted there.

He had spent the last two days traveling with Aaron on runs to Ecuador and Colombia. Aaron had allowed him to pilot the jet even though the FAA had not given him health clearance to do so. However, the risky experiment had gone without a hitch. He'd known instinctively everything about the instrument panel, and his takeoffs and landings had been textbook perfect. It was good to know that when he was declared fit he'd at least have a job again. But still the memory block persisted and somehow he was sure the answer lay here, here inside this Ramapo mountain house that he'd had built when Isabella was his wife.

He moved slowly with his eyes shut, groping like a blind person. In the darkness he heard echoes of the voices two years ago. Every sound. Every nuance. He remembered being tired. He had come home unexpectedly from Panama because a scheduled run to the Canary Islands had been canceled. The moment he had entered the house, he had known something was wrong. He had walked quietly up the stairs and stood on this same second floor landing near the closed door of his bedroom, listening to the uninhibited sighs, heavy breathing and muffled laughter. He couldn't believe it. Didn't want to believe it.

He'd flung open the bedroom door and was met with a gasp and two sets of shocked, guilt-stricken eyes. He remembered it now, as if it were happening at the moment. Isabella was clinging to the beige sheets, her gold hair disheveled, her mouth forming a curious "O" shape. The man's expression reflected both guilt and haughty justification simultaneously. Instantly Noah's attention had riveted on him alone, and Isabella had ceased to even exist.

"Noah, don't," the man had said. "I know how this looks, but face the truth. You knew it all along. I . . ."

"Shut up and get dressed!"

He'd slammed the door on the now strangely absurd scene and stood there, teeth clenched, trying to let go of his rage, trying to control it. It was true; he and Isabella were having problems, and a lot of his feelings for her had died a long time ago, but he was certain it was the factor of who the man was that had fed his rage more than his wife's infidelity.

"Noah, I know this is awkward, but let's be reasonable," the man had said, now dressed and facing him in the living room. "You told me that you and Isabella were getting a divorce. You knew that I was the one she—"

The rage exploded. He hit the man so hard that he slammed into the wall, making a dent in it. The fool tried to escape, but when Noah blocked his way, he cowered in the corner, raising an arm, trying to shield himself from the blows.

Isabella had stayed locked in the bedroom, yelling in vain for him to stop. Her lover had been no match for his strength or the depth of his rage. He'd wanted to kill him with his bare hands. He could have, but he didn't. The voice of reason and conscience had stopped him. He was not a killer.

He'd watched the man stagger, bloodied, to his feet and make his exit like a defeated animal with its tail tucked between its legs.

With his heart racing, Noah opened his eyes and stared into the bedroom. It was now nothing but a large vacant space, dappled with innocuous sunlight and dust motes. He wiped the sweat from his forehead, realizing that he no longer had even the vague trace of a headache.

He remembered who the man was.

Late in the evening, Jasmine was about to enter her apartment, having returned from one of her cleaning jobs, when her name was called. She turned to see Rachel standing in the hallway. The woman had a scarf around her head and was wearing a bulky turtleneck with a pair of black jeans. Her eyes had their usual glaze, but she didn't look as hideous as she had the last time they'd spoken. "Jasmine, we gotta talk."

"What about?" She was not at all in the mood for a conversation with her.

"There's something you have to tell Morgan, 'cause I can't."

"Tell her what?" With difficulty, Jasmine tried not to sound too sarcastic.

"Her grandmother died."

Jasmine's breath caught in her throat. She had known it was coming, but even knowing didn't lessen the impact. "When? This morning?" It was all she could say.

"No, it was about four or five days ago. The aide who took care of her told me and—"

"Four or five days ago!" Jasmine shouted. "And you haven't told her yet? Did they have the funeral already?"

"Probably. Look, I know it sounds bad, but I couldn't tell her, and you know I wasn't going to that woman's funeral. She wouldn't have wanted me there no way."

Jasmine seethed with anger. "Where is Morgan now?"

"She's two floors down, staying overnight with a friend from school."

"Well, I think it's about time you told her. Do I have to keep reminding you that you're her mother?"

"She likes you. If I tell her I'll only make the problem worse 'cause like I said before, I hated that woman. I'm not going to be able to be . . . um . . . sympathetic like you would be," Rachel said stupidly.

Jasmine sighed in frustration. Rachel was definitely right about that. But every day she hated more and more the invasion of her privacy. She loathed the idea of having to tell Morgan such bad news, and she really shouldn't even have to.

"All right, you win. I'll tell her . . . this time. But this whole situation is just going too far. You are going to have to start taking more responsibility for your own daughter. It's not my job. I have a life. I have other things to do."

"I can sure see that," Rachel said slowly, as if tasting the words. "You now looking all pretty like Miss Thang, messin' around with that hunky white man. And don't tell me he's Puerto Rican and he's from around here 'cause I know he ain't."

"The nerve of you! My personal life is none of your business!"

"Maybe it ain't, but does your personal life mean that you're just gonna walk outta here one day and leave that child heartbroken? She can be real difficult sometimes. You know what I'm sayin? She's doing kind of good in school right now; if you decide to shut her out she'll probably go crazy. I might have to put her in a home someplace."

Jasmine was so angry she was almost dizzy from the sting of Rachel's words. How hypocritical could another human being get? "Maybe that's what you should do!" she shouted. "Maybe you *should* put her in a home. She'd probably be better off there than with you. You're the most miserable excuse for a mother I've ever heard of."

The words were out, and how cruel they sounded. She didn't completely mean everything she'd just said— or did she? Somehow during the course of the conversation, her relationship with her own mother had gotten into it. Morgan did not deserve to be discussed in that manner.

Rachel spun around on her heel and marched back to her own apartment, slamming the door. Jasmine lingered in the hallway for a few moments, trying to sort out her feelings. She folded her hands together and clenched them.

"Dear God," she prayed aloud. "Please forgive me. I'm only human and I can't control what goes on in the lives of others. I can't even control my own life. Please, if you're hearing this, please give that little girl the strength to deal with this. Please protect her. I will do what I can."

Jasmine silently brushed Morgan's hair into two short, curly ponytails, helping her prepare for school. She secured the hair with plaid ribbons. Her mind was really not on what she was doing because she was worried about what Morgan's reaction would be upon hearing about her grandmother's death, and she was thinking about Noah. A week had gone by and she hadn't heard a word from him. Had he finally moved on and left her behind as she'd imagined he would?

"Why are you sad?" Morgan asked, jolting her back to the present.

"You think I'm sad?" she questioned, offering a faint smile. "Why do you think that?"

"You're not talking, and you're not smiling at all."

She smiled genuinely now. "Morgan, you know that people aren't happy all the time. Sometimes we feel like the weather. Look out the window. It looks all gray outside, and it's probably going to rain."

"I'm sad, too, sometimes, like the sky," Morgan said. "It's getting ready to cry, but it can't make up its mind if it really wants to yet."

"I think it will," Jasmine said, half to herself.

"But when it stops crying the sun will come out and all the tears will go away and there will be this big, big sparkly rainbow," Morgan said, spreading her arms to emphasize the size of it.

Jasmine hugged her. "Has anyone ever told you what a great kid you are? You're like a little poet."

"Grandma told me that and you told me," Morgan said. "I miss her, but I'm not going to cry."

Jasmine blinked. "You miss her because you can't go to her house?"

Morgan frowned slightly. "No. She's not there anymore. She's dead."

Jasmine exhaled sharply "Rachel told you."

"Rachel doesn't know anything. Grandma told me herself."

"When?" Jasmine asked incredulously.

"I don't remember, but you were gone with Mr. Noah. Grandma whispered to me at night when I was sleeping and woked me up. She told me to be brave and not to cry. She said she didn't feel sick anymore and that things would be okay and special guardians would protect me."

Guardians? The lump in Jasmine's throat thickened. "Morgan, y-you dreamed this?"

"I didn't dream," Morgan said. "Grandma was there."

"I believe you. And your grandmother was right. Guardian angels will protect you." It was all Jasmine could say. There was no logic to it, but who was she to question the child's unwavering belief that she had seen her grandmother? *Thank You*, she mouthed silently to the heavens. *Thank You for not forcing me to be the one to tell her.*

"Jasmine, do you remember that red sweater you bought for me?"

"The special one?"

"Yeah. Can I wear it today? Please?"

"You sure can. Let's go get it."

Three days later, Rachel stood in her doorway. "I know you don't want to talk to me, but I just want to apologize."

Jasmine stepped outside her door because she was not about to invite Rachel in. She had to admit, however, that the woman actually looked sincere for a change.

"Just thought you'd like to know that I ain't got no man anymore. I threw Victor out 'cause he hated my kids, especially Morgan. He told me that she was possessed like that kid in the exorcist movie. Ain't gonna be with no man who don't accept my kids. What I'm saying is that things are gonna change. You were telling the truth when you said I was a bad mother."

"Getting rid of Victor is a good start," Jasmine said.

"From now on, I'm not going to be always sending Morgan over to you. I'm gonna pay more attention to her."

Jasmine took a deep breath and resisted rolling her eyes. She hated always being taken for granted, but at the same time there was no way she could just turn off her own feelings and separate from the child.

"If you're serious about taking responsibility, you should do it gradually. You can't all of a sudden tell Morgan that she can't come to my place anymore."

"I hear what you're saying," Rachel interrupted. "It ain't gonna happen tomorrow. I do know some stuff about psychology. It's gonna take a while before she trusts me."

"It will also help if you do something about your . . . er . . . substance abuse problem," Jasmine said dryly.

"I ain't no junkie, if that's what you're thinking. Sure, I've smoked a little weed, and I drink a little from time to time, but I don't do hard stuff, and right now I'm clean."

Yes, yes, whatever, Jasmine thought. "I'm glad you're willing to work at it, Rachel, but I really can't keep talking right now because I have to go out."

"Oh. I'll come back when you got some time."

Jasmine said goodbye, stepped back inside, and breathed a sigh of relief that the conversation had ended. How could she trust Rachel? The woman probably hadn't meant a word she'd said, and even if she did, how could she just walk out of Morgan's life now?

CHAPTER 15

"I'm so glad to see you," Jasmine exclaimed, joyously enfolding Noah in a tight embrace. He bent his head down and, without reservation, planted a sizzling, seductive kiss on her partially open lips. The magnetic charge of his kiss drew her in and she almost forgot to breathe as she raked her fingers through his dark hair, wishing he'd never stop.

"For a while, I thought you weren't coming back," she murmured.

His eyes twinkled. "You of so little faith." He held her at arm's length. "My, aren't you a sight for sore eyes? I'm pleased you didn't revert to your old ways while I was gone."

"Believe me, I was tempted. Come on . . . sit down. Tell me what you've been doing." She led him into the living room, captivated by the warm, strong grip of his hand in hers. She couldn't help noticing that he looked leaner and tired.

Noah took note of her silvery V-necked sweater and snug designer jeans that molded perfectly to her slender, long-legged body. He liked the breezy, confident way she walked as she held his hand leading him to the couch. There was a difference in the room, too. It looked a lot more inviting with colorful new curtains, a new rug, new lamps and artwork on the walls.

"Did you go back to South Carolina?" she asked.

"No. I was mostly between three airports: JFK, Newark and Stewart."

"Doing what?"

"Trying to acclimate myself. I went on a few international flights with Aaron and discovered that at least I still know how to fly a plane."

"That's great."

"I'm remembering things. The things are not all good, but they're coming back gradually."

"So when does the rational side of your brain ask you what you're doing in this ghetto with this woman?"

"There you go again. When that side returns, it will mean that I'm brain dead. Can we get off this?"

"I was just kidding. You don't have to take everything I say so seriously."

She said the words, but of course he was correct to take her seriously. She would be completely naive to totally trust him at this point. The day she took him completely at his word would be the day his memory was fully restored and he was telling her that he still wanted to be with her.

"How's Morgan?"

"As cute as ever. She's been asking about Mr. Noah a lot. There is sad news, though."

"Tell me."

She told him about the inevitable passing of Mrs. Garcia and Morgan's almost mystical response to it. Noah didn't seem overly surprised by what he heard. He just listened quietly and nodded. Finally he spoke.

"Are you working tonight?"

"No," she said flatly. "I'm off."

His abrupt change of conversation irritated her a little. She had expected him to comment more on the events surrounding Morgan. He had listened with undivided attention, but he was acting as if what had happened was somehow normal and to be expected.

"How about dinner in Manhattan and a show?"

"I can't. It's Friday. I promised Morgan I'd take her to the mall after school."

Noah shrugged. "Oh well, can't say I didn't try."

"I'm sorry. I mean, I really would have liked to go."

"You don't have to apologize. Your child is supposed to be a priority."

"My child? Noah, what are you talking about? You know she's not my child."

Noah didn't say anything. He just laughed. She slapped him. "I do know what *your* priority is, wise guy. You need a decent meal and some rest. You look like you haven't slept for days."

"I don't think I can argue with that," he said.

"Jasmine, do you want to listen to my story?" Morgan asked in the morning.

"Sure. Go get it."

Morgan raced to the bedroom to get her backpack. Jasmine was in the process of washing the breakfast dishes. The TV was on in the living room and Noah was there, stretched out on the couch, half watching. He had spent the night at her place again. He'd slept there, and that was all.

Noah deserved better than what she was offering him, Jasmine thought. She was giving him good reason to walk out of her life because most of her attention seemed to be focused on Morgan and, for that reason, the child's presence aggravated her at the moment. But how could she tell a needy child to get lost?

"My story got first prize," Morgan said, beaming as she opened a notebook. "My teacher thinks I'm smart again."

"I'm glad she does, but we knew that all the time."

"Anyway, she wants me to bring it back to class 'cause she's gonna display it so everyone can see it."

"That's terrific. I'm so proud of you. Read it aloud so I can hear."

"Once upon a time, there was a little girl named Maya who lived on a beautiful island," Morgan began. "Maya's island had a beautiful blue ocean and tall, tall mountains that could touch the clouds. She had a pretty mommy and a handsome daddy who was the king of the island. There were lions and tigers and zebras and they all lived happy together. The sun was always shining and no one ever cried and no one was ever sad.

"One day, bad people came to the island. They found Maya playing in the water with her dolphins and they took her far away. The dolphins cried and the island got dark and ugly. All the people got angry and no one smiled. The mountains began to smoke—"

"The mountains did what?" Noah entered the kitchen with the most intense look Jasmine had ever seen. She turned to stare at him in surprise.

"The mountains smoked," Morgan repeated, pleased to have additional audience.

"Why did they do that?" Noah asked.

"They were very, very angry. Smoke came out and fire—"

"Jasmine," Noah interrupted, his voice a loud whisper, "I have to go now."

"What are you talking about? Go where?" Jasmine stepped toward him with concern and trepidation in her eyes.

"Home. I'm going home."

"Noah, please."

He said nothing. He left the kitchen, grabbed his jacket and swiftly exited the apartment. Jasmine rushed to the door. "Wait!"

"It's all right. He *has* to go," Morgan said behind her, tugging at her sleeve.

Bewildered, Jasmine turned to look at the child. "He has to go where?"

"Back to Cielo Vista," she answered plaintively. "Jasmine, are you gonna finish listening to my story or what?"

Noah was gone. It was as simple as that, and Jasmine didn't have a clue what to do about it besides worry. The following day she tried calling Mariel, hoping that maybe he'd simply returned to South Carolina, but all she got was voice mail telling her to leave a message. She did, but no one ever got back to her. She also considered contacting Aaron at Avian International until it occurred to her that he probably already knew where Noah was, and if she questioned him, he'd no doubt advise her to stop worrying and mind her own business—something she did not want to hear. How could she not worry, especially when she didn't know if Noah was in his right mind?

She began spending most of her free mornings in the library, surfing the Internet for any material she could find about Cielo Vista. The country was described as geographically beautiful, with mountains, beaches and rainforest. Once it had been a major tourist attraction, but now it was off the beaten path because of political instability. In fact, there were only two major hotels, one in the capital city and another on an adjoining island. The majority of people were black Africans from various tribes. They were an impoverished people, dwelling in shantytowns and in the forests. The elite class, mostly Europeans, had beautiful gated homes in the capital city of Montalvo. There was no middle class. She was surprised to read that diamonds were currently the country's most profitable export, although there were indications that the supply was being depleted. The scenario made her cringe because it reminded her of South Africa under apartheid.

Things had been different under the reign of Diego Arias, Noah's father. The country's economy had been driven by tourism and agriculture and the majority of people had been farmers. They had not been wealthy, but not impoverished, either. In contrast, Alejandro Arias's tyranny had amassed great wealth for himself and his allies, but none of it had gone to the people.

Jasmine turned off the computer and leaned back in the chair. Her heart was telling her what she wanted to do. Noah had gone out of his way to find her, and now it was her turn. But how could she when Morgan needed her? She squeezed her eyes shut, searching her soul. Morgan was needy, but maybe she was letting the situation get too out of control. The simple fact remained that Morgan was not her child and her personal involvement could and should be limited. Rachel had said she was willing to work at being a better mother, and so far she was trying. It was also possible that her own interference might prevent Rachel from being effective.

The train of thought stuck with her, justifying her next move. Of course, there was no guarantee that she would even be able to locate Noah, but she was going to make a trip to Cielo Vista. And nothing was going to stop her.

CHAPTER 16

The plane touched down in the capital city of Montalvo. As Jasmine wandered dazedly around the airport, she questioned her own sanity. People of varying nationalities moved all around her, speaking mostly Spanish and French. It was nine o'clock in the morning Cielo Vista time, five hours ahead of U.S. time.

There had been no direct flights from the United States and now she was completely jet-lagged from flying from New York to Madrid, and from Madrid to Cielo Vista. To add to her misery, she'd learned that her luggage was lost. It was a good thing she hadn't packed anything of great value. She consoled herself with the knowledge that at least she had her essentials in her carry-on bag. Her passport was valid and she didn't need a visa for a short stay.

Having gotten her bearings, she stepped up to the counter and exchanged some of her American dollars for the country's currency at the airport's conveniently located bank outlet. After that, using her limited knowledge of French, because it was better than her Spanish, she made a call from the lobby for a taxi to take her to the only hotel in Montalvo.

It was hot and uncomfortably humid as she slid into the waiting cab. A peculiar odor that suggested some kind of chemical burning permeated the air. She felt overdressed, wearing a ridiculous ankle-length floral-printed skirt, a white cotton blouse, sensible-heeled pumps and a silk scarf on her head. She had chosen what she was wearing over jeans and sandals because she'd read that the women of Cielo Vista were expected to dress modestly at all times, and modesty in that country meant traditional women's attire. She had complied because she definitely did not want to attract any attention. Little did they know that she was wearing a pair of white capris under the skirt, which she was dying to remove.

The taxi was a late model European make, driven by a handsome, ebony-skinned African man about her own age who actually spoke heavily-accented English.

"So you are in Cielo Vista on business, no?" he asked.

"Yes," she said, not wanting to engage him in conversation.

"Not many Americans come here," he said.

So it's that obvious I'm American, she thought irritably. "Why do you think that is?" she asked.

"The government," he said. "Your country no longer has any interests here. When I was a young boy, we used to have American and British tourists all the time."

"Is that so?" She fanned herself with a magazine that was on the worn seat near her.

Noticing, he rolled down both front windows. "I am sorry I don't have air conditioning in the car."

"It's all right," she said, offering a slight smile. "Can't have everything."

The business district was actually not much different from any other main street. It was pleasant, with buildings incorporating Spanish architecture. Some of the buildings needed restoration, but nothing was as primitive as she'd expected. People, predominantly Caucasians, walked in and out of establishments dressed in business attire. The women, she noticed, were dressed modestly; no female wore pantsuits.

"Do you live here in Montalvo?" she asked the driver. When he laughed, she realized she had asked something foolish.

"Oh, no. We only come here to work. Only the wealthy live here. I am from Rio Mundo. It's an island outside of the city. Perhaps you will find time to visit there."

She now remembered from her reading that only the Europeans lived in the capital city and its suburbs.

"I would love to visit Rio Mundo," she said, finding herself warming up to him a little. "I'm not going to be here very long, but I'd like to squeeze it in."

"You will find it a very interesting island," he said. "It is beautiful, too, if you like beaches. Most of my family are fishermen. My name is Hassan, by the way."

She told him that her name was Angela, not sure why she chose not to tell the truth. They had pulled up in front of a large, modern hotel, which was actually walking distance from the airport. As she reached into her wallet to pay him, a warm gust of wind brought the peculiar scent back to her. She wrinkled her nose.

"Hassan, what *is* that smell?"

He looked puzzled at first, and then he laughed. "You mean that odor in the air like something burning?" "Yes, exactly. It's like sulfur."

"That's from good old Mount Cielo. She is a volcanic mountain, and every now and then she lets off some steam."

"Isn't that dangerous?"

"Oh no, not at all. She has been doing it for hundreds of years. The last major eruption was probably back in the seventeenth century. Geologists go up there from time to time to check. There is nothing to worry about."

He came around to open the door for her. She paid him and gave him a good tip. Nervously, she entered the hotel's lobby. The frigid blast of air conditioning was welcome.

"Could you tell me if Daniel Viera is staying in this hotel?" she asked the clerk at the desk, using Noah's bogus name.

The clerk, a man of mixed heritage, looked bored. "I'm sorry, mademoiselle, but I am not able to give out that information."

"I'm aware of the hotel's policy, but he is expecting me. I have very important business with him. There was a mix-up over where we were to meet." She showed him a significant amount of cash.

Instantly, the man's eyes registered interest. "Room 500 on the fifth floor."

Jasmine's heart skipped a beat as she gave him the money. It had been a long shot, but it had worked out— or had it? Maybe there was another Daniel Viera in the hotel. She was just going to have to find out. After all, who was to say that God wasn't maneuvering things?

She was escorted to her own room on the second floor. It was a basic room with a bed, a bath and a small kitchenette. She scowled, remembering that she had nothing to unpack since she was minus her suitcase. She should probably stop at one of the boutiques in town to pick out some clothes.

The first thing she did was indulge in a long, hot shower. After that, she collapsed on the bed. She figured she would take a quick nap and then go up to room 500 in about an hour to find out if Noah really was there.

The hour turned into several. By the time she woke up, the room was dark. Alarmed, she switched on the bedside lamp and at first had no clue where she was. When it finally dawned on her, she shook her head in dismay. The clock announced that it was approaching midnight. Something had to be wrong. But the clock in the kitchenette said the same thing. She really had slept for almost twelve hours.

Noah stirred restlessly on the bed in his hotel room. He had spent the entire week traversing the country, a country he now remembered as clearly as his own reflection. He also remembered his purpose and the fact that Mariel had been right about everything. There wasn't much time before the window of opportunity God was granting him would close.

Normally only an occasional social drinker, he'd indulged in quite a few earlier in the evening and was now regretting it because the effect of the alcohol was disorienting. It made him feel angrier and more vengeful than he could afford to. It didn't matter that his rage was justified. He knew from past experience that strong emotions only got in the way and were capable of sabotaging even the best-made plans.

Just being here in Montalvo was a risky move because the chances of having his cover blown were much greater here than anywhere else in the country. It would have made more sense to have remained at the much preferred, low-key family-run hotel in Rio Mundo. Even when he was a child, he had always hated the capital city and its governmental estate, preferring the vast natural beauty of the sea, the land and its indigenous people.

He was taking the risk because the next day, President Alejandro Arias and his cohorts were hosting a media-crazed political rally at the hotel, and out of malicious mockery and perhaps a bit of masochism, he wanted to be in the crowd so he could look at the man who had defiled the land and stained it red with his father's blood. He especially wanted to cast his eyes upon Isabella for the last time and truly see her for what she was, a traitor and the wife of Rafael Arias, a murderous piece of scum.

The most devastating blow—even more devastating than finding his wife in bed with Rafael—was coming to grips with the fact that the murderous piece of scum in her bed was his own half-brother, the son of his father's first wife. Aaron's theory was not a theory at all, but a fact. Rafael had tried to kill him. It all made sense now.

Possessing a completely different personality, Noah had never been particularly close to his older brother when they were children, but he'd never taken Rafael's jealousy or their subtle rivalry seriously enough either. It had begun when his father had chosen him to be the heir instead of his older son, for reasons that had been rather obvious. Rafael had been academically challenged and had shown little interest in the important things his father had wanted to teach him about the country. He liked the material fringe benefits of being a prince, but felt there was no responsibility that went along with the title.

Now Noah realized that Rafael must have harbored a burning hatred for their father and could have been secretly pleased when he was assassinated. And all along he'd probably been coveting Isabella, feeling that she rightfully belonged to him, due to a family agreement that stated she would marry the heir. That heir would have been Rafael, had he not been rejected.

Noah felt a surge of exhilaration thinking about what was going to happen in the near future, but along with it there was also a deep sadness, the sadness of knowing that in his previous state of amnesia he had lied to Jasmine. The chances of his actually returning to her were decreasing because there was the very real possibility that he wouldn't even survive.

He closed his eyes and pictured her, a beautiful woman who had been through so much agony and self guilt, yet still managed to retain a powerful dignity and grace—a woman so deeply caring that she had practically adopted a stranger's child. Amidst the coldness and atheism of many in the world, she still wanted desperately to believe in God, even if she didn't understand His ways or His purpose. There were also her feelings for him. Out of all the patients in the nursing home, she had singled him out.

A muffled sound outside the door disturbed his thoughts. He sat up abruptly and listened. It was definitely a knock. He had no friends in Montalvo. There was no reason why anyone would be knocking at the door unless it was one of the hotel staff. Instinctively, he reached for the gun he kept beside the bed. He approached the door sideways, gun drawn. "Who's there?"

"Me," an apprehensive and very familiar female voice answered.

"Jasmine? What in the—" He flung open the door and seized her by the arm, yanking her into the room.

Jasmine gasped in shock at being rudely manhandled by a very strong, unshaven, blond-haired man who looked like Noah. And he was pocketing a gun.

"What *are* you doing here?" he demanded angrily, his gray eyes blazing.

"I . . . I . . ." She swallowed. "What's going on? Your hair? Why do you have a gun?"

"Never mind about that. I can't believe you would do something this stupid."

Recovering from her shock, Jasmine pulled out of Noah's grasp and gave him a look that was nearly as fierce as his own. "I came here because I was worried about you, and I see I have every reason to be. What on earth are you going to do? Do you really think you can take down a government with a stupid gun and a disguise? You . . ."

"Keep your voice down," he said tautly. "What I do is not your concern. What *you* will do is turn your pretty little self around and go right back to New York."

"And suppose I don't?"

"You will. There's nothing for you in this country. You don't belong here and you never will."

"You're going to do something crazy, and you're probably not even in your right mind," she argued.

"Jasmine, look at me."

He seized her by both forearms and their eyes met dead on. "This is not a game. I no longer have amnesia. I remembered everything the day I left . . . the day Morgan read her story. Things have changed between us."

She was silent. He sounded slightly delusional, but the coldness of his eyes was new and penetrating. They resembled Aaron's eyes.

"So," she hesitated, "what you're saying is that we're strangers now?"

"Exactly."

"But . . ." She hesitated again. His icy hands on her arms made her shudder, and she yanked away for the second time. She was beyond hurt and she could feel her eyes welling up with, of all things, tears.

"Go back to your room and make your arrangements to leave in the morning," Noah said. He opened the door.

She did not want him to see her cry. How could she have allowed her heart to make her so stupid? She had known all along that this was going to happen, and now that it had, she was still unprepared for it.

She left the room abruptly without looking back.

CHAPTER 17

Hours later, Noah could not sleep. He felt heartsick, and the reason was obvious. His negative response to Jasmine's arrival was intentional because he wanted to protect her, but his alcohol consumption had done the talking and had contributed to his coming on even more harshly than he'd intended.

He could still see the distraught and stricken expression on Jasmine's beautiful face as she'd left his room. How could he have done such a thing to her after she had been through so much and had traveled so far to find him? He paced the room and then sat down hard on the bed, burying his face in his hands. Was it always necessary to hurt someone you loved in order to protect them? And he did love her. He wasn't even sure what he would do without her. She had become the heart and spirit behind his ambition.

Noah headed for the shower. There wasn't much time left before dawn. He had to move quickly.

At sunrise Jasmine stood in line at the airport, waiting to purchase an earlier return ticket to New York via Madrid. She felt desensitized and hardened. After leaving

Noah she had succumbed to tears in the privacy of the room, but they were long gone and now she felt as cold and empty as the look on his face.

Ironically, it was almost the same feeling she'd had when she'd first moved into the slum in Brooklyn, trying to punish herself for causing Dawn's death. But the focus of her pain was much different this time. This time she was angrier at him than she was at herself. He was nothing but a demented, lying traitor, running around like a fool with a gun—certainly not the kind of person she should associate with. She had known way too many people like that in the past. Oh, it was crazy but she still wanted him—still did, even after what had gone down, but she knew for a fact that she was not going to fall apart over the loss. She could not prevent him from doing whatever he was planning to do. The only thing that really puzzled her was why she had felt so strongly that God wanted her to come here. She guessed she could chalk that up to treachery of the heart and temporary insanity. Yes, the heart could be treacherous. There was a scripture about it in the Bible. She even remembered that it was in Jeremiah 17: 9. Ida Gordon had frequently quoted it to her when she was young.

It didn't matter. She would return to New York, and Noah would be just a bittersweet memory. She would reconnect with Valerie, have that talk with Natalie and try to move on with her life. She would still visit Morgan and try to help her, but she did not plan on remaining in Brooklyn. She would find a better apartment in

Manhattan or the suburbs, and she would possibly try to resume her career. The ache in her heart for both Noah and Dawn would go away eventually. What didn't kill her would make her stronger.

The line was not moving. A man at the counter was arguing loudly with the ticket clerk over his seating arrangement. Jasmine frowned impatiently. A woman in front of her juggled an infant who had just woken up and was starting to scream.

"Excuse me, señorita, your luggage was found."

With a start she looked to see a tall, handsome, blond-haired man holding the familiar suitcase, which had apparently found its way out of some black hole. But it was not the suitcase that held her attention; it was the man who held it. Noah.

"This arrived at the hotel," he said, hesitating slightly. "The concierge gave it to me because you had left already."

"Thank you," she said coldly, taking it and moving farther up in line.

"I didn't come just to deliver a suitcase," he said. "We have to talk."

"I have nothing to say," she replied. "You told me where to go. You were right, and I'm going."

"I wasn't right. I was dead wrong. Please."

She looked at his face. The eyes were no longer like steel; they looked sincere, vulnerable even.

God help me, I'm about to fall again, she thought. She was also aware that it could be potentially dangerous to create a scene in a public place, and if she kept denying him, that's exactly what would happen. Already some people were looking at them curiously. Furious at herself for complying, she stepped out of line and they walked swiftly through the lobby.

"This had better be good," she fumed once they were outside in the parking lot. "Did you see the size of that line? Now I'm going to have get back in . . ."

He kissed her. The kiss was deeply passionate and promising, leaving her silent and breathless.

"I thought about last night," he said slowly. "It would probably still be better if you went home immediately . . ."

"Then why," she interrupted, having found her voice, "why did you stop me? You know how I feel about you. I can't keep playing these games. I'm not going to."

"I can't play games, either," he admitted soberly. "I love you and I want you to know more about this country and why it means so much to me."

"Noah, I don't care about Cielo Vista. I care about you."

"You can't separate the two of us. Now that my memory is back, this country and I are entwined." He slid his arm around her. "If you really care about me, you will stay a little longer so I can show you why this land is in my blood . . . why I can't just walk away from it."

"All right, I'll stay." *I'm going to live to regret this,* she thought.

But the truth was, she knew she had traveled too far and spent way too much money to just turn around and go back home. Plus, he had admitted that he loved her. Would a few more days actually complicate the situation any more than it already was?

Noah had taken her suitcase and was escorting her to his rented Jeep. She somewhat resented the presumptuous way he so quickly assumed that she was going to give in, and resented even more that he was right.

"I'll give you a major tour of some of the scenic spots tomorrow," he said.

Once they were in the Jeep, she looked at him long and hard. "You know, I really liked you much better with black hair."

He laughed. "You'll get used to the weird blond guy while we're here."

Jasmine rubbed her eyes worriedly, still contemplating how foolish she was being. She'd assumed they would be going back to the hotel, but Noah pointed the car in the opposite direction. The road dipped slightly downhill and she gaped at the towering ridge of mist-shrouded mountains that loomed in the distance, the highest peak casting its giant purplish-blue shadow over the city.

"Awesome, aren't they?" Noah commented.

"Spectacular." She took a deep breath. "I've been told that they're volcanic mountains. Yesterday, I could even smell sulfur."

Noah smiled. "The highest peak, Mount Cielo, is the volcano. It's calm today. You don't smell anything now, do you?"

She sniffed the air. "No. I understand that there hasn't been an eruption for hundreds of years, but I can't help thinking that it's really foolish to have a major city right in the path of a volcano."

He smiled again with a hint of mockery. "This city is a good fifty or so miles away, but I agree with you. It is foolish." His eyes twinkled. "Don't write that up as third world mentality, though. Remember that some cities in the United States, in Washington State, for example, lie under Mt. Rainier, which *is* an active volcano."

"That's true," she admitted. "Sometimes I don't understand the mentality of people at all."

Noah nodded, keeping his ironic smile. "I'm being a pessimist, but in due time the whole human race might become extinct because of its own arrogance."

He was driving slower now. "Cast your eyes upon the grand palace."

They'd traveled only about a mile from the airport. Jasmine looked to her right and noticed that they were passing a high stone wall with an elaborate iron gate. Wearing stoic expressions, military personnel stood outside the entrance. In the distance beyond the gate she could see a stately white mansion.

"That's Cielo's version of the White House," Noah said. "Home of Uncle Al, the murderer."

"So this is it? This is the same place where everything happened?"

"Yes. It hasn't changed much. At least not from what I can see of it."

He sounded bitter and she could easily imagine exactly how he was feeling. A feeling of helpless awkwardness overtook her. She glanced toward the mountains again.

"Noah, what was your father like?"

"He was a fool."

Her eyebrows arched as she looked at him questioningly.

"I'm not saying that he wasn't a good person," Noah said. "He was a fool in the sense of being a hopeless dreamer, and dreamers don't always make good rulers. In a leadership position one has to be able to deal with the reality of the moment and at the same time possess the ability to adapt to change. My father couldn't move beyond his own vision and he stupidly fell into the pattern of trusting people because they were family."

Jasmine shook her head. "That's sad. I mean, in an ideal world we do like to think that we can trust family."

He flashed another mocking smile. "I guess you can say the apple doesn't fall far from the tree. I made the same mistake, but it's never going to happen again."

She waited for him to continue, but he focused completely on the road ahead, and she guessed that he was referring to Isabella's betrayal. Isabella. The question lingered in her mind. She wanted to keep it buried there, but it was burning like a hot lump of coal on her tongue.

"Have you seen your ex since you've been here? I mean secretly, without her knowing it."

"I'll get a glimpse of her later this evening."

"What?"

"The president and his flunkies are having some kind of public rally at the hotel. She'll probably be there with her . . . husband."

"I don't believe you," Jasmine exclaimed, disappointed. "Why would you put yourself at risk attending some stupid rally just so you can look at her?"

"They won't recognize me in a crowd of people. I'm also supposed to be dead, remember?"

Jasmine swallowed hard, resisting the urge to tell him to turn the Jeep around and head right back to the airport.

"It's not what you're thinking," he said. "I'm not attending so I can drool over my ex-wife. It's more of a confirmation, a reckoning with everything that's happened in my life. Besides, we'll be together." He reached out with one hand and lightly touched the side of her face "You're just the insurance I need to keep me from doing something reckless."

Something reckless? The words chilled her. She remembered last night in the hotel, his eyes, the gun.

"Noah, you *weren't* really planning to kill . . ."

"I don't know," he interrupted. "I was a bit deranged last night, and I'm still dealing with a lot of anger . . . the vengeful side of me wants payback. I probably wouldn't have pulled anything that suicidal, but now I know for sure I won't."

In the evening, after dinner at a local restaurant that catered to European tastes, Noah and Jasmine returned to the hotel, joining the throngs of people who were standing in the crowded lobby trying to get a glimpse of the president. From their position, which was well in the back, Jasmine scanned the spectators and could pick out only a handful of native Africans amongst them. On the recently erected flag-draped platform, the president stood at the podium with his dignitaries seated behind him. She felt angry, angry for Noah.

The president looked deceptively benign with his silver hair and dignified, polished-for-the-media stance. However, she was sure she would observe some of the coldness lurking within if she were standing closer and able to look into his eyes. She prided herself on being able to read people's hearts by what was in their eyes.

Two women sat with the men behind the president. One of them was older, probably the first lady. The other woman was strikingly beautiful with blonde hair worn in an upsweep; she was wearing an elegant suit. The expression on her face was bland, mannequin-like. Interestingly enough, she did not appear happy.

"Who's the person near Isabella?" she asked, observing the dark-haired, stern countenance of the husky man beside her. "Is that the husband?"

"Yes, that's Rafael Arias, recently appointed deputy minister of the treasury. Never mind that he can't count his fingers and toes."

She felt dizzy. "Rafael?" she whispered. "Rafael is your brother. You . . . you didn't tell me that Isabella ran off with your brother."

"Half-brother," he corrected. "I didn't tell you back in the States because I didn't remember it myself. It was part of my mental block, part of what I didn't want to remember, and what my mother was afraid to tell me because she was worried about what I might do."

Jasmine wanted to turn around and drag him right back upstairs to the hotel room. His rage was even more justified knowing this, and just standing there watching the culprits was borderline masochistic. There were probably even more revelations, and she felt she had a right to know the whole truth about everything if they really were going to have any kind of meaningful relationship. Noah knew just about all there was to know about her personal life, and now it was her turn to learn about his.

The two biggest questions in her mind at the moment were how an exile like Rafael had found his way back into the government and why Isabella had betrayed Noah for his own brother—a brother who didn't appear to be very appealing. She remembered Mariel's hinting that Isabella was interested in marrying into political prominence. Deputy minister of the treasury was a governmental position, but it was hardly lofty. In some ways it sounded like a trumped-up, token slot.

The president was speaking, but she wasn't interested in even trying to understand what he was saying. It was all political propaganda anyway. Her eyes were fixed on Noah.

Noah stood silently watching, surprised by the sudden calm that had befallen him. He no longer felt the all-encompassing rage that had plagued him ever since he'd arrived in Cielo Vista. It was gone. The people elevating themselves on the platform looked like puppets in a children's stage show.

He thought about the biblical account of Daniel, when the errant king of Babylon was about to be overtaken by Medo-Persia. He remembered the writing on the wall and the interpretation: *God hath numbered thy kingdom and finished it. Thou art weighed in the balances, and art found wanting. Thy kingdom is divided and given to the Medes and Persians.* His mother had made him read that account many times in childhood, and it resonated with him now. He smiled knowingly.

He felt Jasmine brush lightly against him and silently reach for his hand. He took her hand, squeezing it gently, reassuringly. The lovely woman at his side looked like a beacon of light in the sea of misguided humanity crowding the room. She literally glowed with hope, genuine concern, and sincerity. It was the first time he'd ever felt that kind of love. It had never really been there with Isabella. Never.

He bent slightly and kissed her. "Let's go," he whispered. "I've seen enough."

"Please don't tell me you can't discuss it because I have to know," Jasmine said. "I need to understand how . . . why Isabella ended up with your brother."

Noah shrugged. "It's very easy to explain. When you come from a lying, traitorous family like my own, I guess it comes naturally."

She flinched. "That's not entirely true. Your mother and your sister aren't like that."

They were standing beneath a pale amber streetlamp in a small circular park because Noah had refused to discuss anything confidential within the hotel or its surroundings.

"At least tell me how and why Isabella and Rafael returned to this country," Jasmine pressed.

"It's a long story," Noah said. "I would have to start at the beginning."

"I have time. I'm not going anywhere. Unless you decide not to tell me," she couldn't resist adding.

He told her about Rafael's jealousy over being rejected as heir, as well as the reasons he'd been rejected. He also told her why Rafael felt that Isabella belonged to him, even though she didn't love him.

Jasmine cringed. *"Belonged?* How could she *belong* to him? She's a person, not a possession."

"Unfortunately, this country has always had a narrow, primitive view of women," Noah admitted. "Isabella was the only daughter of Miguel Rios, who was vice president at the time. He and my father agreed that as an adult, she would marry the one chosen as heir. Her earliest years were spent being groomed and programmed to become first lady or queen."

"That's outrageous. I always thought planned marriages were cruel. Didn't you have any say in that?"

"It probably wouldn't have been enforced if I'd been dead set against it, but as it happened, Isabella and I did like each other. Rafael, on the other hand, developed a twisted obsession over what he couldn't have."

She shook her head. "A twisted obsession that lasted down 'til today. So why did the tables turn?"

Noah stared up at the sky. "After the coup and our exile, it was assumed by most of our supporters that when I grew up I would somehow return and take Cielo Vista back. You've heard all this talk before."

She nodded, listening intently. "Please go on."

"Isabella always believed I would. Our marriage was primarily based on our original destinies. In her mind, I fell short. She never quite managed to fit in with the Western world lifestyle. She was beautiful and she had talent, but she refused to channel it. Her only goal was to return as first lady to Cielo Vista, and she hated that I seemed content to remain in the United States running Avian International. She was miserable, and started nagging me day and night."

"How ridiculous and cruel," Jasmine said. "She completely ignored the fact that you could get killed sacrificing your life for her."

"Not just for her," Noah said. "For the country. That's not really so strange, is it? Soldiers do it all the time."

He's right, she thought glumly, *but why was it assumed that he was destined to be a soldier?*

His eyes narrowed as he continued. "From childhood, I have known a lot of secrets about the geography and resources of Cielo Vista. The economy of this corrupt regime is boosted by its trade in diamonds, but they are rapidly depleting the mines. A while back, when we were very young, I foolishly trusted Isabella with just one of those secrets."

"What secret was that?" Jasmine asked.

"I told her the exact location of an untapped source of diamonds. She kept the secret until she became convinced that I was going to remain in the United States. Then she revealed it to Rafael."

Jasmine clenched her hands together. "And Rafael contacted the government and used the secret to secure a position and win Isabella."

"Yes," Noah said. "He also collected a huge financial reward."

Jasmine was silently reeling from the story. "Did Isabella really think Rafael was capable of overthrowing the government?"

Noah laughed mockingly. "No, she's not that stupid. She just wanted to be back in the country. Knowing her, she's probably planning to dump Rafael for someone more powerful. Isabella can be very persuasive. She's been known to wrap even strong men around her little finger."

"She may not be stupid, but she is evil." Jasmine's eyes met his. "And how does your . . . accident tie in?"

"I'm getting to that. Isabella was driving me crazy with her whining, and I was thinking about leaving her but still trying to work things out. Around that time, I came home unexpectedly one day and caught her and Rafael in bed together."

Jasmine closed her eyes and rubbed her forehead, picturing the scene. "And I suppose you confronted them and there was a fight."

"It was more than just a fight. Maybe there's something wrong with my head that I never suspected they could betray me, but when I saw my brother and my wife together I was completely shocked." He hesitated for a second before continuing. "Rafael and I were never that close, but we grew up together. We were family, and I thought that was supposed to mean something. Anyway, I was so angry that I almost beat him to death." He took a deep breath. "I'm sorry I didn't."

She put her hand on his shoulder. "Please don't say that. I know you. You have every right to be angry, but you're not a killer."

Noah looked at her directly, his eyes piercing the darkness. "Maybe I'm not, but Rafael is. You've probably guessed by now that I didn't have an accident. Rafael planned to kill me. He *had* to in order to assure the president that I would never return to claim my place."

Jasmine was silent. It hurt to hear how easily people could be bought—even family. She realized, however, that she shouldn't be surprised. After all, the history books, and even the Bible, were filled with all the horrific things people had done throughout the ages in their quest to attain wealth and power.

All of a sudden she was gripped by a chilling, almost paranoid fear. She looked around. There was only silence and gathering dusk. No one was following them.

"Maybe . . . maybe you shouldn't talk about this anymore tonight."

"Relax. No one can hear us," Noah said. "There's no danger here."

She laughed weakly. "You're right. Maybe I'm just overwhelmed. Go on, tell me the rest."

"Aaron's people did a private investigation and they reached the conclusion that I was knocked unconscious by a blow to the head and stuffed into the driver's seat of the car, which was sent careening down the cliff, that same cliff I showed you when we went to visit my place. Remember?"

She shuddered. "Yes."

"I know when it happened now. It was a week after the fight. Isabella had gone wailing back to her aunt in Spain and I was getting ready to go to the airport on business. I walked out in the driveway to get in the car and it's the last thing I remember. Rafael probably ambushed me at that point."

Jasmine shivered despite the muggy night air, and Noah slid his arm around her, drawing her close.

"I agree with you now," he whispered. "No more talking about this tonight. I promise, we'll have a better day tomorrow."

They began the trek back to the hotel. Jasmine felt so numb that she was hardly aware of her own legs moving. The numbness was coming not only from what he had told her, but her fear of what could happen in the near future. She didn't want to admit it, but things had been a lot less complicated when he had amnesia.

"Noah . . ." she began warily.

"Yes."

"Suppose there had never been a betrayal. Were you at some point really going to try to overthrow . . ." She stopped, afraid to finish.

"Isabella didn't wait long enough to find out, and I thank God she didn't," he said. "I have no desire to spend the rest of my life with a woman who's all ambition and no heart."

CHAPTER 18

The jade green of the jungle spread out before them as they trekked slowly through the rainforest to the sounds of birds, the rustling of foliage in the humid breeze and the occasional chatters, shrieks and howls of camouflaged primates. The light from the sun was almost obliterated by the dense canopy of trees.

Noah knew instinctively where to go, and around every bend or trail formed by passing herds of elephants and zebras there were new discoveries. As they wandered deeper and deeper into the forest, Jasmine marveled at God's creations and at Noah's natural ability to navigate the twisted labyrinth of trees and shrubs.

They paused at the top of a hill and looked down a ravine to watch a herd of African elephants moving remarkably silently in their search for water. Noah said that the elephants were smaller than their cousins in the savannah, but to Jasmine they were still enormous and awe-inspiring.

She marveled at the cute colobus monkeys huddled in trees, the large, brightly colored exotic birds and the giraffe-related okapis with their zebra-striped hind legs that she spotted in the distance. Although she was not exactly at ease with poisonous snakes, she had to admit that even they were fascinating. From the pale, slender green of the African vipers to the thicker brown and yellow-toned puff adders, they all contributed to the complex ecosystem of the rainforest, and as long as they remained mostly hidden under rocks and in hollowed-out tree trunks, it was fine with her. She would never even have noticed them if Noah hadn't pointed them out.

Billions of reddish-colored ants swarmed the branches of the trees. She could see why she had been warned not to touch anything, because the insects were capable of inflicting painful stings on unsuspecting victims. The most annoying were the mosquitoes, but in exchange for the view of wildlife in its natural habitat she was ready to forgive even them.

She was appalled to learn that most of the animals they were viewing were on the endangered species list. Noah told her about the illegal poachers who slaughtered and killed many of the animals for meat and sold it on the open market. He explained that most of the problems had begun with Western logging companies cutting down trees, destroying the natural habitat for both humans and animals, forcing the humans to rely solely on meat to survive when centuries ago they had lived mostly on fruit and fish.

Jasmine loved the sounds of the forest. If she held her breath and closed her eyes, she felt as if she could actually blend in and become a part of it. The really strange thing was the sense of *déjà vu*, as if she'd somehow been here before, in another time, another place. But that was plain impossible and crazy to dwell on. Maybe it had been in one of her dreams. She started to mention it to Noah but decided against it.

She glanced at him in awe. He was an intrinsic part of the forest. Even when he walked, his footsteps were in sync with the rhythm and motion of the big cats, centuries-old dwellers in a land that had existed long before humans.

"Noah," her voice was barely a whisper. "Are there any people living in this rainforest?"

"Yes, the Baka people. Most of them are barely five feet tall. You'd feel like a giant among them."

"Pygmies? I've read about them."

"Some refer to them as Pygmies, but I prefer to call them by their tribal name. The village isn't too far from here if you want to see them."

She hesitated. "I . . . I don't know about that. Are they friendly?"

"Not to everyone, but they are to me. The Baka like to live the way their ancestors did. They don't generally associate with so-called civilization."

"After some of the things you've told me, I don't blame them," she said. "I guess I'm not really prepared to see the village now, but I would like to someday."

Noah smiled. "A wise decision. If we did go to the village, we would be offered a meal and I don't think you'd appreciate what's on the menu."

She frowned. "Bush meat?"

"Probably."

"How is it that they're friendly with you? Didn't you tell me that no one in Cielo Vista knows you're still alive?"

"Everyone living in so-called civilization believes I'm dead. But don't worry, there is no danger in the Baka knowing otherwise because they don't associate with the outside world. Believe it or not, they've elevated me to mythical status. They think I'm going to liberate the forests from the loggers and give it back to them so they will be blessed by their forest god."

She flinched. "That belief is almost tragic. It's also unfair that so much has to be expected of you." She didn't want to add that it was also making her angry because she resented having to share him with a country. Why couldn't they simply be a man and a woman exploring an exotic place? She sighed. There was no escaping the truth. "How did your relationship with these people start anyway?" she asked.

Noah jammed his hands into the front pockets of his khakis and gazed skyward. They were moving into a flat clearing where the foliage was less dense, and he was starting to feel the weight of the knapsack strapped to his back. "When I was a boy, I wasn't your typical little prince," he said. "My father gave me a great deal of freedom . . . freedom which I used to explore the country and its people. I learned to speak the language of not just the Baka, but of many tribes."

"That's impressive," she said.

"My best friend was an African kid named Simon Baraka," Noah continued. "His dad was secretary general during my father's rule. Anyway, Simon was as anti-civilization as I was back then, and we were holy terrors, always getting into mischief. We ran away from home for three weeks when we were maybe ten years old because we got this notion that we wanted to live in the wild." He laughed. "You should have seen us. Those were the days."

"That must've created quite a royal scandal, not to mention it probably worried your parents to death," Jasmine said. "What happened?"

"We wanted to witness the exclusive coming-of-age rite for Baka boys and we hid in the jungle at night trying to watch." He closed his eyes and smiled, remembering the moment. "They discovered us."

"Weren't they angry?"

"A little, but they knew we were only kids. They took us back to their village and let us live with them. We went through the rite."

"Was it painful?"

Noah looked at her with an enigmatic smile on his face. "There is this god that they call Jengi, otherwise known as the spirit of the forest. It is their belief that this spirit kills you and then brings you back to life anew as an adult."

Jasmine brushed lightly against him. "It sounds fascinating. Primitive, but fascinating. What actually happens during the rite?"

"It's pure mysticism, like nothing I'd ever experienced before or ever will again. But Simon and I promised that we would never tell the secret. In Baka culture the ritual is never shared with women."

She slapped him lightly on the arm. "Oh, you guys and your deep, dark secrets. I'll bet the Baka women know all about it anyway. They just don't let on."

Noah's eyes twinkled now. "If I know anything about women, you're probably right, but you'll just have to humor us."

"When you finally did get back home, weren't you punished?"

"A little. Nothing drastic, though Simon's father was much more of a disciplinarian. He sent Simon away to a boarding school in England." Noah's eyes darkened. "That's where he was on the night of the coup."

"But Simon's father was native African. You'd think he'd be less upset than yours about what happened."

"You would think it, but his father was schooled in Europe and he viewed the people of the bush and forests as ignorant."

"I guess the irony is that Simon never did learn discipline," Jasmine said. "I noticed a picture of you and him back at your mother's house and I remember hearing things about him in the news years ago. He was quite a champion for human rights." She hesitated for a moment, recognizing the disturbingly familiar gleam in his eyes. "Mariel told me that he's in prison here."

"That he is," Noah said.

And she could tell that he wasn't going to elaborate on it.

The ground began to rise and she knew without asking that they were no longer in the rainforest because the canopy of trees had lifted and the sun was intense. It was around noon, and they'd been hiking since early morning.

"Just a little farther to reach that picnic spot," Noah said. "I promise you the walk will be worth it."

"Oh, I'm not complaining," Jasmine said. "I've been so overwhelmed by all God's creations that I didn't even realize 'til now that it's noon."

After a few more minutes of walking she could hear a rushing sound, and instantly they were upon a gorgeous waterfall. She looked up to see that the foaming white water cascaded about one hundred feet over a cliff into a pool-like basin below. She stared, mesmerized, while Noah unharnessed his backpack.

"How deep is . . ." She turned to address Noah, and then completely forgot what she was going to say because he had stripped his shirt off and was unbuckling his belt. She was relieved, somewhat relieved, to see that he had navy swim trunks on. But the sight of him barely clothed was almost as impressive as the waterfall. He looked like a sculpture of an ancient Greek god. His hair, although still annoyingly blond, was slightly longer and wavier than usual. His muscular biceps were toned and sculpted. Add to that a narrow waist, a flat ridged stomach, and he was even better looking than she'd imagined.

"Now you know why I asked you to bring a swimsuit," he said, smiling, oblivious to her blank stare.

Snap out of it, she thought, and busied herself opening the backpack that contained their lunch, some supplies and a large beach towel, which she spread out on the grassy embankment above the crystal pool.

"Will you be joining me?" Noah asked.

"Yes. Go on in. Give me a few seconds."

Instead of walking farther down to the pool's basin as she expected, he strolled to the ledge and dove in. Her breath caught in her throat as he soared gracefully through the air in a dive worthy of the Olympics and splashed into the water. Her question was answered. It was deep.

As she methodically stripped down to a plain black bikini, her nagging conscience warned her that there could be repercussions to this moment, but she didn't want to listen. Instead, she wanted to keep pinching herself to make sure she wasn't dreaming and to continue focusing on her increasing awareness of how much Noah belonged to Cielo Vista—to the mountains, the rainforest and the waterfalls. It didn't matter that he wasn't African or indigenous to the land; it was in his blood as much as it was in the blood of the majestic elephants and the graceful zebras.

The big question was, where did she belong? Definitely not in a gloomy urban housing project, that was for sure, but now, surrounded by the natural beauty of Cielo Vista, even her previous single career woman suburbia seemed insipid and unappealing.

Why do you always have to think so much? she chided herself. Why couldn't she be just a little like some other people who seemed to have perfected the art of living for the moment? It was what she was going to do right now. She was not going to let anything ruin her current state of utopia.

With no intention of imitating Noah's dive, she carefully picked her way down the incline until she was almost level with the pool.

Treading water, Noah observed Jasmine. She was magnificent. From the arch of her neck to her long, slim legs, she moved with the quiet stealth and purpose of a lioness. Her head, tilted slightly downward, caused her long braids, anchored with tiny shell-like beads, to brush against each other. He could almost hear the faint music of the beads. She hesitated for just one second at the pool's edge and then slid in.

The water felt cool and refreshing after the long walk through the muggy jungle. It washed away the physical grime, along with the thoughts of problems lingering on the horizon. They swam together, frolicking like children, splashing each other with water. They skirted the rocks on the shallow edge and moved cautiously toward the fringes of the falls. Jasmine was delighted to discover that there were actually two falls, the thundering powerful one and a smaller trickle from lower down the cliff. They stood under the smaller one and let the water shower them. It was truly what paradise had to be like.

Facing Noah under the cascade of water, Jasmine felt an all-encompassing sense of liberation that she had never been aware of before. She felt deliriously giddy. "This place is just too beautiful for words!" she exclaimed.

"So why are you talking?" Noah asked.

He kissed her, sliding his arms tightly around her, igniting an inner fire that even the cold crystal falls could not put out. She returned his kiss with equal ardor, reveling in a sensation that somehow made her a part of him and a part of the beautiful, exotic land. She wanted all of him, and her voice of reason had vanished as ripples of desire coursed through her body.

It had been such a long time since he'd been with a woman. Noah wanted her as desperately as she wanted him, and the hot, pulsing sensation was nothing like he'd ever felt with Isabella. This feeling was new. This feeling was wonderful. With Isabella, their love had been almost perfunctory, but with Jasmine it felt complete. He wanted to please her. He wanted to protect her. Protect her?

Noah realized that Jasmine was spellbound, swept away. By taking her to this spot he'd made it very convenient to satisfy his own desire, which was increasing by the second. On the other hand, maybe she was ready to embrace whatever happened.

But nothing was going to happen. As much as he wanted to, he couldn't let it. His feelings for her were too strong to risk hurting her. She had been through too much hurt in the past. Even though he desperately wanted to make more of a commitment to their relationship, there were reasons why he shouldn't, the most obvious being that he couldn't promise anything beyond the moment. He wouldn't be able to promise her anything until Cielo Vista was back in the right hands and he was still alive.

Still alive. That thought alone made him gently disengage himself from her embrace.

"Noah." Jasmine's voice quavered slightly as she looked questioningly up at him.

He placed his palm gently on her cheek. "It's getting late. We have a long walk back and we haven't had lunch yet."

Lunch? How can you possibly be thinking about food at this moment? she wondered. "But . . ." Her eyes shimmered with uncertainty.

He didn't let her finish. He swooped her up in his arms as if she weighed a mere ten pounds and carried her, speechless, back to the shore. No one had ever done such a thing to her before and it made her feel vulnerable, childlike and a bit resentful.

"What was *that* about?" she asked when they were both on solid ground, facing each other. "If I'm out of sync and getting all the wrong vibes, just tell me."

"You're definitely not out of sync," he said gruffly. "I feel exactly the same way you're feeling."

She looked confused. "Well, then—"

He looked directly into her eyes. "Look at me and tell me if that's really what you want or need right now."

She looked at him and sighed. He was bringing her back to reality whether she wanted to be brought back or not. And he was right, partially right. She did desire him, but she definitely did not need casual intimacy. After all, she was the one who had told him earlier that she didn't want another pointless physical relationship, and she had even had the nerve to tell him that God wouldn't approve—God, whose mysterious ways she still couldn't quite come to grips with. Why had she told him that? Why had he taken her words so seriously? Most men, lesser men, probably wouldn't have.

"Are you a believer?" she asked, avoiding his gaze, allowing her body to recover from what could only be described as feeling like a balloon rapidly deflating. "I remember asking you that a while back, but you still had amnesia and you were kind of vague . . ."

He smiled slowly, ironically, a smile that illuminated his whole face. "I am," he admitted. "I may not be quite as devout as some are, but I don't see much wisdom in deliberately breaking God's commands, either." He studied her intently. "Just don't forget that I'm only human. The good that I wish isn't always what I do."

"One of the apostles said that, I think," Jasmine murmured. She exhaled slowly. "Tell me, did you wait for Isabella? Was she a virgin when you married?"

"No," he said bluntly. "I slept with her long before we married. Maybe that's part of what went wrong with our relationship."

What exactly does that mean? she wondered. Was he seeing her on a higher level? Did they actually have a future? She wanted to ask him directly, leave nothing to chance, but fear over his response, and her own, caused her to refrain. She could only handle so much reality at this moment.

"I guess there's really no point in dwelling on what we can't do." She took his hand. "You know, I really am starving. Let's get dressed and have lunch."

As they began the trek back up the slope, Noah thought about how different Jasmine was from his ex-wife. The purely physical side of him had wanted and expected her to throw a temper tantrum and insist he finish what he'd started, but he loved her even more for responding the way she had.

In hindsight, he was also grateful for what could have been divine intervention on the night when he'd subconsciously called out Isabella's name, preventing him and

Jasmine from the inevitable. On that night he'd thrown every precaution to the wind and would have gone all the way if she had been agreeable. Even her mentioning having traces of Christian scruples, despite disillusionment about faith, could only be a sign from above.

One thing was very clear: God would have no reason to show him favor on big issues if he broke His commandments on small things. He had waited long enough for the right moment to return to Cielo Vista, and now that he could almost taste the victory, he knew he would have to wait for Jasmine too.

After lunch, they backtracked through the rain forest using a shortcut. Jasmine viewed a passing herd of zebras from the distance and they spotted a family of mountain gorillas. It was nearing evening by the time they had reclaimed his Jeep and were rolling along a dirt road. She had no clue where they were heading now, but she was trying not to succumb to exhaustion because she was still enjoying every moment.

"We'll be staying on the island of Rio Mundo tonight," Noah informed her. "It's much better there than in Montalvo."

"Sounds good. I'm sure I won't have any trouble sleeping tonight."

He smiled. "I hope I haven't worn you out too much. It's just that you won't be here very long and I'm trying to give you a crash course on the splendors of Cielo Vista."

She smiled back. "You've definitely succeeded. I may not understand everything about you, but I don't think I'll ever question why you feel the way you do about this place again."

There was a long silence as he drove. The Jeep seemed to hit every rut and crevice on the dirt path. The jolting of the vehicle was doing a fine job keeping her awake. If they had been riding on smooth asphalt, she probably would have dozed off a long time ago.

"Are you awake?" Noah asked.

"Yes. I'm just thinking."

He rolled his eyes. "Haven't I warned you that thinking is dangerous?"

"Many times. Obviously, I don't take advice."

"I assume you're about to tell me, so what is it?"

"Is there a specific date for the . . . er . . . military action?"

His eyes focused on the road ahead. "Yes."

It was her turn to roll her eyes. "Will you tell me what that date is?"

"No."

"You are *such* a pain. Of course I *knew* you were going to say that."

"So why did you ask?"

She glanced at his face as he focused on the road. The corner of his mouth was slightly upturned, indicating humor.

"I *have* to ask," she said, frowning. "How could I not? Do you honestly think I can just erase this from my mind? I'm worried. Our . . . I mean, *your* life is hanging on this." She swallowed hard, wondering if he had caught her little slip with the word *our*.

Noah didn't notice—or pretended not to. "I understand you're worried, but I can only assure you that this plan has been in the making for years and it involves many intelligent minds behind a skilled military force. Everyone has been subjected to psychological profiling, and none of them have anything to gain by betraying the cause. These people are loyal."

A familiar chill swept over her. Would her already damaged psyche be able to withstand the blow of losing him? "I . . . I'm glad you're so confidant. It's just that people are people and so many things could happen." She hesitated. "And don't take this the wrong way . . . you have your overly macho virtues, but I just don't see you as a killer."

He looked straight ahead. "Do you remember any of these verses: 'A time to kill and a time to heal; a time to break down and a time to build'? I don't remember them in order, but it later goes on to say, 'A time to love and a time to hate; a time for war and a time for peace.' "

She scowled. "Everyone knows those verses, but I wish you wouldn't put the Bible in this."

"Why not? I believe the statements are true." He seemed amused again.

Jasmine remained silent.

Noah took a deep breath. "Whatever the case, I'll do what I have to do, but if things go exactly as planned, I won't have to kill anyone."

Jasmine wearily twined an errant braid around her finger. "Are any other countries backing this coup? Is the United States behind it?"

Noah laughed outright now. "You're very persistent, aren't you? I told you, no more detail."

Exasperated, she sat silently and stared at the headlight beams piercing the darkness ahead.

"Military might is not the only key to winning this battle," Noah said in a conciliatory tone. "Right will prevail if God wills it."

If God wills it. There was nothing left for her to say, but some fervent prayers might help.

CHAPTER 19

The air was dense and the pungent ground felt soft and springy under her feet as she moved quietly through the jungle, ducking under sagging tree branches. An African gray parrot squawked.

"Dawn," she called. "Dawnee, are you here?"

The brush parted and a tiny ethereal form stepped out, beaming radiantly. "Auntie Jammin, look."

The little wood sprite, wearing a headband of garlands and dressed in a sparkly white fairy dress with delicate rainbow-hued wings, held out an exquisite bouquet of white and lavender orchids.

"They're beautiful, Dawn, where did you find them?"

"In the garden," Dawn said, smiling angelically. "They for you."

"Oh, what a little sweetheart you are," Jasmine exclaimed, accepting the offering. "Thank you so much. I'll keep them forever and ever."

She gently set the bouquet down against a tree, lifted the child in her arms, and began to dance to the music of the forest. Dawn giggled, delighted by her suspension in mid-air, spinning around and around.

"Forever and ever and ever," Dawn repeated.

"Always," Jasmine said, lifting her even higher.

"That's not true." Dawn's voice became more defined, more mature. "You can't keep flowers forever and ever. They die."

"What?" Jasmine responded, taken aback, realizing with a start that Dawn suddenly weighed a ton and she could hardly hold her up. Gasping, she set the child down.

"You can't keep them always," Dawn repeated. "Flowers don't live long. They die soon. Everybody knows that."

The once-gentle sounds of the forest grew louder, aggressive. "Stop it!" Jasmine's voice rose above the cacophony. "Don't you ever say that, Dawn. Don't—"

"You stop it! I'm not Dawn, I'm Morgan," the child interrupted, stamping her foot impatiently.

The girl looking up at her was still wearing the winged fairy gown, but she was larger, older.

Disappointed, Jasmine glared at her. "What are you doing here again? I didn't call you. I don't want you. What did you do with Dawn?"

Tears shimmered in Morgan's eyes. "But I . . . I thought you liked me."

"Go away!" Jasmine shouted. "I don't want you."

Crying, Morgan turned and started to run away from her. Jasmine's heart ached. "Wait! she called. "I didn't mean that—"

But her words had no impact. She shouted again, but she couldn't even hear her own voice because the roaring in the forest was now deafening. She watched, paralyzed, as Morgan, blinded by tears, ran straight toward the slanted yellow eyes of a lion crouching in the bush.

"Morgan, no! Don't go that way!" Jasmine tried to run after her, but her legs wouldn't move. Her feet felt leaden. Morgan hesitated, turned and ran back to her. She grabbed the little girl's trembling hand and faced the opposite direction. It was too late. They both stood unprotected in the center of the jungle arena, and everywhere they looked they were surrounded by the tawny, muscular forms of crouched lions, their amber eyes gleaming, tasseled tails twitching, and mouths open in snarling anticipation of prey. They could feel the desperate beating of their own hearts as they prepared for their last moments. And a most bizarre thought entered Jasmine's mind—how beautiful the lions were.

"Jasmine." A familiar voice called her name in the distance. It seemed very far away. A knocking sound followed the voice. Her vision clouded and the jungle shimmered eerily and then dissolved into a strange blue light, causing the lions to dematerialize in a wisp of smoke. She sat up with a start and nearly tumbled out of bed.

"Just . . . just a minute," she stammered.

"Take your time," Noah said from outside the door. "I just wanted to know if you felt like taking a walk on the beach before sunrise."

A walk? What? She groped for the small clock near the nightstand. "It's still dark out," she protested.

The illuminated dial told her it was five o'clock in the morning, and she remembered that they had crossed by private ferry to the tiny island of Rio Mundo and spent the night, a very short night, in separate rooms in a small bed and breakfast inn.

"I know it's early," Noah said from outside her door. "But the sunrise is really spectacular from this location. You won't regret it."

It was crazy. She was still disoriented from the dream, but there was no way she was going to lose the opportunity. This was, after all, her last day in Cielo Vista. "Give me a few minutes. I'm coming," she said.

She literally tumbled out of bed, blindly groping for her clothes and feeling grateful that she had taken along a change. She pulled on a simple knee-length denim skirt, a snug-fitting yellow T-shirt and sandals. Rushing in childish anticipation, she stumbled into the tiny connecting bathroom and splashed cold water over her face.

Despite having survived an attack by a pack of lions and another bizarre metamorphic appearance from Dawn, she thought she looked none the worse for wear. She quickly dabbed on some lip gloss, shook out her braids and rushed to open the door.

She found Noah waiting in the dimly lit lobby of the inn dressed in beige khakis and a black T-shirt. The sight of him caused her to involuntarily suck in her breath. No matter what he wore, he never failed to impress her with his tall, sinewy demeanor that was reminiscent of a certain dark and brooding actor from a past TV show called *The Highlander.*

He smiled. "You're getting really good at these spontaneous adventures."

She smiled back. "Keeping up with you *is* an adventure. Never mind that when you called me I was in the middle of a dream and had no clue where I was."

"Sorry. Was it a good dream?"

"Actually, it was a nightmare. I'm glad you woke me."

"My timing is impeccable."

"It is," she agreed. "It's almost eerie."

They stood in the sand at the chiseled mouth of a cave overlooking a beach which was sheltered by towering cliffs that jutted out into the sea, forming a protected inlet. The sun had not yet risen, but the sky was lightening into a shade of mauve, splotched with wispy gray clouds chasing each other in slow motion across the horizon. The naked masts of anchored fishing boats reached for the heavens as the boats rocked gently on the waves.

"Gorgeous," Jasmine said. "Does this place have a name?"

"It's called Puerto Alba," Noah said. "This was my favorite spot when I was a kid. I used to explore the cave, but mostly I liked coming here to be alone, to watch the sun rise or set." He inhaled deeply. "No matter what kind of mood I was in, this place always made me feel peaceful, made me feel close to the Creator. This place was also my last connection to this country. Aaron snuck us out through this harbor."

Jasmine closed her eyes and leaned against him. "I knew you when you were a boy. I ran with you through the forests and I swam in this sea, too. When I wanted to be alone, I would come here to Puerto Alba and watch you from a distance."

His eyes twinkled. "I knew you were there. You were a little girl with long, curly black hair that you rarely combed. You belonged to no one but the wind and the tides and you used to run around wearing some kind of costume, a white dress, I believe." He reached out and touched the tip of her nose. "You had wings and they sparkled."

Jasmine's breath caught in her throat. "How did you know about the sparkly wings?"

He laughed. "I told you I saw you."

She stared at him incredulously. "Noah, stop . . . this game is too weird."

"You started it. Anyway, what's so weird about wings? Most little girls seem to like that stuff. Morgan probably would, and I'll bet you were a lot like her when you were small."

Jasmine shook her head as remnants of the bizarre dream with Dawn and then Morgan wearing the fairy dress drifted back. The whole thing was unnerving and she wondered what it was all supposed to mean, if anything. A tremor went through her body. Noah's arm slid protectively around her.

"Are you cold?" he asked.

"No. It's just goose bumps. I was thinking about the past and an eerie dream I had last night."

"Do you want to talk about it?"

"It was about Dawn." She hesitated and then shook her head. "No. I can't talk about it now. Maybe another time."

Noah didn't insist. She looked at his eyes and she could almost see the sky reflected in them. He seemed to be far off. When he spoke his voice had an enigmatic resonance.

"Don't live in fear of the past. Learn to embrace it and move ahead." He studied the clouds. "Cielo Vista's going to be a good place again. I can feel it."

She leaned against him. "I'm praying that you're right."

He smiled. "You keep doing that."

She could see the sun taking shape now, an opaque orange glow rising out of the sea. The sky had transformed from violet to pink with hues of tangerine and lemon.

"Jasmine, are you aware of what Puerto Alba means in Spanish?" Noah asked.

"My Spanish is even worse than my French," she said, still watching the sky. "I know puerto means port or harbor, something like that. I don't know about Alba."

What does it mean?"

"Alba means dawn," he said softly.

Her mouth dropped and she stared at him for the second time. "Dawn," she repeated. "Dawn's harbor. Oh, my God." The words throbbed like a pulsating heartbeat and then caressed her in a warm embrace. "She's here, Noah. She's really here and she's okay."

"Of course she is," Noah said simply. "And she's waiting for you to complete your journey."

She was not going to question anything. She just wanted to stay with the mystical, peaceful feeling, even if

223

it wasn't logical. Noah's arm tightened around her and they moved out onto the sand.

The sun was up now, a big red ball of fire suspended over the azure sea. Jasmine could hear the music of the tide as the waves gently brushed the shore and she and Noah faced each other. He guided her into a waltz position and they moved in rhythm with the waves—a dance she wished would never end.

CHAPTER 20

The doldrums of reality came around all too quickly as soon as Jasmine's plane touched down at Kennedy. The depression followed her into the limo that whisked her down dirty urban streets, crossed bridges and took her back to Brooklyn.

Darkness surrounded her as she entered her apartment feeling completely disoriented. When she had left Cielo Vista it had been early in the morning. Now the cover of darkness was welcome because it numbed the effect of her return somewhat. She left her luggage sitting in the living room and paced, trying to get her bearings.

The building was deceptively quiet, which was a good thing. Exhausted, she tumbled onto the bed and lay there, but sleep did not come because she could not get Noah and Cielo Vista out of her mind. She could still see the frolicking waves on the Rio Mundo beach and hear the calls of birds in the rainforest. What was going to happen in Cielo Vista? What kind of historical drama was about to be played out? Would Noah succeed? Would he live? She squeezed her eyes shut and prayed that he would be victorious, that the country would go back to leaders who would respect it and its native people.

When daylight intruded, exposing the raw bleakness of her surroundings, Jasmine remained lying on the bed.

She thought about Morgan and guiltily hoped the child wouldn't come knocking on her door to see if she was back. She was not ready to interact with her at this point because the little girl represented a reality she was not yet ready to deal with.

At around seven-thirty there was a muffled knock at the door, but the sound did not persist and she ignored it. The next time she looked at the clock it was noon, so she got up, showered, dressed in jeans and gulped down a slightly stale English muffin with the dregs of a container of orange juice. She needed to go shopping, but she didn't want to. What she really wanted to do was to move out of the apartment right then and there. She thought about Valerie in New Jersey. Maybe she could stay with her.

"Oh, don't be ridiculous," Jasmine muttered aloud. There was no way she could come crashing in on Valerie, especially since they hadn't seen each other in over a year. She thought about Natalie. She knew that very soon she was going to face her again. They would talk. She should call her—maybe now. No, it could wait.

She stepped out into the hallway and gagged on the scent of stale air and urine. The ceiling light bulb flickered as usual, and out of the corner of her eye, she caught a glimpse of a figure looming outside Rachel and Morgan's apartment door. Aware of her presence, the man turned to glare at her with serpent-like, beady black eyes, and she recognized with disappointment and anger that it was Victor Morales. He opened the door and vanished inside. Apparently, Rachel was involved with him again. Thoroughly disgusted, she took the elevator down to the vestibule to check her mail. She had just finished fishing the mail out of the box when she sensed another person watching her. She turned to look.

"Hi," the woman said. "I'm just wondering if you might be Jasmine."

She was unfamiliar, ebony-skinned, in her late thirties or early forties, petite, with dark hair styled conservatively in a pageboy. Her smile was pleasant.

"I suppose I could be," Jasmine said, smiling back. "Depends on why you're asking."

The woman laughed outright. "My ex-husband used to always tell me to mind my own business, but I never took his advice. My name is Pat Kendall from the tenth floor. My granddaughter Leah is friends with Morgan. She slept over at my place last night. Got the two of them off to school this morning."

"That's great." Jasmine breathed an audible sigh of relief. "I'm really happy to hear that Morgan has friends." As she spoke she wondered how Pat Kendall knew about her connection to the child.

"I heard you've been taking care of her," Pat went on. "She's such a cutie. Drives me crazy to think about all the good people in the world who'd love to have a child like that, and instead she's got that crazy drug addict for a mother. Anyway, I'm glad you're back 'cause she talks about you all the time. I was hoping you hadn't moved out of the building without telling her. It would break her heart."

"I would never do that," Jasmine said, concealing her irritation that a complete stranger was also inflicting the responsibility of Morgan on her.

"I guess you must be wondering how I knew who you were even though we've never met till now," Pat said.

"It did kind of enter my mind."

"What happened was Morgan described you so well that when I saw you I knew you had to be the Jasmine she just couldn't stop talking about."

"I'm sorry about that." Jasmine inspected her mailbox once more to make sure she hadn't missed anything. "Kids have a habit of going on and on, sometimes even about the most insignificant things." She closed the box door and locked it. "You know, I'm surprised. For a while it seemed like no one in the building even noticed what was going on with Morgan."

Pat moved closer and glanced around, apparently to make sure no one else was in the lobby listening. "I and a few others noticed a while ago. It's just that sometimes it's dangerous to get involved in other people's business. You know what I'm saying?"

"Definitely." Jasmine pushed the button for the elevator and they both stood waiting.

"Before you started looking out for her, I used to see her roaming around the halls late at night," Pat said apologetically. "Got to wondering what kind of idiot parents would allow their kid to do that. I almost called Social Services, but then I was afraid they wouldn't keep the call confidential, and I can't afford no trouble from drug addicts. I'm all alone here raising my daughter's child."

As the elevator door opened and they both stepped in, Jasmine wondered where the daughter was, but she didn't ask. She was pleased that Pat and others were at least aware of Morgan's plight, but she was still exhausted and waging a war with her own feelings. The main thought on her mind was Noah. She wanted to get back to her privacy and think about what she was going to do next.

"You're gonna laugh at this," Pat continued, oblivious to Jasmine's inner turmoil. "When Morgan first started coming over to play with Leah, she told me that you were her real mother."

"She what?" Jasmine repeated, jolted back to the present.

"That little girl can tell some stories," Pat continued. "She told me you were her real mother, and that the state took her away from you and made her live with an evil foster mother."

"Oh, God. You're right. She really *can* tell some tall tales. Did she give you a reason why the state supposedly took her away from me?"

"Uh huh. She said you had a terrible illness and you could only come out of the house at night because the sun could kill you."

Jasmine laughed in spite of herself. Pat laughed too. "I'm going to have to talk to Morgan about that imagination of hers. But could you please do me one big favor?"

"If I can."

"If you see Morgan this afternoon, please don't tell her that I'm back yet. I just got home from a trip to

Africa and I'm really, really out of it. I absolutely have to have this day to get my act together."

"Africa?" Pat hesitated for a moment. "Girl, that's some kind of traveling. Don't worry, I won't tell her."

"Thanks, Pat." Jasmine breathed a sigh of relief. "It was good to meet you. Maybe we can talk sometime."

"Yes, I'd like that," Pat said, hesitating slightly even though the door had slid open on her floor. "Well, see you around." She stepped out.

Jasmine realized that Pat had most likely expected her to elaborate on her trip to Africa and she was probably disappointed that she hadn't. Whatever the case, she couldn't think about it right now because there were too many other things on her mind.

Staring numbly at the letters in her hand, she listened to the elevator's noisy ascent upward, hoping no one else would get in. One letter stood out as though illuminated amidst the bills and junk mail. That letter was addressed to Jasmine and Noah Arias. What in the world? She stared at the white envelope with the black-ink hand-writing. What kind of joke was being played on her? The return address was from A. Garcia in St. Albans, Queens. She frowned. Mrs. Garcia was dead. Then she noticed that the letter had been postmarked weeks ago, a week before Mrs. Garcia's death.

Shaken, Jasmine placed the letter in her purse. If she could bear the suspense, she would wait to read it. Mrs. Garcia might not have been in her right mind at the time she'd written it and the thought of what it might reveal was unnerving to say the least. *Jasmine and Noah Arias.*

As the elevator door shuddered open on her floor, she laughed at the thought and nearly collided with a scowling man stepping in. He glared at her as though he'd like to wring her neck, but she barely noticed him and didn't even bother to apologize.

The helicopter hovered over the pit and Noah leaned toward the window to look down into the mouth of the abyss. Red flames of molten lava simmered in the caldron of the volcano, creating a scene that was as close to the biblical description of Gehenna as he'd ever care to witness. The volatile mountain looked as though it were about to blow at any moment. In reality, it could be weeks. It could be days. Whatever, it was going to be a very unwelcome surprise to some people. Montalvo would not suffer a catastrophic hit because it was at least fifty miles away, but the city would get inundated with ash fallout and heaven only knew what else.

"Spectacular, isn't it?" pilot and geologist Rob Hernandez said.

"Yeah," Noah agreed, adding a grin. "Got that date yet?"

Rob chuckled at the ongoing joke between them. "How many times must I tell you that predicting the date of an eruption is not an exact science?"

"An educated guess then." Noah quizzed. "C'mon Rob, you're the expert."

"How does November fourteenth sound?" Rob said, focusing on the controls, increasing the chopper's altitude.

Intensely aware of the pungent sulfur smell in the atmosphere, Noah blinked at the irony of Rob's guess. "I'll take it," he said. November fourteenth was only a few weeks away, and the exact date he and Aaron had planned for their action.

The corrupt government officials of Cielo Vista didn't know about the imminent danger. They believed things were exactly as they'd always been at Mt. Cielo. Unbeknownst to them, the volcanologists they thought they'd hired from the university to routinely monitor all active volcanoes were working undercover with Avian International for the liberation front. The scientists were deliberately giving them false information.

But it was only part of the plan to overthrow the government. It would be a beautiful thing if nature cooperated, but the takeover was not contingent on nature's assistance, at least not from Aaron's strictly military point of view.

The helicopter circled once more, affording them both a second look, and then it headed off toward the clearing and the geological center ten miles from the smoking mountain.

Something was wrong. He knew it the minute he touched the doorknob and it turned freely in his hand. He had locked the door before he went out and now it was unlocked. Maybe one of the maids . . . maybe nothing; it was almost midnight and they didn't work nights. Jasmine had left the previous day. He'd seen her board the plane, so there was no reason why she would be back in his room.

Adrenaline pumping, he drew the gun from his concealed shoulder holster and opened the door. The light was on. He curled his finger around the trigger.

"Noah, don't!" a terrified voice cried out. He stared into the face of a shockingly familiar woman with flaming red hair and petrified blue eyes. "Please put the gun down. I'm alone. Nobody else here knows you're alive, only me. *Please . . .*"

He didn't lower the gun. Instead, he continued to stare at her, not wanting to believe who was in front of his eyes. *Kill her,* the voice inside his head commanded. *Do it now.* But he couldn't

"I'm so, so sorry for everything. I should have trusted you." She backed up, but the bed in her path impeded her progress. "I can make things right . . . I swear. Give me a chance."

"Shut up!" The words erupted venomously from his mouth. Still holding the gun, he caught her none-too-gently by the arm with his free hand and spun her forcibly around to check for weapons. She was clean. He yanked at the coppery curls and the wig dropped to the floor, allowing her gold hair to spill out over her shoulders.

"You . . . you don't have to treat me like a common criminal," she stammered, trying to regain her footing.

He ignored her and forcefully dragged her along with him as he checked the closets, the bathroom and the hallway. Satisfied that they were alone, he returned to the front room, slammed the door and released her roughly. She sat down hard on the bed.

"How did you find out?" he demanded.

She hesitated, recovering slightly, her fear slowly being replaced by outrage and humiliation.

"Tell me, Isabella. Now!"

"Stop yelling at me!"

"How did you know?"

"I . . . I never accepted that you were dead. It was like an intuition kind of thing because we've been together for so long." Her words rambled, collided. "I never wanted you to die. Please believe me. I had absolutely *nothing* to do with that part. Rafael caused the accident. I had no idea he would go that far."

She blinked, hesitating again. Noah wasn't buying it. His expression was cold, fierce, unlike any she'd ever seen before. It was quite possible that if she didn't level with him, she could be in imminent danger.

"I almost didn't go to your fake funeral because I simply couldn't believe you were dead," she babbled. "I forced myself to attend because I thought it would help me accept what was supposed to be reality . . . but it didn't. Because . . . because when I came, they told me that you had been cremated. The fact that there was no body made the whole memorial even more unreal. I kept thinking that you would appear in the room at any moment." She gestured dramatically. "I thought I was losing my mind. For the longest time after it was all over, I kept hearing you, seeing you.

And all this was because I wanted desperately for you to be alive. The—"

"So it was quite all right with you that I was in a coma for years. It was just the dead part you couldn't deal with," Noah interrupted sarcastically.

She flinched. "No! That's not true. It was horrible seeing you like that, but as horrible as it was, there was still the hope you might recover. And you did, Noah. You did."

The vulnerable, wounded side of him wanted to ask her why she never came to the hospital if she really cared so much, but he refrained. It didn't matter. She didn't matter.

"The feeling that you were still alive got so strong that Rafael tried to talk me into seeing a psychiatrist . . . I didn't, but when he was away on business two, maybe three weeks ago, I went back to South Carolina because I wanted to talk to your mother."

Noah glared at her with contempt. "My mother can't stand you. She wouldn't have told you anything."

"I never saw your mother. It was your sister who confirmed that you were still alive. She may be young, but she's smart enough to realize that you and I still belong together."

"Gianna? You spoke to my little sister?" Noah's voice rose again.

There was no way Gianna would ever willingly betray his trust, but at the same time, no one had told her the whole truth about his divorce, or anything, and the breach could have occurred. The girl had largely been left in the dark because she was young. Whatever inaccurate knowledge she'd acquired had probably come from her own sleuthing and eavesdropping on Mariel's conversations. And some of that was indirectly his own fault because while in his confused, traumatized state of mind, he'd made the abrupt journey to Cielo Vista, without telling her that his memory had returned.

"Noah, you mustn't be angry at Gianna," Isabella was saying. "She's a kid, a young, romantic dreamer. You *know* how she is. She was only trying to help, and I was very persistent."

She continued to talk, but in his rage, the words did not sink in. But his anger was not directed at Gianna. She believed he still had amnesia. Maybe she had wilted under Isabella's badgering because she felt if they got back together that he would remember everything.

But Gianna's gullibility aside, the weighty question remained: Could the plans for the coup be salvaged? The voice inside his head grew louder, telling him that there were still two ways out of the mess. He could silence Isabella permanently by killing her, or he could play the game.

"Gianna didn't really tell me anything I didn't already suspect," Isabella continued, uncomfortable with Noah's silence and the fact that he was still holding the gun. "She only confirmed what I already believed. Anyway, does it matter? I've told you before, no one else knows. Our secret is safe."

Noah said nothing. He returned the gun to its holster.

She breathed a slight sigh of relief. "I realize that you have every right to be angry at me, but you must know the truth. I don't love Rafael. Never did, and I never will." She shuddered. "Just thinking about him is repulsive."

"Liar! You didn't seem repulsed when I caught the two of you together."

She squeezed her eyes shut and opened them again. "Please . . . please try to see beyond that. What I had with Rafael was nothing. We, well . . . we used each other. I just wanted so desperately to go back home. Besides, the whole thing got started because you were so obsessed with living in the United States and running Avian International. Your actions convinced me that you had turned your back on our country, and I felt as if you were also rejecting me." She took a deep breath. "Rafael wanted the same thing I wanted, and he took advantage of my desperation."

"How interesting that you're blaming my *obsession* with Avian International for all of this. Am I supposed to believe that Rafael raped you?"

"No, no. Of course not. What happened was he took advantage of my despair, my vulnerability."

She was about as vulnerable as a cobra, he thought. But he allowed her to ramble on.

"I'm not really blaming you for anything. It was me. Oh, I was such a fool for not trusting you. I should have been patient. I promise you I'll never make that mistake again. We can still be together, Noah. We belong together. Your father wanted us to be."

He resisted the urge to slap her for even mentioning his father's name.

"Gianna mentioned something about you and another woman," she continued. "But that woman is nothing . . . just a poor substitute for the real thing. Forget about her. She is to you what Rafael was to me. You must forgive me. We're all human and we make mistakes. I'm still the one who should be your wife."

How wrong she was, and how dare she compare his relationship with Jasmine to that debauchery she shared with Rafael. He wondered how he could ever have been in love with such a cold, mercenary woman; but as much as he wanted to lash out at her and tell her what he was really thinking, he had to keep his mind fixed on the bigger picture.

"What do you know about my so-called future plans?" Noah said, trying to sound as casual as possible.

"Nothing," Isabella admitted. "But I don't have to know details. It serves me right that you probably won't tell me anything politically confidential again. All I know is that you are finally going to get our country back."

"How do you know that I'm planning anything? Maybe I just came here to visit," Noah said.

"I *know* you. I can see it in your eyes. You're a man of your word. God, if only I could take back all the stupid things I've said and done to hurt you. You're far from being a coward. You had a plan all along. You stuck to it, and now the time is right."

Noah felt his blood pressure decrease a little. He was convinced that Isabella was telling the truth. She really didn't know anything about the details of the plan or who else was involved. The hope of salvaging the mission was still alive.

"Do you really think I can forgive you that easily?" he asked. "It's only through God or fate that I'm alive. What were you planning to do in the future if I'd actually been dead? Tell me what you expected to get out of marrying Rafael? I know you weren't crazy enough to think he could take over the country."

"Rafael? Of course that idiot could never have done it, but as I've said before, he was just my means of getting back. Even if you really were dead, I had no intention of remaining married to him. My hope was for the next generation." Her eyes locked poignantly with his. "My hope was that maybe our son could take the country back."

His heart stopped cold. "Our what? What did you say?"

"It's true." She bit down on her lip. "We have a son. He's two years old and he's living in Spain with my aunt."

Noah's head spun. "I don't believe you!" The words exploded from his mouth. "If there really *is* a child, it's probably Rafael's."

"I know this is a shock," Isabella said slowly. "But I haven't been with anyone else, and I know for a fact that Rafael can't have children."

His ears were ringing. He couldn't believe it. "Why didn't you tell me?"

"Because . . . because of the accident, I never had the chance."

"*Accident?*"

She flinched. "I mean the murder attempt. You know . . . you were in a coma after the car was sent over the cliff. I discovered I was pregnant the day after you found Rafael and me together. You remember how it was with us then. We were both angry, avoiding each other. I never had the chance to tell you."

He felt dazed, shell-shocked, as if he were about to go into another coma. "What is this child's name?"

"Noah Diego Arias. I named him after you and your father," she said, fumbling with her wallet. "I have a picture. He's beautiful. You'll see. He looks like you."

Noah stared vacantly at the picture of a handsome, smiling toddler. He was blond like his mother, but the eyes were gray like his own and the shape of his face was unmistakable.

But it didn't change anything. Even after DNA confirmation, there was no way he could ever reconcile with Isabella. He just couldn't let her know that right now.

"Why isn't the boy living with you?" he asked.

"Rafael didn't want him around."

And neither did you, Noah thought. "Are you his mother in name only?"

There was an uncomfortable silence. "I see him when I can."

"When was the last time you saw him? Tell the truth."

"Last year. But I talk to him on the phone often."

She was a stranger to her own child, and that was no surprise because Isabella had never exhibited any maternal instincts. For all intents and purposes, Noah Diego Arias was an orphan.

Isabella read his mind. "We'll change all that. When we're back together and this country is ours, we'll be a real family."

With eyes sparkling, she rose from the bed and stood face-to-face with him, her fingertips stroking his neck, her lips dangerously close to his own. He could feel the warm penetrating sweetness of her breath brush seductively against his face. The familiar, the predictable.

"Things are all going to work out just as destiny and the stars planned. I have always loved only you, our country . . . and our son."

Her lips met his.

At midnight, in the dimly lit warehouse office of Avian International's Houston branch, Aaron paced grimly. His expression did not need words, and Noah felt the weighty impact of the silence.

"I realize that the risks have increased substantially," Noah said. "But we can still be successful."

"There was only one way to avoid compromising the mission and you refused to follow through," Aaron responded coldly. He knew he could still eliminate Isabella himself, since Noah wouldn't do it, but her being the mother of Noah's child complicated the maneuver and would damage, or even sabotage, their alliance if he went ahead. "It's too risky," he concluded. "My hands are just about tied."

"It's not over!" Noah shouted. "I know what I *could* have done, but for me that was never an option." He jammed his hands into his front pockets and met Aaron's intense glare. "Trust me, man, I can use Isabella the same way she tried to use me. I know her *modus operandi*. I will make it work."

Aaron's dark eyes blazed. "I *do* trust you. But it's not just about us. Other lives are involved. Your sense of righteousness and humanity may serve you well in public service, but as a soldier in a war it's a major liability. The odds are too high."

Noah took a deep breath. "I hear you, and under different circumstances I would totally agree, but time is running out. We *can't* abort. This is the last opportunity we're going to get." He gestured emphatically. "Where is your faith, Aaron? This isn't just about strategy and military prowess. Don't you believe that God will allow justice to prevail?"

Aaron seized the blueprints and maps lining the desk, balled them up and sent it all flying into the trash. "I've been alive a few years longer than you have. I've seen many things, and not all of them were positive. Justice does not always prevail. All one has to do is look at the history books to prove that."

"Where is your faith?" Noah repeated.

"My faith is in my own hands and those of our allies. Only the weak and hopeless turn to God."

A silence fell in the dusty and shadowy warehouse. "Is that how you see me, as weak and hopeless?" Noah asked.

"That statement was a generality which doesn't apply to you," Aaron said. "If it did, we wouldn't be friends or business partners. It's just that I have never come to grips with your spiritual side. I believe in what I can see and touch. I believe in logic and rationality."

"I know where you're coming from, and I realize that I'm asking a lot from you, but trust me, Aaron, even as I trust in God. We're *not* going to fail."

Another long silence ensued, and then Aaron raised his hands in mock surrender. "That being the case, who am I to argue with you and your God? It's your call, Noah."

Noah smiled grimly and clasped Aaron's shoulder. "You won't regret this."

"I hope not. I've had enough regrets in my lifetime."

CHAPTER 21

"You're back!" Morgan exclaimed. "Did you find Mr. Noah?"

"Yes, I did find him," Jasmine said, hugging the small girl. "He has a lot of things to do in his country, but I'm sure he'll tell us all about it when he returns."

"Will he be back before Halloween?"

"I don't think so. Halloween's only a week away."

"How about Thanksgiving?"

Jasmine laughed. "I can't really answer that, Morgan. I hope so. We'll just have to wait and see."

"Can I stay with you in your 'partment?"

"Well, yes, sometimes. Like you did before."

Jasmine held her at arm's length. Morgan's boyish haircut was already growing out. The tousled curls framing her pixie face were starting to touch her shoulders. By summer her hair would probably be down her back once again. She looked healthy although her clothes were shabby. The green plaid skirt she wore was too big and was held up by a safety pin. Her shoes were scuffed and her knee socks were covered with lint. The sight of her made Jasmine flash back to the days of her own childhood—the childhood that always identified her as one of the *poor* kids in school.

"How was school today?"

"It was all right," Morgan said, shrugging. "But I'm glad it's Friday and you're back, so we can do something fun."

Never mind about my life, Jasmine couldn't help thinking with ironic amusement. Children's needs were very linear—they didn't consider an adult's desire for privacy. Still, there was no way she could shut Morgan out any longer. Her plans would just have to include the child if possible.

"Tell you what, Miss Morgan, I don't know if this is exactly going to be a fun weekend, but if Rachel says yes, I'll take you with me to visit my sister in upstate New York."

Morgan's eyes widened. "I didn't know you had a sister. Is she big or little?"

"My sister's name is Natalie. She's a grown lady like me, and she has a little boy named Damon who's about two and a half years old."

"She doesn't have a little girl I can play with?"

Jasmine hesitated for a moment, the image of Dawn passing through her mind. "Sorry. Natalie might be having a little girl or another little boy soon, but the baby hasn't been born yet."

"That's all right," Morgan said quickly. "I want to go with you anyway. Boys are okay when they're small."

The minute she caught the view of the George Washington Bridge in the rearview mirror, Jasmine experienced the lure of the open road. Driving alone in her rented Toyota, she felt completely relaxed with no feeling of trepidation or sense of impending doom, only a heady exhilaration that had eluded her for a long time.

Morgan was not with her because Rachel, who appeared to be in sound mind, had informed her that the child had been naughty and as part of her punishment was not allowed to go. It was good in a way, since Jasmine knew it was a trip that was better taken alone, but she was disappointed because it would have been enjoyable to have someone with her to share the beauty of the autumn scenery, which was now at its peak upstate.

Once in the beautiful and quaint town of Clintonville, Jasmine didn't know what to expect. The serene, almost pastoral beauty of the small-town setting did not tie in with the Natalie she knew. The curious feeling grew when she found the house at 35 Ashford Street. It was a homey, remodeled Victorian with a wrap-around porch, set amidst crimson and gold maple trees. A minivan was in the driveway. Was that actually Natalie's car, or did it belong to her husband?

"Jasmine!" Natalie cried, running out to meet her.

"Natalie!"

The two sisters hugged with difficulty. Jasmine laughed deliriously as she stretched her arms to encircle her sister. Her massive belly, which was encased in a balloon-like red T-shirt, inhibited the embrace.

"Look at you!" Jasmine exclaimed. "Are you having twins?"

"No. Just one very large baby, as far as I know."

Natalie's hair was up in a disheveled topknot, and she wore denim stretch pants and a wide, genuine smile.

"Do you know if it's a boy or girl?" Jasmine asked.

"Nope, Michael and I want it to be a surprise." Natalie's eyes shimmered. "I can't believe you're actually here. God, Jas, it's been such a long time."

"I know, but it's over. Let's go forward from here," Jasmine said.

"Yes, let's. Come on in. I've got so much to tell you."

I'll bet you do, Jasmine thought.

"I'm sorry Michael's not here. He wanted to meet you, but he had to go out of town for a seminar," Natalie said as they entered the house. "He's been praying that we would get back together."

The living room was large, rather old-fashioned, but tastefully furnished and neat. A few toy trucks were lined up in the corner, but nothing like the kind of chaos normally associated with Natalie's lifestyle. She seemed like a different person.

"So, where's my nephew?" Jasmine asked.

Natalie took a deep breath. "He's been running me ragged. I finally got him down to take a nap. Come on, you can take a peek at him if you want."

Jasmine followed her up the stairs and glanced into a typical boy's bedroom with blue walls, fire engines and rocket posters on the wall. The owner of the room lay sound asleep in his race car-shaped bed. Jasmine sucked in her breath. He was a handsome boy with skin the color of a Hershey's kiss and tightly curled black hair in need of a trim. The last time she'd seen him, he'd been sleeping in a crib.

"I know he needs a haircut," Natalie whispered, "but it's so hard taking him to the barber for the first time. I would braid it, but Michael doesn't like braids on little boys."

Michael doesn't like it? Jasmine thought. No doubt about it, this was definitely a changed Natalie. In the past, she'd parted company with every man who'd even dared to disagree with her on anything.

When they were back downstairs sipping coffee in the cozy kitchen, Natalie fell silent and Jasmine could almost read the unspoken words. She gazed at the rooster-faced clock ticking away on the wall above the sink. There was so much to say, it was hard to know where to start.

"I'm sorry," Natalie finally said, startling her. "I'm so sorry for all those awful things I said to you at Dawn's funeral."

"You were upset," Jasmine said, exhaling slowly. "Who wouldn't be?"

"Don't defend me. What I did was horrible, and it wasn't even your fault. Dawn was my baby. She was only two years old. If I'd been watching her—"

Jasmine started to speak, but Natalie waved a hand to silence her. "There's no excuse. Back then I was a horrible mother, an evil, selfish, irresponsible witch. What happened that day was an accident, but I could have prevented it. I blamed you, but it was really because I couldn't stand myself." Tears formed in her eyes. "I still think about her."

"I do, too," Jasmine said slowly, wondering if Natalie sensed what she had been going through.

"But sometimes terrible things happen for a reason," Natalie continued. "I mean, it's crazy, but if I hadn't lost Dawn, I'd probably never have met Michael and found God. I . . . I probably would have ended up just like our mother. Maybe I might have lost Damon, too."

"We can't bring her back," Jasmine said.

"I know, but can you forgive me?"

"If you can forgive me." Jasmine reached across the table and took her sister's hand. They both held on tightly, bridging the tumultuous sea between them. It seemed like an eternity before Natalie spoke again.

"Do you ever think about our mother—ever wonder what really happened to her?"

Jasmine shuddered. "Sometimes. I imagine she's dead now. Maybe she died a long time ago."

"You're probably right." Natalie brightened now. "You know, Jas, it's not like I deserve it, but the Lord's been really good to me. Michael's like the best thing that ever happened in my whole life. He's taken over his father's church, and our congregation is really growing. There are so many young people and—"

Jasmine laughed. "I'm sorry. I'm not making fun, but I guess it's just kind of odd to hear you talk this way. You were never religious before."

"Yeah, I suppose it does sound weird coming from me," Natalie admitted, "but things really are different now. Sure, I remember all the negative things I used to say about God, but then I met Michael and he's really helped me so much with faith and everything. I prayed for forgiveness and God has blessed me. I feel His power. He is merciful."

"I'm happy for you," Jasmine said sincerely.

"And now enough about me. What are you doing? Are you still living in the city?"

Jasmine looked up at the ceiling. She couldn't begin to tell Natalie about her life as a recluse and about how Noah and Morgan had entered it. "Let's just say I'm working my way back to my life."

"Is there someone special?"

"Maybe." Jasmine stirred the coffee in her cup.

"What does that mean, *maybe*? We're sisters. Aren't you going to tell me?"

"I'd like to, but I can't. The relationship isn't completely defined yet."

Natalie rolled her eyes. "You're still the same Jas, complicated. What does he look like?"

"He's gorgeous," she said without mincing words.

Natalie blinked. "Gorgeous as in Shemar Moore? As in Terrence Howard?"

"No. Ruggedly so. Maybe if you could combine Benjamin Bratt and Clive Owen."

Natalie's eyes narrowed. "In other words, as in white guy?"

"Natalie, don't look at me like that. We're not about color."

"You told me after the thing you had with Drew Larsen that you'd never date outside your race again."

"Obviously, I was wrong," Jasmine said. "Anyway, it wasn't deliberate. I'll be able to tell you more later, but right now our difference in skin color is the least of my concerns. There are so many other complications going on that it just doesn't matter."

Natalie shook her head. "Well, I hope you know what you're doing. But it should be okay if you let God into the relationship."

Jasmine bit down hard on her lip to keep from laughing again. She still couldn't get over her sister talking to her in that way. "Noah is a believer," she said.

"Noah?" she quizzed. "Don't tell me he's Jewish."

"So what if he is?" She took a deep breath. "No, he's not Jewish. He's actually Spanish by way of Barcelona, but he was born in Africa."

"You mean he's one of those white South Africans?"

"No. He's from a small country called Cielo Vista. It's a string of islands kind of near Cameroon."

"And?" Natalie said.

Jasmine smiled. "And what?"

"What else about him? Why do you have to be so secretive? It's like I have to practically wring your neck to get you to talk about this guy."

"Just let it go," Jasmine said, still smiling. "I realize that the tables have turned. I was always giving you advice, and now it seems that I'm in need. But you're right . . . if God wills it, the relationship will grow."

And then they talked and laughed for hours about the nearly three years they'd missed from each other's lives. The conversation was mostly about Natalie's growing family and her husband's church, but Jasmine didn't mind because it was such a positive metamorphosis for her sister, and it empowered her own wistful sense of hope—her fragile belief that miracles actually could happen and that it really was possible for a person who was heading down the wrong road to turn around and discover the right path while they were still young enough to enjoy walking it.

CHAPTER 22

Three weeks flew by. It was now early November and Jasmine had not heard a word from Noah. He had warned her that she probably wouldn't hear from him for a while because he wouldn't be able to get back to New York anytime soon and he didn't want to make too many calls that could be traced. Jasmine understood that it was always better to err on the side of caution, but the worry was driving her crazy.

Every day she tuned into the world news reports, waiting, always waiting, for some news about events in Cielo Vista. It was as if her life was permanently on hold pending the final outcome.

She was so absorbed with thoughts of Noah that she felt a growing impatience with Morgan, who on this day was dawdling, whining and complaining of not feeling well because she didn't want to go to school. Jasmine took her temperature, and as expected, it was quite normal.

"I'm sorry," she said, "but you don't have a fever and you're not coughing or anything. Did you tell Rachel you weren't feeling well?"

Morgan's lower lip formed into a pout. "I did, and she said that I have to go. But if I do and get really sick, the nurse will send me home anyway."

Jasmine sighed. "Morgan, what makes you so sure that you're going to be sick? I thought you liked school. Did something happen there?"

"No, but I want to stay here with you 'cause I'm scared."

Jasmine slid her arm around the child's skinny shoulders, drawing her close. She thought about Victor Morales. "Scared? What are you scared of?"

"That . . . that you're going to go away and I'll never see you again."

"Morgan, I'm not going to do that."

"Rachel said so. She said that you're tired of me . . . that you don't want to be bothered with a stupid kid anymore. She . . . she said you're going to move far away."

Jasmine closed her eyes and took a deep breath. "Morgan, listen to me. Rachel's wrong about that. It is true that one day I will leave this building, but that doesn't mean I'll forget about you. I'll still come back to visit you to see how you're doing."

Morgan didn't want to comprehend any of what she'd said. Tears filled her eyes. "I won't be bad . . . ever. I'll do everything you tell me to. I won't talk too much or break things."

Jasmine held her and let her cry. She felt guilty and the truth was she really didn't know what to say. The letter Morgan's grandmother had addressed to her and Noah was still unread in her drawer because she was afraid of what it would reveal. How could anyone keep a promise like that? It would be different if Morgan really was an orphan, but she still had a mother and there was nothing legally she could do to change that. However, it hurt to realize that the child felt that her behavior could determine the outcome of things, and it reminded her of similar feelings she'd had when young. She'd often thought if she and Natalie had been better behaved then maybe their mother wouldn't have abandoned them. She knew better now.

"Honey, you *are* a good girl, and even if you weren't, it wouldn't change anything. You just can't control what other people do. When I leave, it won't be because I don't want to be near you. It's because grownups have to work. We have bills to pay and a whole lot of other responsibilities. I need to find a better job, and when I find it the government will tell me that I'm making too much money to live in this building and they'll make me move."

"Can't I move with you?"

"I wish you could, but you're Rachel's little girl, not mine. I can't take you away from her." She squeezed Morgan tighter and added quickly, "But I'm not going anywhere yet. It won't be today, tomorrow or even next week. When it actually does happen, I promise I'll come to see you often, most weekends if you like. We can still go places and do things."

"You'll still be here tomorrow and the next day and next week?" Morgan asked, her voice choked out between sobs.

"Yes."

"Do I still have to go to school today?"

"Yes, but if you stop crying, I'll walk you there. I'll even stop by to walk you back home."

Morgan wiped her eyes with the back of her hand. "Okay," she said.

The discarded leaves of October were everywhere. They carpeted the ground and crunched under her feet as she walked. The skeletal limbs of the mostly naked trees were etched against the pallid sky. On her way back from walking Morgan to school, Jasmine took the route through the old abandoned park that she had visited with Noah months ago. It seemed more like years. She stopped near the fountain of the headless statue and looked up.

The statue offered no hope, of course. Its prospects were as bleak as ever. As bleak as the stagnant, green-colored water in its moldering, leaf-choked basin. Leaning against the fountain, she whipped out her cell phone and punched in Mariel's number, certain this call would be like all others. Noah's mother was never at home and she never responded to messages. Jasmine had long since stopped leaving them. The phone buzzed once, twice. She waited for the machine to pick up and was startled by a click and an actual human voice saying hello.

"Hello," Jasmine responded quickly. "May I speak to Mariel?"

"She's not home. Is there a message?"

Jasmine recognized the voice. "Hi, Gianna. I'm Jasmine Burke, remember me?"

"Oh, hi." Gianna's voice sounded flat and apathetic.

"I've been calling and calling, trying to reach your mother because it's impossible to contact Noah. I'm wondering if you've heard anything from him?"

"Well, I haven't exactly heard from him yet," Gianna said. "But since he's back with his wife, I'm sure things are better."

Back with his wife! "What?" Jasmine shook the phone, thinking she had a bad connection. "I'm sorry, I didn't quite understand what you said. Could you repeat it?"

"I *said* Noah's probably okay." Gianna sounded testy. "He's back with Isabella and they're out of the country."

Jasmine laughed, despite the bitter, metallic taste forming in her mouth. "Back with Isabella? How can that be? I was under the impression that she didn't even know he was alive."

"She knows it now. She's known for about two weeks."

Jasmine was speechless. There had to be some kind of misunderstanding. Maybe Gianna didn't know what she was talking about.

"Look, I'm sorry I have to tell you this," Gianna continued. "I mean, I suppose you really liked Noah, but you knew he had amnesia and that he was married . . ."

"Isabella and Noah were *divorced*. She's married to someone else," Jasmine interrupted. "How did she find out that he's still alive?" Her words were curt and edged with emotion. They seemed to be coming from a mouth other than her own.

Gianna hesitated. "Well, I told her. She came to see me and she kept asking questions and it didn't seem right not to tell her the truth."

"But you *don't* really know that they're back together, do you? You just know what you told her."

"That's true, but of course they're back together. Why wouldn't they be? She doesn't love whoever she's with now. It's always been the two of them since they were kids."

Jasmine struggled to contain her emotions. What had actually gone down in that short period of time since she'd left him in Cielo Vista? If Isabella knew the whole truth, how could Noah proceed with the military plans? Had he foolishly decided to trust her again? What was going on?

"Gianna, does your mother know what you told Isabella?"

"No. My mother hates Isabella, but she doesn't have the right to keep them apart."

Anger and fear painted the world crimson. "You shouldn't have done that! Don't you realize that secret was kept for a reason?" Jasmine didn't want to hear anything else the misguided girl had to say. Clearly, she had no clue of the dire ramifications of her ignorant actions. She didn't even realize that she had possibly put Noah's life in jeopardy.

Gianna's voice rose. "Why are you yelling at me? I know everyone thinks that Isabella tried to kill Noah, but it's not true. She loves him and she'd never do that. You must be upset because you love him too, but it's not *his* fault. I'm sure he didn't mean to hurt you, but you're just an outsider and you know *nothing* about our family. There's a lot more going on than—"

"I *know* I'm an outsider, but you were still wrong!" Jasmine shouted. "I'm sorry, but I can't talk about this anymore."

She ended the call and stood there dazed, looking at the fountain. What was she going to do now? She had to find Noah. She had to talk to him. She hesitated. But what if she had just been a mere diversion in his twisted world of family betrayal, foreign intrigue and amnesia? Her brain fogged. She didn't know what to think. She didn't know what to feel.

A solitary leaf drifted off a tree, brushed against her nose and made her jump as though she'd been pelted with a stone.

Maybe Noah was in prison right now.

Maybe he was dead.

CHAPTER 23

The night was hot and still as Jasmine stepped out of the taxi in front of the hotel in Montalvo. She felt clammy and slightly nauseated due to the heavy, stifling scent of sulfur in the air, a scent that was much stronger than she recalled it had been a few weeks ago. It was amazing how the natives acclimated themselves to the city's acrid aroma and thought little of it.

Feeling an oppressive sense of *déjà vu,* she inquired about Daniel Viera at the reception desk in the lobby, but there was no such person registered under the bogus name. No surprise. It would have been just too miraculous had he actually been there. It was too late to search for him in Rio Mundo, so she figured she'd head out there in the morning.

Once checked into a room, she dropped down wearily on the bed and perused a local newspaper she had picked up in the airport. Much to her relief, there were no reports of high profile arrests or hints of anti-government conspiracies, but it didn't remove the feeling of doubt that once again she might have been used, betrayed and tossed aside.

She closed her eyes briefly and thought about how futile and ridiculous her decision to return to Cielo Vista was. Of course, some of that decision had been fueled by confusion, anger and fear, but whatever the case, she simply could not have stayed back in New York agonizing and waiting for answers that weren't materializing. At least here there was a slim hope that she might actually find him again and learn the whole truth firsthand.

She had gotten over her anger at Gianna because the girl couldn't possibly have known what she had done. It was probable that she didn't know a thing about Noah's military plans. After all, why would he, Mariel, or any adult have shared such confidential information with a minor? Gianna had probably been left in the dark about matters, and like most children growing up in the shadow of family secrets, she had probably resorted to eavesdropping, hearing half truths and forming her own opinions without solid evidence.

Something else caught her eye in the newspaper. The society page reported that today, November 14, was the president's seventieth birthday, and a big bash was being thrown in his honor at the estate. The party was probably going on right now. *Long live the dastardly Alejandro Arias.* She grimaced at the thought.

Restlessly, Jasmine stood up and paced. She knew she should be exhausted, but it was impossible to sleep. In fact, it was impossible to stay in the room. Nervous energy was driving her insane. No longer concerned with what the locals would think, she dressed in Nikes and a pair of jeans with a yellow sweater. She didn't know where she was going, but she had to take a walk outside.

It didn't seem possible, but the air was even thicker and more odorous than when she'd arrived. Frowning, she gazed toward the blackness of the distant mountains, but they offered no excuses or apologies.

There wasn't much traffic moving about and very few people walking. The silence of the city puzzled her for a moment. *Silly,* she chided herself. *What do you expect? You're not in Manhattan. People actually do stay indoors after dark here.*

She continued walking until she realized with a start that she had come as far as the service road leading to the airport, which was almost three miles from the hotel. The road jogged her memory of an earlier tour with Noah, the moment when they had driven past the governmental estate. If she kept walking in this direction it would take her there. She stopped and stood still. Why did she want to go past the estate? No cut and dried logical reason, only that it was a place of reckoning, and for all she knew, maybe the last connection she'd have with Noah. Her feet propelled her forward.

Would losing Noah to Isabella really be an unbearable thing? Should it be? There was no doubt she was in love with the man and that she desperately wanted him, but she also knew that in no way, shape or form was she ready to play the role of first lady, or for that matter, leave the United States and make Cielo Vista her home. The truth was, she wanted it all—her sanity, her old occupation as an architect, her country of birth, her surrogate child and the man she loved. She wanted it all in a neat package tied securely with a gold ribbon and delivered at her doorstep.

She laughed aloud in order to mask the silent scream building inside her. Even if God helped her to attain some of those wishes, it would all feel empty without Noah.

As she approached the estate, Jasmine's thoughts shifted abruptly to the present. The massive iron gates were wide open. *Strange.* Where were the armed guards? Anyone could just walk right onto the grounds. Puzzled, she moved closer for a better view.

There were sounds coming from within the compound, sounds like war. She distinctly heard muffled shouting and muted gunfire. There was movement. Dark forms were advancing in the night, people were running toward the gate.

A petrifying chill swept over her. It couldn't possibly be happening. It *couldn't*, but it was, right here, right now. Before she could even react, there was a flash of light and something sharp and hot whizzed past her, grazing her forehead. Fighting shock and panic, she flung herself headfirst into a thick row of hedges bordering the gate. The ground trembled and a disembodied scream emanated from her as a deafening roar penetrated the night and the earth convulsed violently. Afraid to look, she sensed without seeing it that the whole sky had ignited.

Upon raising her head cautiously, she felt something hot and sticky trickle down her forehead and make contact with her left eye, partially blinding her. Blood. But she could still move and there wasn't much pain, so in terms of the larger picture, the injury didn't alarm her. Trying to remain camouflaged, she awkwardly pulled a handkerchief from her pocket and dabbed at her forehead as she tried to glimpse the sky from her awkward position beneath the thick hedges.

All she saw were flames. Oh, no! They couldn't have—no way. No military force in some little banana republic had the capacity to deploy nuclear weapons. And then the logical side of her brain clicked back into gear. Of course it hadn't been a nuclear explosion. Mt. Cielo had just blown its top, and she had no idea what she was supposed to do or where she was supposed to run.

Feeling as detached as if in a theatre watching a disaster movie, she continued to lie still. Lights were flashing, people were screaming and running. Cars were moving. A steady stream of vehicles exiting the estate rumbled by, a convoy of some sort. Noah. Where was Noah? Was he in there somewhere? Did he realize what was going on outside? She had to find him. They had to get out of the city before they all died. Visions of the cataclysmic destruction of ancient Pompeii played in her head. As she tried to stand, the earth shook again, bringing her to her knees. She made a second attempt to stand and succeeded. Dazed, she staggered, half walking, half crouching, through the gates and toward the building.

Noah moved stealthily down the dimly lit hallway, gun drawn. He could hear the reassuring static of the walkie-talkies from the remaining back-up commandoes securing the building. The now-deposed president, Rafael, and the rest of the former dignitaries were at this moment being flown out of the city to a prison miles away.

Almost every aspect of the plan had gone perfectly: from the sequestering and eventual control of the media, to Aaron's brilliant orchestration of the prison takeover, right on down to the final attack on the estate. Simon Baraka was once again a free man, and the winds of change were swirling in Cielo Vista.

Noah struggled to contain the powerful surge of adrenaline and awe within him because he could not quite savor the victory yet. There was concern for the welfare of the civilians who were right now being evacuated from Montalvo to the next city, and there was still danger from possible lingering resistance as well as earthquakes and ash fallout from the volcano.

The main complication thus far, which had him still searching the building, was that Isabella, realizing she'd been betrayed and was about to be arrested along with the others, had managed to elude the commando force. He didn't know for sure if she really was still hiding in the estate, but if she was, he felt a moral obligation to find her because her life was in danger. Another earthquake could cause serious structural damage to the building, not to mention the suffocating ash and gases that were in the air. Conditions were worsening outside. He knew there wasn't much time.

"Noah, the chopper's waiting. We have to go!" one of the men shouted in the distance.

"Five more minutes. Just five!" he answered.

"Isabella!" he yelled as a last resort.

Of course there was no response. She knew what awaited her, but could the threat of punishment be worse than dying? She would have to stand trial with the rest of them, but she would get leniency from the court and do very little prison time, if any.

The first thing he planned to do once he flew out was to call the person he missed most. Jasmine. His memory shifted to her last day in Cielo Vista, the day on the beach in Puerto Alba. He could almost see her gold-hued eyes looking into his and hear the singing of the tide as they waltzed on the shore.

As he moved outside the banquet hall, a shadow materialized before him and he was quickly jolted back to the present. He instinctively pointed his gun in the direction of the shadows.

"Isabella!"

Nothing. Perhaps it had been his imagination. The electricity had gone out all over the city and emergency generators, which were no doubt about to fail at any moment, were providing the feeble light that remained in the estate. It was definitely much dimmer than it had been just a few seconds ago. He reached for his flashlight.

The floor shook suddenly under his feet and he braced himself against the wall to maintain his balance. When the shaking ceased, he realized it was time to give up. He could no longer risk other lives in his search for Isabella.

"I'm coming," he barked into the walkie-talkie.

Jasmine knew she shouldn't have gone inside the estate, and had she not been dazed and disoriented, it would have never entered her mind. But here she was inside the dimly lit, rapidly darkening labyrinth of a building, unable to find her way out. And if that wasn't bad enough, she was also a moving target. What on earth had made her think that Noah could still be here? He'd probably left, along with the convoy or the helicopters she'd heard swirling around outside.

She was inching along slowly, back pressed up against the wall, searching for light, any light, when a rumbling sound overwhelmed her and the floor shuddered under her feet. Dropping to her knees, she tried to shield her head against beams that would surely come crashing down. *You're going to die here, you idiot,* she thought, and in a flash of twisted irony, she recalled how just last year at this time she had been an anonymous cleaning woman shuffling about a nursing home with a mop and a broom. Now here she was in a foreign country possibly about to be buried alive in an earthquake.

And suddenly, like a beacon of light, she heard a voice in the distance. Noah's voice.

"Noah!" she screamed.

The quaking stopped and the building trembled once more and then composed itself. She stood up straight, looking, listening. It was pitch black now. "Noah!" she called again. "I'm over here!"

"*Jasmine?*" His disembodied voice sounded shocked, as well he would be.

"Over here! Over here! I can't see you," she shouted.

She heard his footsteps and saw a beam of light illuminating the darkness. Just as she recognized his formidable, weapon-bearing presence and was about to cry out in relief, an arm sprang serpent-like from the shadows and encircled her throat. Shocked, she tried to turn around, to struggle, but felt the cold, hard metal of a gun pressed against her temple.

"You move and you're dead!" a high-pitched, female voice hissed in her ear. Jasmine could feel the gun's muzzle trembling against her and realized that her captor was as terrified as she was. If it weren't for the weapon, she could probably overpower her, but an attempt right now might cost her life. Instead, she found herself staring helplessly, incongruously, at Noah. His hair was black again, black and gleaming, his eyes piercing, panther-like.

"Isabella, put the gun down and let her go!" he commanded, his voice terse but amazingly controlled.

His gun was pointed directly at Isabella—or was it pointed at her? Jasmine couldn't tell. She *could* tell that Isabella reeked ludicrously of some kind of nauseating, expensive perfume, and that she was wearing a gem-studded tennis bracelet, because she could feel the hardness of it biting into her neck.

"No, I won't!" Isabella shouted back, her voice strained with emotion, her free arm tightening around Jasmine's neck. "I can't believe what you're doing! You're throwing away all we have for this, this nobody? What about our future . . . our son? What about us?"

"Listen to me, Isabella. We're divorced, and those days are gone. There is no *us* and there never will be. But if you drop that gun right now, I can get you a pardon and you won't have to go to prison."

Son? Jasmine wondered, shell-shocked. *What son?* Noah had never told her anything about a child. Why was it even registering? She was going to die. Maybe he was going to kill her and spare Isabella instead. Before squeezing her eyes shut, she realized that others were in the building. She could see more shadows.

"Pardon! I don't care about a pardon!" Isabella shrieked, outraged. "We're destined. We belong together and you know it. I'm sorry, Noah, but you don't need this. You can't have it both ways. She has to go!"

"This is the last time, Isabella. Drop the gun now! Don't make me do this."

The nightmare wasn't going to end peacefully. Jasmine sensed Isabella's trembling finger curling around the trigger and imagined a click. No way was she just going to submit helplessly to fate. No way was she ready to die! With all her strength, she rammed her elbow into the madwoman's rib cage and simultaneously catapulted herself forward, away from a flash of light that heralded the deafening crack of gunfire. Despite her own singular focus on survival, her peripheral vision revealed Isabella crumpling to the floor.

"Jasmine!" Noah's face was as white as a sheet as he grabbed her, dropping his gun. "Are you all right?"

"Yes. I . . . I . . ." she stammered, lost in his embrace. She was totally losing it now, her eyes filling with tears. "I'm sorry, Noah. I'm sorry," she sobbed.

Through the blur of tears, she saw men in the background descend upon the scene and one of them bend over Isabella. Noah didn't move. His arms were still tightly wrapped around her and she could feel the intensity of his heartbeat. "Is she dead?" he asked, his voice hollow.

"She's still alive, but barely." Jasmine vaguely recognized Aaron's voice. "We have to evacuate immediately."

She went numb. The voices, the sounds faded to nothing. Later she didn't remember being carried out of the building into the suffocating ash from Mt. Cielo or the harrowing ride on the helicopter to the refugee city.

CHAPTER 24

"Well, Jasmine, here I am again. Can you hear me? I know you can, so I'll just keep talking. Everything is working out perfectly. I know you're happy to hear this. We can finally be together the way God meant for us to be. No more complications, no more drama. It's just us now, you and me."

The lighting in the room appeared blurred, distorted—beiges, whites, pale yellows all swirling around abstractly. But one focal point was very clear. She was staring into a pair of misty, sea-swept gray eyes that were guiding her back. Back from where? She allowed his eyes to lead and she became cognizant.

"You and me? Something's wrong with this picture," she murmured, her voice thick. "I'm supposed to be sitting where you are and you're supposed to be in bed."

Noah laughed. His laughter sounded unbridled, emotional. "You're right. However, I can gladly arrange it so we're both in bed this time."

"Really, Noah." She blushed and wondered where that reaction was coming from.

"All kidding aside, you do realize that you're in a hospital, don't you?"

"Yes. Where?"

"We're still in Africa."

A rush of anxiety consumed her. "Oh, no! Don't tell me that a lot of time has gone by!"

He laughed again, a deep, throaty chuckle, and it struck her just how much she loved that laugh.

"Don't worry," he said. "It's only been two days, not two years."

She slowly raised her hand to her forehead and felt a bandage. She was starting to recall, but it was almost as if she didn't want to.

"It seems you were hit with a piece of shrapnel," Noah said. "But you were really lucky. Other than being traumatized and in shock, the doctor said it's nothing serious. You've got a few stitches, and you were pretty heavily sedated."

She remembered the exact moment of the injury. It had happened when she'd taken her first step onto the estate's grounds, right before the volcano's eruption. The enormity of the past events hit her like a freight train. For a moment, she felt breathless and panicky as images of gunfire and Isabella replayed in her mind. She was afraid to ask. She didn't want to know, but the question spilled out. "Noah, what happened to Isabella?"

"We took her here to this hospital. They tried to save her, but she didn't survive the surgery."

Jasmine averted her eyes and stared toward the open window. The sunlight streaming into the room seemed mocking. "I don't know what to say. I can't begin to tell you how sorry I am for causing . . ."

He leaned forward and silenced her with a kiss. "No. You are *not* going to play the 'blame yourself' guilt game again. What happened to Isabella was caused by her own actions. I feel terrible for what I had to do, but it would have been far worse to lose you."

She searched his eyes again and the sincerity was palpable, possessive even. She inhaled deeply. God, she loved him, but she still wasn't sure of the ramifications of that love.

She toyed with the bed sheet. "I realize how hard that moment must have been for you, and I do owe you an explanation as to why I was there. It . . . it was because I learned from Gianna that Isabella knew everything, and she also told me that you and she were back together again. I didn't know for sure what that meant and I thought you might be in trouble—"

"Your being there at that time really shocked me, but I understand why you did what you did," Noah interrupted. "It was *beyond* dangerous and the whole thing could have had a terrible ending, but God didn't allow it. I just don't want you to think for one second that I ever considered going back with Isabella."

"But is it true that you and Isabella have a son?"

"Yes. I would have told you if I'd known, but it was a shock to me, too. He's about two years old and he's temporarily living in Spain with Isabella's relatives. I haven't even met him yet."

"And now you'll have to tell him that his mother's dead."

Noah took a deep breath. "That's going to be hard, but by her own admission Isabella was no textbook mom. She pretty much dumped the kid on her relatives and only called him a couple of times a year. He hardly knew her."

She toyed with the sheet again and shook her head as if to clear it. "Noah, is this . . . this whole military thing really over?"

"The most dangerous part, yes. The reconstruction has just begun."

"I'm just so glad that you're okay, that you're alive."

"I told you we would do it. God willed it, Mt. Cielo cooperated and the timing was perfect. If it weren't for the volcano, there would have been a lot more bloodshed. When it erupted, the president and his flunkies were drinking and partying. They were caught off guard and they panicked. It made our job easier."

There definitely had to have been some sort of divine intervention, Jasmine thought. She was convinced of it. No way could all of those events have just coincidentally come together on that night. "Could you tell me how you got all those soldiers to cooperate?"

"A lot of the people involved were working for the U.S. Avian International has a huge military contract with the United States Air Force. A lot of our pilots are also ex-military."

"But why the interest? I don't get it. Surely the United States wouldn't be that interested in diamond exports."

He laughed. "Cielo Vista has something a lot more valuable than diamonds." He lowered his voice. "It has oil deposits. I'm the only one who knows exactly where they are located. Even Alejandro Arias knew nothing about that. We plan to trade with ally nations, but the profit from exporting the oil will be used to benefit our own citizens right here instead of just lining the pockets of corrupt politicians."

For a second, Jasmine was dumbstruck, just taking all the information in. "Was Montalvo destroyed?" she finally asked.

"No. Most of the buildings are still standing, but some collapsed under the weight of the ash. The volcano has calmed down, and a big clean up is underway at this moment.

"It's all just, just so awesome," she said, sounding and feeling like a giddy teenager. "Well, I guess I can get back to New York now without having to worry about you. I didn't plan to be here this long. There are issues with Morgan again, and I'm kind of worried about her."

"I know," he said. "You might have to remain here in the hospital for a few more days, but when you do return, I'm going with you."

She looked puzzled. "What? How can you do that?" She unconsciously fluttered her fingers over the sheet again and found herself staring at her own hand. What she saw there made her gasp. On her ring finger was a beautiful gold band spangled with gems—diamonds.

"Oh, my God." She raised her hand. "Noah, what is this?"

"Some people call it an engagement ring. I was hoping you would be pleased, not shocked."

"I *am* pleased, b-but it's too soon. I mean, I haven't really thought about this since so much was going on. I don't think I can live in Cielo Vista. I'm from New

York. I want to feel whole again, work as an architect again. I don't know anything about being first lady to a president."

"President?" he repeated, laughing again.

She couldn't understand why he was laughing. She stared at him incredulously.

"Apparently you missed a few things," Noah continued. "Let me take the time to tell you, my love, my fiancée, that I have no intention of staying here to be president of this country. My mission was to get the country back into the right hands. I never said those hands were mine. The presidency will go to Simon Baraka."

"Simon Baraka." She mouthed the words, hardly able to believe them. "You and Aaron risked your lives for Simon?"

"Simon is a man after my own heart, and even better, he's a native African. My dream has always been that this country should be returned to those whom it rightfully belongs. I will have to be involved here for a while during the reconstruction, but make no mistake about it: I am no politician and I never will be. Aaron and I have our hands full running Avian International, and my home is in the United States with you. I want us to be a family, Jasmine. I mean to marry you. Do you want the same thing?"

"Yes, but—"

"No buts," He cupped her chin with his hand, raising her head so they stared directly into each other's eyes. "We've come a long way. I don't want anything else between us, not countries, not ghosts, not the past."

He had her attention. She sat up straight, her heart bursting at the seams. Could this be real? After all the trauma—all the sorrow—she was getting exactly what she wanted handed to her with no strings? She laughed to keep from crying and reached out to him. He held her in his arms and they remained locked in an embrace for a long time.

Jasmine didn't get out of the hospital until four days later. Noah took her on a helicopter tour of Montalvo and she saw firsthand the results of the volcano's meltdown. The city was still standing, but most of the buildings were buried up to their windows in a fine gray ash. The airport was temporarily shut down and only emergency flights were going out on a much smaller runway in Rio Mundo. Surprisingly, the picturesque seaport had suffered little damage at all.

The towering mountain, which had returned to its peaceful slumber, seemed to be gloating. Noah told her that it had diminished a bit in height after literally blowing its top, but she didn't notice any significant change in its appearance.

There was panic of course, mostly among the supporters of the ousted Alejandro Arias regime. They were trying to get out of a country that no longer spread its welcome mat for them. Arrangements were being made for this, but it wasn't going to happen overnight. The remaining citizens were supportive and hopeful even though armed soldiers patrolled the streets and there was a temporary curfew at night.

Jasmine had the feeling that Noah held back on telling her all the details. He didn't have to. She could well imagine the difficult path ahead of him, and even more for Simon Baraka, who barely had time to embrace his freedom from prison. Despite this, he was up to the task.

There had been some initial confusion among the people because they had expected, as she had, that Noah was going to be president, but he had skillfully introduced Simon at the televised press conference, and from then on everyone observed the incredible persuasive powers of Mr. Baraka, and Jasmine acknowledged first-hand everything Noah had told her about him. He was stalwart, powerful, a motivational speaker, and even more significantly, she could see the sincerity and heart of the man. Simon Baraka was no stereotypical career politician who read his lines from a script. He believed in everything he said and was willing to work hard toward the goal of making Cielo Vista a better place for its people.

On the morning of the day she was scheduled to leave the country, she, Noah and Aaron had breakfast in the dining room at the charming bed and breakfast in Rio Mundo. Noah was very attentive to her, but politics dominated the conversation and she welcomed it. She didn't want to be left in the dark as to what was going on. The only dicey moment came when he left his seat to converse with the inn's owner, leaving her sitting with Aaron.

"I must admit you've turned out to be something of a surprise to me," Aaron said, stirring his coffee.

Jasmine managed a smile, although she found being alone with him disconcerting. "How is that?"

"You have a loyalty and determination that's unusual for . . ."

"A woman," she interrupted, unable to resist.

He smiled. She blinked. The smile was a little bit mocking, but it was a real smile, and it looked good on him.

"I wasn't going to say that. I was going to say for a person born in the United States with no military background."

She smiled again. "That's still kind of offensive, but not quite as if you had said the other."

"I'm not trying to offend you." He inadvertently glanced at the engagement ring on her finger. "I just want to congratulate you. I believe Noah's made a good choice this time."

She didn't want to admit that she felt pleased by his acceptance because even half of a compliment was nice coming from Aaron. "Thank you," she said quietly. "But you shouldn't hold Isabella against Noah. She was never really his choice anyway. His family kind of determined that."

"I suppose we often do fall victim to our circumstances."

She blinked again, wondering if he was talking about her and Noah, himself, or a combination of all. It would be nice if he revealed more of his inner thoughts because, as much as she hated to admit it, his cool cynicism was intriguing. But today was clearly not going to be the day. Maybe he would at some point. If not to her, perhaps to some woman in the future, a unique woman who would find the key to his heart. She almost laughed. What was she thinking? The notion of Jasmine Burke as match-maker was beyond ridiculous.

Noah returned to the table and sat down. "Are you two kids playing nice?"

Jasmine laughed. Aaron didn't.

"There's something I failed to mention to you," he addressed Noah.

"What's that?"

"I looked over the autopsy report on Isabella,"

Jasmine frowned, wondering why he had to bring that up now. She glanced at Noah, who looked impassive.

"And?" Noah said.

"At the time of the confrontation, we both fired at her, but it was my bullet that killed her. I just thought you'd like to know that."

Jasmine exhaled sharply as she felt Noah's emotional release. Silence settled over the trio, a long silence.

"I'm glad you told me," Noah said finally.

CHAPTER 25

Back in Brooklyn, Jasmine coughed as a nauseating, smoky odor drifted out into the hallway from the partially open apartment door, followed closely by an ominous phantom figure that seemed to materialize from the haze.

"I ain't seen you in a while," Rachel said.

Jasmine restrained herself from recoiling. The woman looked horrible. Her dried-up hair was literally matted to her head, her skin blotchy and bruised. Two of her front teeth were glaringly missing, and one eye appeared to be swollen shut. She looked like a battered homeless person.

"I had to go away on business," Jasmine said, taking a deep breath. "I know it's not quite noon and Morgan must be in school, but I was wondering how things are going."

The minute the words escaped she felt foolish. It was pretty obvious how things were going.

"They going fine. I don't have no time to talk 'cause see, I been real sick. Lots of viruses going round this time of year. Got the kids all sent off with my sister. They down in Newark. All 'cept Tamara and her baby. She living across the street with her boyfriend and his mother."

Jasmine's eyebrows rose. "Morgan's in Newark, too?"

"I *said* the kids, didn't I? She one of them."

"Look, Rachel, I'm sorry you're not well, but I only asked because you told me a while back that your sister didn't want to be responsible for Morgan."

"Well, things change, okay?"

"But what about school?"

"They in school there. I gotta go now. Bye."

The door banged shut and Jasmine remained standing in the hall. Morgan was in Newark? Somehow she couldn't comprehend that. If Rachel was telling the truth, how was she going to find her? She knocked half-heartedly on the door again, not expecting a response.

"Could you at least give me your sister's phone number?" she asked in vain.

No answer. Frustrated, Jasmine returned to her apartment. "Noah, what should I do now?" she murmured aloud. Maybe she was typically overreacting. It was, after all, a good thing that Morgan was in Newark right now because Rachel looked like death warmed over and obviously wasn't even capable of taking care of herself, let alone her children. Under different circumstances, she would have felt sympathy for the pathetic woman, but it was just too obvious that her *virus* came from crack addiction and the swollen eye was probably courtesy of Victor Morales.

She missed Noah already. He hadn't been able to catch the same flight out with her, due to his involvement in Cielo Vista, but he'd promised that he'd join her as soon as he could. She wasn't expecting him right away because she knew the tasks that lay ahead of him were monumental.

Next on her agenda had been plans to start packing and disposing of things so she could vacate the hideous apartment as soon as possible, but not knowing Morgan's status was throwing a damper on those plans.

Think, Jasmine, think. She sank down on the sofa. Maybe Rachel's oldest daughter would give her the sister's number in Newark, if she could find the daughter. She sighed.

A pile of unopened junk mail lay on the coffee table. On the top of the pile was the letter from Morgan's grandmother. Jasmine picked it up and couldn't contain her sudden smile of irony as she again scanned the name of the recipient. *Jasmine and Noah Arias.* The concept was no longer a jest. Mrs. Garcia had known all along.

No longer intimidated by the letter, she opened it and read exactly what she'd suspected would be there. It stressed over and over again, in no uncertain terms, that they were to have custody of Morgan. There was even the name of a lawyer who she claimed would fight for them. She put the letter down.

It didn't seem logical that it could happen, but a few months . . . a few weeks ago, it didn't seem logical that she would be engaged to Noah either. The truth was that there was nothing she could do for Morgan right now except pray for God's direction. Since she had already seen on a very large scale just how powerful prayer and positive thinking could be, she was not about to wallow in anxiety. That road was well worn and marked with ruts and potholes.

Besides, she was so happy she felt delirious. Good things were looming on the horizon and she wanted to share them with someone. She would call Natalie and Valerie right now to tell them about her engagement. They were going to be shocked.

"You're here!" Jasmine exclaimed, literally pulling Noah into the tiny foyer, mesmerized by how tall and handsome he appeared with his sun-tanned skin and raven-black hair.

"Told you I would come. Never mind it's after midnight."

She kissed him on the mouth, inhaling his cool, breezy masculine scent, enjoying the tangy taste of him. She immediately began helping him out of his coat, which dropped to the floor at his feet.

"Wow! That's quite a welcome," he teased. "I guess that means you're glad to see me."

"You bet it does," she replied, fingering the buttons on his shirt. "How'd you get here?"

"I flew out two hours after you did on a non-commercial flight. There are advantages to co-owning a cargo airline."

He allowed her to unbutton his shirt halfway, and then he held her at arm's length and chuckled. "Nice pigs."

She glanced down at the ridiculous, oversized pig slippers on her feet and laughed too. Between that and her long purple robe, she was quite a sight.

"Sorry, I've never been into making fashion statements after midnight. I've had these for a while. Dawn loved them. She picked them out for me on my birthday. Natalie said I needed something silly because I was just too serious."

It suddenly occurred to her that she had actually mentioned Dawn with fond remembrance as opposed to pain and sorrow. The feeling enveloped her like a warm, gentle breeze and invoked a smile.

"I'm looking forward to meeting Natalie soon," Noah said, sliding his arm around her as they walked into the living room. He noticed that she had the television on. "I can see why you couldn't sleep. Your friends next door are carrying on. They're so loud I could hear them while I was coming up on the elevator."

She sighed. "I think they're just starting to calm down now."

"Doesn't anyone ever call the cops?"

"Oh, please." Jasmine rolled her eyes. "It wouldn't do any good . . . not in this neighborhood."

"I'm assuming Morgan's sleeping over with you." He glanced toward the bedroom.

Jasmine sighed. "She definitely would be if I had any say in it, but Rachel told me that she and the other kids are in Newark staying with her sister. It's awful, Noah. Rachel's really off the wall. She needs to be in rehab."

But even as she mentioned her, she did not want to dwell on Rachel's issues. What she was really thinking about was how silly it seemed that Noah probably intended to sleep on the couch even though they were engaged. What difference would it make if they shared the bedroom at this point? She stopped herself. It seemed like a trivial technicality to wait for the actual marriage, but acknowledging God meant obeying his commandments fully, not just picking and choosing what to obey and what not to. *As long as you don't push my buttons, Noah, we'll be okay,* she thought.

"Guess we've got some plans to discuss and some packing to do in the morning," Noah said. "I'd like to see you out of this place as soon as possible." He'd sat down on the couch and was about to remove his shoes. "Might as well try to salvage some of the night."

She'd opened her mouth to speak when a muffled thump outside the door silenced her. Noah cocked his head sideways. "Do you normally have visitors at this time?"

"Uh, Jasmine . . . I mean, Ms. Burke. I know it's late but I need help," said a voice, that of a young woman from out in the hallway. And it didn't sound like Rachel.

Noah stood up as Jasmine went to the door.

"Who are you? What do you want?" she asked without opening it.

"I'm Tamara, Morgan's sister."

Immediately, Jasmine unlatched the door, admitting the teenager who was dressed in a hooded black parka with a scarf around her neck. She looked extremely nervous and even more so when she saw Noah.

"Are . . . are you a cop?" she asked.

"No. He's my fiancé," Jasmine answered for him. "What's wrong, Tamara?"

"They . . . my mother and her friends . . . they're all passed out from drugs and drinking and stuff, and it's Morgan. She's really sick. I can't get her to . . ."

The blood drained from Jasmine's face. "Morgan! Isn't Morgan in Newark?"

"No. The other kids are. They got her here locked up in the closet. I've been sneaking food and stuff to her when I could, but I think she's hurt. She's been in there for about a week. She's not moving. She . . ."

Before Jasmine could say anything else, Noah was out the door. She rushed after him, forgetting all about Tamara. Her heart hammered inside her chest. *Oh, God, please no . . . not again . . . not another child. Not Morgan.*

The door to 12C was wide open and the usual smoky fumes drifted out. Inside, strangers were lying supine and entwined on the couch and sprawled out on the floor. Deranged laughter came from an interior room. No one confronted them or even noticed their arrival.

"In here," Tamara murmured from the shadows.

The hall closet had an outside chain lock on it. Noah opened it and was hit with the stench. In the darkness, Jasmine could just make out the form of a filthy, half-naked child tangled up in rags and dirty clothing lying unconscious on the floor. Unconscious, but breathing.

Despite the squalor, Jasmine dropped down on her knees and cradled the child in her arms. She began rocking back and forth, tears streaming down her face. "Morgan, it's me. I'm here. It's all right, you're going to be—"

"Jasmine, let me take her. We've got to get her to a hospital now," Noah said urgently. He was beyond shocked and angry by the appalling abuse of the innocent child, but he sensed that Jasmine's trauma was even greater.

"No. It's okay. I'm okay. I've got her." Trying not to tremble, Jasmine covered the child with an old coat and lifted her carefully, aware that her arm was positioned at an unnatural angle, obviously broken.

As they were about to leave the asylum, footsteps sounded and someone yelled, "Hey, what you think you're doing!"

Noah spun around to face an enraged, glassy-eyed man charging at them like a bull. Without the slightest hesitation, he hauled off and slammed the man square in the jaw. Morales dropped to the floor like a ton of bricks.

On the way to the hospital, Noah dialed the police on his cell. They would have to deal with the rest of the fallout from apartment 12C. Jasmine cradled Morgan in her arms all the way to the emergency room, unaware that Tamara had pulled a complete disappearing act, unaware of anything except her own prayer that Morgan's body and spirit would heal.

CHAPTER 26

The story made headlines in a city still reeling from past child abuse cases where the children ended up dead. Victor Morales was arrested on child endangerment and drug charges, and Rachel was about to be once she got out of the hospital where she had been taken for a nearly fatal overdose.

Jasmine spent the rest of the night in the hospital with Morgan, who'd undergone surgery to fix her fractured arm. The child had cuts and bruises and was also suffering from dehydration, but the doctors said that she would recover. The emotional damage would probably take longer to heal.

Noah couldn't get Jasmine to budge from Morgan's side, so he ended up returning to the apartment to answer questions for the police and to get her some appropriate clothes. He'd had to remind her that she was still wearing a purple bathrobe and pig slippers.

When Morgan woke up at the gleaming of dawn, the first person she saw was Jasmine bending over her bed.

"Jasmine?" Morgan said. Her angelic voice sounded weak and shaky but hope was still burning in her beautiful brown eyes. She even had a faint smile.

"It's me. I'm here, baby. You're in the hospital," Jasmine said. "The doctors had to fix your arm."

Morgan gazed, detached, at her left arm encased in a white cast.

"It's not so bad having a cast," Jasmine said. "Actually, it can be kind of cool. You can have other people draw pictures on it and sign their names. See, mine's there already. Noah's going to sign his, too."

Morgan looked down again and smiled at the purple inked name with hearts surrounding it. Her mouth puckered. "Do I have to go back with Rachel?"

Surprised that she would ask that so soon, Jasmine responded emotionally. "No. Never. You belong to me and Noah now."

All traces of sadness vanished from Morgan's face. "I can live with you always?"

What was I thinking? Jasmine bit down on her lip. "Here's what's going to happen. We're going to do everything we can to make that possible, but in the meantime there are people from this place called Social Services. They might temporarily have you stay with another nice family until . . ."

Her lip trembled. "I don't *want* another family. I want you and Noah. Grandma promised!"

A tear trickled down Jasmine's cheek. "If your grandmother promised you, then we *are* going to help keep that promise, too. It's just that in this crazy grownup world, there are a lot of papers to fill out and lawyers and stuff like that."

Morgan's attention faded. She clutched at the pillow with her good hand and squeezed her eyes shut. "I was really scared. They wouldn't let me out. It was dark in

there." Her voice turned to a sob. "There were m . . . m
. . . monsters. They hurt me."

Jasmine sat on the bed and gathered the child in her
arms. "I know. I know. But the monsters are gone now.
It's all over. They'll never hurt you again. Noah and I are
going to fix everything."

She continued to hold her until she was suddenly
aware that Morgan was trembling slightly and giggling.
Giggling? Jasmine looked puzzled and followed where
the child's eyes were focused. They were centered on the
enormous, fuzzy pink pig slippers still on her feet.

In the following weeks, no one had time to even
think about relaxing. Noah was continually flying back
and forth between Africa and New York, while Jasmine
remained living in the Brooklyn project to be near
Morgan, because once released from the hospital, the
child welfare agency had had her placed in a state-run
orphanage that was located in Brooklyn. It was similar to
the one she herself had grown up in.

In the meantime, the custody battle had begun.
Things were looking good because in her will, Morgan's
grandmother had named her remaining son as heir, but
had requested specifically that Jasmine and Noah should
raise Morgan. That son was obviously in no position to
raise a child since he was deployed overseas in the military, and therefore was in total agreement and willing to
do whatever he could to support the decision. The most

positive thing of all was that a contrite Rachel, now in prison, was agreeing and hinting that she was going to allow them to permanently adopt Morgan because she couldn't take care of her. Jasmine was also increasingly aware that she and Noah should get married soon because it would cement their relationship and possibly solidify their grounds for adoption.

During all that, Jasmine managed to accompany Noah to Spain, where he got acquainted with his son and immediately bonded with him. Diego was an adorable, curly-haired toddler, very much the typical two-year-old. Shy at first, once he adjusted, he transformed into a perpetual state of mischief, charm and activity. As Noah had predicted, the little boy didn't have much of a reaction to being told about his mother's death. Jasmine found it sad in a way, but it made it easier for her to love him on sight because she didn't have to contend with the ghost of his mother even though he resembled her.

Isabella's elderly relatives, who had mostly delegated his care to an *au pair*, gladly relinquished the boy and he was taken to stay with Noah's mother in South Carolina. She would temporarily care for him until they married and decided on a place to live.

Morgan and Diego met for the first time when Noah and Jasmine took both kids on an outing in Manhattan. The administrators at the orphanage where Morgan was temporarily placed allowed her to spend the day with them. The little girl had been very subdued in the last few weeks, but Jasmine was delighted that today she was her old self. Most of that she attributed to Diego's presence.

As the four of them strolled the avenues, gawking at the city's seasonal holiday displays, Morgan was totally captivated by the little blond, curly-haired boy. He couldn't speak a word of English, but it didn't seem to matter in the least. The language barrier didn't concern Jasmine either. At two, he didn't have an enormous vocabulary anyway, so it would be easy for him to adapt to English.

They entered a festively decorated, overpriced toy store just to watch children, big and small, run amuck. Shoppers were everywhere with their little ones in tow. Choruses of "I want this and I want that," rang through the air. A harried mom loudly disciplined her pouting son in the middle of the aisle while her twin babies screamed in their stroller.

"This is crazy," Noah said. "So this is what being a parent is like?"

"I'm afraid so," Jasmine said with a smile. "And it gets worse."

"Diego, look at the train!" Morgan shouted.

Distracted from reaching for a stuffed lion, which tumbled to the floor, leaving Jasmine to pick it up, Diego scampered over to where Morgan was. Noah lifted him so he could get a better view of the encased display, which contained a miniature winter village featuring Lionel trains winding through tunnels and mountains and fields white with fake snow.

Jasmine watched the child's eyes light up. In his toddler phase, he resembled a tiny cherub with gorgeous gold curls that needed trimming. He would have made a beautiful girl.

"I love this train," Morgan said, pressing her nose against the display. "I wish I had one just like this."

Noah smiled and tugged playfully at the fuzzy ball on top of her red knitted cap. "You'll need an awfully big room to set this up in, but maybe one day you will."

"Diego likes it, too," Morgan beamed.

Diego wanted the train. Now.

"Sorry, sport. Not today," Noah told his whining son. "You can have one thing in the store, but it has to be something you can carry."

Jasmine gulped. The baby's eyes were scrunched up and his angel face was turning red. She recognized the signs from when she used to take care of Dawn. Little Diego was about to have a meltdown. Apparently, Morgan sensed it, too.

"I'll help him pick something," she offered eagerly, as Noah set him back down on the floor. She quickly took his hand. "Let's look over here, Diego. Wow! Look at the cool airplanes."

"Good girl," Jasmine praised as the situation was defused. She took Noah by the arm. "Daddy, I think you've got some things to learn about kids," Jasmine teased him. "Never take a two-year-old to a toy store and ask him to select just one thing."

Noah shook his head and laughed. "You're right. Running a country is a piece of cake compared to this. I definitely have a lot to learn, but it looks like Morgan's willing to teach me."

"Hmmm, I think she's teaching us both."

They finally left the store with a silver replica of a 747 jetliner for Diego and a holiday edition Barbie doll for Morgan. After leaving the packages in the car, they walked to Rockefeller center and joined the skaters on the ice rink. Jasmine skated with Diego and Noah with Morgan. She still had her arm in a cast, so he was careful that she didn't fall.

It turned out to be a special, enjoyable family day.

Late in December, Jasmine and Noah stood outside the mountain house in the Ramapo hills surveying the scene. Snow was falling gently around them. In the pristine silence of the woods, she could hear its whispery sound. As she inhaled the strong aroma of the pines, she felt she couldn't have conjured up a more beautiful, seasonal setting. The place seemed to be drawing them in, offering peace and a strong desire to shelter them.

"So what do you think?" Noah asked, glancing at the realtor's For Sale sign.

She smiled. "You know what I'm going to say. Let's keep it."

"Are you sure? I mean, I want you to be able to make it yours."

"Oh, I definitely can. Anyway, you told me that Isabella hated this place, so I don't associate it with her. It's you I'm concerned about. Can you live here with memories about the accident and all?"

He smiled. "If things hadn't happened the way they did, we wouldn't be standing here together now. I'm seeing a clean slate. I don't hold the house responsible."

She rubbed her hands together enthusiastically as a buffer against the cold. "Morgan and Diego will love it here," her eyes sparkled mischievously, "as well as whatever other little person we might add in the future."

"Then it looks like we've got ourselves a home." He yanked down the For Sale sign and turned to kiss her.

They had a very small, private wedding in January, which was attended by Natalie and her husband; Noah's mother and sister; Aaron; and a few other friends. Jasmine was highly entertained to observe her friend Valerie acting like a smitten teenager around Aaron. It was true that he actually was attractive in a glacial kind of way, but the idea of them as a couple was totally ludicrous.

Soon after the wedding they were assured custody of Morgan in a few months, and Jasmine permanently freed herself of the apartment in Brooklyn. She considered signing on as a partner with an architecture firm in Manhattan, but decided she'd hold off on her career a little while longer so she could focus on her new family.

Rachel's other kids remained living with her sister, and Tamara, the older daughter, remained in Brooklyn raising her baby, attending school and living with her boyfriend's family. It turned out that she was actually a good student with aspirations to be a teacher. Because they were grateful that she'd been courageous enough to help save Morgan's life despite knowing the decision would cost her mother jail time, Jasmine and Noah set aside a scholarship fund for her, in hopes that she would stay in school and not repeat her mother's lifestyle.

EPILOGUE

Jasmine, Noah and Morgan stepped out into the sunlight, leaving Brooklyn's children's home in the shadows.

"Are the people of Cielo Vista happy now?" Morgan asked.

"Very happy," Noah said.

"The animals, the trees and the mountains too?"

Noah laughed. "Yes, Princess Morgan, everything, including the snakes and spiders."

"I'm glad," she hesitated, "even for snakes and spiders 'cause it's awful to be sad all the time."

"It is," Jasmine agreed, hugging her. "But our family is going to be very happy."

They had just signed Morgan out of the home permanently, and it was the most beautiful spring day Jasmine could remember in a long time. A warm, gentle breeze caressed them as they walked hand-in-hand down the block with Morgan in between them.

"Noah, I think we just passed the car," Jasmine said.

His eyes twinkled "I know. We're going for a walk."

"Where?" Morgan asked eagerly.

"Oh, it's no big deal, but it's a place Jasmine likes."

Jasmine frowned. "But we're almost near the old projects. There isn't any place around here that I could actually say I like."

"Just keep walking."

They were getting closer to her old stomping grounds, but then he swung right and they rushed across the street. Morgan was laughing and skipping lightly about like a butterfly in her bright yellow jacket and short denim skirt. Jasmine laughed now. They were heading straight for the dilapidated park where she and Noah had shared their first defining moments.

Something was different. The grass looked greener, more luxuriant. There was no stumbling on the stone path because all the stones had been reset. Every bench they passed was freshly painted and restored so people could actually sit on them. She could hear birds trilling in the treetops and the distant, lyrical sound of water flowing. The path led to the fountain, and Jasmine looked up at the stone cherub, which was no longer headless. Its sculpted facial expression appeared blissful as it stared up into the sunlit heavens with its hands clasped in thankful prayer to the Creator. Water spouted from those hands and trickled into the marble basin below, a basin that now possessed only a few aesthetically patterned vines creeping up its sides.

"It's beautiful! I can't believe they actually fixed it," Jasmine exclaimed, turning to look at Noah. "How did you know?"

"Because Avian International donated the funds for the restoration, and the city has agreed to maintain it." He dipped his hand in the water and shook a little bit on Morgan, who laughed and leaped back.

Jasmine stared at him in wonder. "You're something. You never cease to amaze me."

"This park is actually much bigger than you'd think," Noah continued. "If you keep walking, you'll end up down near the Hudson River shore, so it's kind of like a harbor. We've christened it Dawn's Harbor, like Puerto Alba in Cielo Vista."

Overwhelmed, Jasmine flung her arms around her husband and embraced him tightly. "I love you so much. I wish every woman on earth could have a man like you."

Slightly embarrassed by their display of affection, Morgan giggled and ran a few paces ahead of them.

Noah's eyes twinkled. "Careful, Jas. I don't know if every woman on earth would appreciate that. You know I can be pretty obnoxious sometimes."

"Even obnoxious is a virtue with you." She brushed back a stray lock of hair. "What a gorgeous day it is. I just can't wait to pick up Diego so we can all go home together as a family." She glanced over his shoulder. "Morgan, come here."

"I'm coming. I'm coming," she said, skipping back to them.

They gathered hand-in-hand around the fountain, heads bowed, and mouthed silent prayers of gratitude to the Creator of all things good.

ABOUT THE AUTHOR

Kymberly Hunt resides in Rockland County, New York. A life-long lover of music, history, and creative writing, she has been inventing stories since early childhood. She is also involved in spiritual pursuits and is currently at work on her third novel. Please visit her web-site at *www.KymberlyHunt.com.*

Coming in March, 2008 from Genesis Press

Crystal Hubbard's
Blame It On Paradise

CHAPTER ONE

"Hold onto your chairs, soldiers, and don't let your eyes deceive you." Reginald Wexler, co-founder and CEO of Coyle-Wexler Pharmaceuticals, punctuated his admonition with a sly smile. A slight bob of his rectangular head spurred his personal assistant into motion at the far end of the cavernous executive boardroom. The fidgety young man jerked open a pair of double-wide mahogany doors and stepped aside.

The executives of Coyle-Wexler operations—save the dearly departed Gardner Coyle—and a fleet of attorneys turned to watch an elegant, shapely woman make a cheerful and gracious entrance.

"Gentlemen," Reginald started, "and ladies," he added, acknowledging his trio of female executives: the Puerto Rican vice president of marketing, the African-American vice president of communications and the Korean vice president of customer service. "I'd like you to meet the new Mrs. Reginald Wexler."

Jackson DeVoy sat back in his plush leather chair, slowly swiveling to follow the new Mrs. Wexler's long and stately walk from the doorway to her husband's side at the head of the gigantic conference table. Jackson's heavy eyebrows met in the incisive scowl he normally reserved for opposing attorneys as he thoughtfully took his chin between his thumb and forefinger. He studied the woman. The new Mrs. Wexler looked like Ann-Margret, circa *Grumpy Old Men*. A red knit dress flattered her curvaceous figure, hugging it in all the right places, making her look like a belated Christmas present. Her auburn hair was swept into a simple twist that accentuated her cheekbones, and her makeup had been applied with a light and careful hand. Her coffee eyes were her most striking feature, and they seemed to laugh while her mouth merely smiled.

The *new* Mrs. Wexler? Jack cocked a suspicious eyebrow.

She responded to his expression with a surreptitious wink.

"Mr. Wexler, I'd like to be the first to congratulate you on your surprise nuptials. I don't know about anyone else here, but I wasn't aware that your excursion to the South Pacific six months ago was a honeymoon trip." Edison Burke bumped Jack's chair, hard, as he vaulted out of his seat to approach Reginald and his wife. His skinny arms and legs encased in an ill-fitting striped suit, he scurried to the head of the room and clamped Mrs. Wexler's hand between both of his, shaking it so hard that his frameless glasses bounced on the bridge of his nose. "I believe I speak for everyone in this room when I say that we had no idea that you were contemplating divorce, never mind remarriage."

Edison brought Mrs. Wexler's hand to his face and pressed his lips to the back of it. She absently wiped her hand on the skirt of her dress when Edison turned his silvery blue eyes on Reginald. "May I also say that your new wife is a vision of sheer loveliness, truly an upgrade, compared to the former Mrs. Wexler." He guffawed, shoving an elbow into Reginald's ribs.

In a gesture of infinite patience, Reginald passed a claw-like, liver-spotted hand through the white floss covering his head. "Burke. Sit."

"Yes sir." The word left Burke in a humble whisper as he backed toward his seat.

"I suppose you're all wondering why I've called you here this morning." Reginald addressed the forty-five people seated at the conference table, but he kept his gaze on his wife. "It was to meet my wife, yes, but—"

"Not your new wife," Jack said.

Mrs. Wexler's face broke into a smile, and then she chuckled. "Jack, how did you know?"

He stood, straightening his exquisitely tailored jacket as he did so. His presence alone commanded the attention of every man in the room, and his dark, golden good looks captivated Wexler's trio of female veeps.

"Your eyes." Jack neared Mrs. Wexler, still not quite believing what he was seeing. "You can change the body, but the eyes . . . they can't hide." He allowed Wexler's wife to give his hands a brief squeeze, and then he set a chaste kiss on her cheek. "You look wonderful, Millicent."

Reginald gave Jack a proud pat on the back. "Very good, Jackson, my boy. Once again, you've shown why you're my number one."

Millicent Wexler—the first and *only* Mrs. Wexler—beamed. She clapped her hands to Jack's face and gave him a grandmotherly smooch full on the lips. "Jack, you're such a smart cookie!"

"Okay, Millie, enough's enough." Reginald impatiently ushered her into an empty chair. He picked up a remote control and used it to simultaneously dim the lights overhead and lower a projection screen at the front of the room. With the click of another button, an image appeared on the screen. Jack took his seat.

"This is Millicent Wexler, one year ago." Reginald paused to give his audience the chance to absorb the sight of Millicent Wexler's pale, doughy flesh spilling over the confines of a floral bathing suit. "Millicent topped the scales at an all-time personal high of two—"

"Must you, Reginald!" Mrs. Wexler's voice drowned out the rest of the number.

He rolled his eyes skyward and took a deep breath before continuing. "Honestly, Millie, everyone in this room knows you used to be—"

Jack felt the heat of the fiery stare Mrs. Wexler pinned on her husband.

Reginald snorted impatiently. "This is a scientific presentation," he stated gruffly. "Full disclosure is key here, and that includes your weight."

Mrs. Wexler stubbornly crossed her arms.

"Would *you* like to handle this presentation, Millie?"

"Actually, I would," she said, standing. "Thank you, Reginald." She plucked the remote from his palm before taking his shoulders and guiding him into her unoccupied chair.

"Ladies and gentlemen, that indeed is a photo of me from last year." Millicent began a leisurely stroll around the conference table. "That's me in the pool at our house on Cape Cod on our thirty-fifth anniversary. I weighed in the neighborhood of two hundred pounds. As many of you know, I've tried every weight loss aide offered by Coyle-Wexler and every other pharmaceutical company in the Western Hemisphere as well as all the diets on the bestseller lists, every homeopathic remedy, hypnosis, acupuncture and even a few things that aren't legal within the United States.

"Nothing worked for me. I tried low-carb, low-fat, all-vegetable, all-liquid, citrus, cabbage, soy, fasting, water binging . . ." She stopped to catch her breath. "I'm an older woman, but I'm not an old woman, no matter what you young hotshots might think. I wanted to improve my health as well as my looks, but nothing helped me manage my weight. Just when I began considering drastic surgical options, I discovered something better."

She clicked the remote. A leafy green plant appeared on screen.

"What's that?" Edison snickered. "The parsley diet?"

"It's mint," Millicent said. "It grows half a world away, in the mountains of Darwin Island. I spent six weeks on Darwin with Reginald, my sister and her husband. While we were there, we were served a delicious mint tea that's brewed from freshly picked young leaves. By the end of our third week, my sister and I had each lost nearly twelve pounds, and we weren't dieting. On the contrary, we gorged ourselves on every delicacy the islanders set before us.

"By the end of the six weeks, I'd lost twenty pounds and my sister had lost sixteen. I brought some of the tea back with me, and once it was released from quarantine, I resumed drinking it. Within five months, I'd lost another sixty pounds, and I'd never felt better. I *ran* the Susan G. Komen Race for the Cure a few months ago, I took the 55-and-over doubles title in my indoor tennis league, and I've reached my goal weight. I'd fit right in on Darwin now. The women there are exceptionally fit and healthy, and we were told it was because of this mint tea. The women drink it the way we here in the United States drink soda."

Millicent switched photos, now showing a beach shot featuring a sampling of the island's female residents. Every man in the room sat up straighter, some shifting from side to side to get a better, unobstructed view of the screen.

"The women on Darwin are beautiful as well," Millicent said, "which probably has more to do with the various ethnicities of its residents rather than the tea."

Other than a slightly quirked eyebrow, Jack showed no outward reaction to the smiling, nubile figures on screen. Dressed in skimpy bathing suits, simple cotton dresses or topless, the women of Darwin ranged in complexion from strawberries and cream to ebony. Jack's eyebrows drew together in curiosity as he picked out a very fair-skinned woman with very full lips and a broad, flat nose, and then a dark-skinned woman with straight, honey-blonde hair. Jack knew that Aborigines could be born with blonde hair, but he'd never seen such a thing, even in photos.

Edison openly leered at the attractive nubile figures in the photo. "It's like that scene in *Mutiny on the Bounty*, the one where the native women choose their mates from among the English sailors."

Reginald grimaced. "Keep it in your pants, Burke. Millie, may I take it from here?"

She handed over the remote. Reginald raised the lights, drowning the image of the island beauties in fashionable track lighting. "According to Darwin's Ministry of Health, the average woman on the island is five-foot-seven and weighs 135 pounds. Her measurements are 35-24-36, and she lives to be 84 years old. On Darwin, obesity is unheard of for the natives."

The stout vice president of new developments raised a pudgy pink hand. "Does this Darwin mint have the same effect on men as it does on women?"

"Yes." Reginald nodded his appreciation for the question. "In fact, the tea's effect seems to work even faster."

"Figures," muttered the female vice president of marketing.

"People, my wife has given you a firsthand testimonial as to the effectiveness of Darwin mint, but as you know, our stockholders and the Food and Drug Administration require far more than that." Reginald clasped his hands behind his back.

Edison's snort resounded through the room. "You intend to market that weed under the Coyle-Wexler trademark?"

"That's exactly what I plan to do." Thirty years of sharpening his claws on pipsqueaks like Edison Burke put a gleeful shine in Reginald's eyes as he braced his hands wide on the glossy tabletop. "Do you have any objections, counselor?"

"N-No, sir." Edison's hands trembled slightly as he straightened his already straight tie.

Jack bowed his head to hide a grin.

Reginald directed their attention to the folders set before them on the table. "Over the past few months, I've had our research department working to chemically synthesize this tea. So far, we've had no success in reproducing it. In fact, our trials have been dismal failures. One of the women in our initial test study gained twenty pounds in eight days. Another version of the tea had side effects of, and I quote, 'temporary blindness, irritable bowel syndrome, acute sleeplessness and episodes of speaking gibberish.' Either the sample we're working with is too small, or there's something in this tea that cannot, and clearly should not, be duplicated in a lab."

"Why can't we just buy the rights to Darwin mint from the growers on the island?" Jack asked.

Reginald, grinning smugly, narrowed his eyes and pointed a finger at Jack. "That's where you come in, my boy." He greedily rubbed his hands together. "The mint grows exclusively in the Paradise Valley region of the Raina Mountains on Darwin Island, which is privately owned by J.T. Marchand, who has ignored all of our inquiries regarding Darwin mint tea and its outright purchase. Now, gentlemen—and ladies—clinical trials on the tea are ongoing, even as we speak. But once we get clearance from the FDA to market the tea, Coyle-Wexler Pharmaceuticals fully intends to be the sole producer and distributor."

Reginald strolled to the expanse of one-way glass forming the east wall of the boardroom. He gazed at an unparalleled view of Boston from sixty stories up as he said, "Darwin mint tea is what the world has been waiting for. It's a weight loss aid that has no discernible side effects. It's impossible to overuse it, as it seems to paradoxically act as an appetite stimulant if consumed in massive quantities. This tea will change the face, and the figures, of the world. J.T. Marchand is idling on the gold mine of the millennium, and I want in on it."

Reginald turned away from the wall of glass. "I'm sending my best man to work out a deal with J.T. Marchand. Burke . . ."

Surprised, Edison sat taller and offered the room a gloating smirk.

"I want you on standby, in case I need a second down there," Reginald finished.

His smirk morphing into a petulant pout, Edison sat back heavily in his chair.

Reginald issued his closing command. "Jack, pack your bags. You leave for Darwin today."

By the time he had departed Boston's Logan International Airport and arrived in Sydney, Australia, where he'd boarded a chartered flight bound for Wellington, New Zealand, Jack felt comfortable in his knowledge of Darwin Island. He'd read the comprehensive report Coyle-Wexler's research department had prepared and now considered himself a walking encyclopedia of trivial information about Darwin.

J.T. Marchand was another subject entirely. In an Internet-driven information age, Marchand had a canny knack for staying out of newspapers, magazines and web sites. The hasty Internet search Jack had conducted on his own in the air above the Rocky Mountains had yielded only the most basic information.

Marchand, a descendant of the French, English and Aboriginal settlers who colonized the island in the late 1700s, inherited the whole of Darwin at an early age. Like the Vatican and the tiny country of Malta, Darwin Island was a sovereign entity under international law, which made Marchand the closest thing to a genuine potentate Jack ever hoped to meet. What most intimidated Jack was the fact that Marchand was a summa cum laude graduate of Stanford Law School and a corporate attorney with an undefeated record.

A perfect winning record was one thing Marchand and Jack had in common, and he mused on that as he stepped off of the charter from New Zealand to set foot on Darwin for the first time.

"Welcome to Darwin, the pearl of the South Pacific," greeted a woman with a bright smile, flawless terra cotta skin and a clipboard bearing the passenger manifesto. A warm, fragrant breeze made her long, black hair dance and shimmer about her shoulders and upper arms. It played in the wispy grasses of her low-slung skirt, which revealed a considerable expanse of her taut, honey-dark abdomen and rounded hips. The five male passengers disembarking after Jack trained their eyes on their hostess's exposed flesh and the straining contents of her floral bandeau top while she stamped Jack's passport and visa.

Jack had eyes only for the nearest taxi. "I need to get to the Warutara Hotel." He took off his double-breasted Burberry trench coat, which was no longer necessary now that he'd left the brutal New England January on the opposite side of the Earth. He pushed back the cuff of his left sleeve to set his watch to Darwin time, which was nineteen hours ahead of Boston.

"The Warutara, Mr. DeVoy?" The hostess returned his passport and visa before gently taking his arm, much to the envy of the other male travelers who had been on Jack's flight. She guided him toward the compact terminal attached to the small airstrip. "Are you sure that's where you—"

Speaking over her, Jack tactfully extracted himself from her grasp. "I'm in something of a hurry and I'm quite sure of my itinerary. If you could just point me in the direction of the rental car center, I'd really appreciate it."

The pretty native's mouth tightened before relaxing into its former welcoming smile. "Well, then, Mr. DeVoy, if you have any items to declare, you may do so at the customer service center inside the terminal. You'll find transportation waiting at the front of the terminal, Mr. DeVoy. I'm afraid if you need assistance with your luggage, you'll find that—"

"I have everything I need right here." He impatiently indicated the leather garment bag slung over his shoulder and the valise and briefcase gripped in his hand. "This won't be a long stay."

Jack's helpful hostess seemed relieved. "Even so, welcome to Darwin Island, and I trust you'll have a memorable visit."

Jack grunted his thanks and hurried into the terminal, shouldering his way through a colorful mix of tourists and locals as he searched for the customer service center. There had been a mere ten passengers on his flight from Christchurch, New Zealand, to Darwin, and Jack spared little more than a glance as the arms and smiles of chattering family and friends swallowed his fellow passengers.

With his travel-rumpled business suit and his decidedly pale Boston pallor, Jack stood out as he paced in front of the terminal, wondering which vehicle and driver could possibly be his. He was accustomed to seeing stone-faced drivers bearing placards with DeVoy printed on them, but here and now, forced to choose among an open-topped Jeep with bald tires and no passenger seat, a wooden cart drawn by two extremely bored yet diabolical-looking long-haired goats, a rusting Stingray with a flat rear tire and a minivan already filled to capacity with cheerful, laughing locals, Jack decided to retreat into the bustling terminal to find customer service.

At the far end of the terminal, between a humming vending machine and the men's lavatory, Jack spied a high counter manned by a portly fellow wearing a splashy shirt printed with exotic birds. Jack's long, hurried strides carried him there quickly, and he marched directly to the front of the long line. "Excuse me. My name is Jackson DeVoy and I have an important business meeting in the city in less than an hour and I need to get to my hotel. I just flew in—"

"Your arms must be tired!" the desk clerk cut in. His golden-brown cheeks puffed with laughter at his own goofy humor as he slapped the desktop.

"—and I was told that transportation would be waiting for me." Jack clenched his jaw. "Where might I find my car and driver?"

"Do you have a reservation for a car and driver?"

The clerk's accent was odd, something between Australian English and something Jack couldn't quite place. Whatever it was, "reservation" came out as "riversation."

"Of course." Jack withdrew an envelope from his inner breast pocket. He opened it and yanked out his itinerary, which included the confirmation numbers for his flight, transportation and lodging. He set the paper before the counter clerk, who studied it as though he were auditing an income tax return.

The clerk smiled and cheerfully handed the paper back to Jack. "This reservation is no good. Next!"

The short woman who'd been first in line stepped forward, making a point to give Jack a small shove, and set a live chicken on the countertop. The bird escaped the woman's grasp and frantically scrambled across the counter before leaping at Jack, who jerked himself clear of the bird's awkward flight path. The frenzied fowl hit the tile floor and began zigzagging through the terminal, much to the counter clerk's amusement and Jack's annoyance.

After shunting aside the next person in line, Jack again stood directly in front of the clerk. "Look. I need transportation. Why is my 'riversation' no good?"

The counter clerk watched the chicken's mistress chase her charge. "You booked Nathan's Limousine Service. Nathan himself drives the one car, but Nate will be on his back for the next few weeks. He slipped a disc yesterday, trying to land a striped marlin out on his boat. She was a beauty, about seventy kilograms, but she got the best of our Nate."

Jack drummed his fingers on the desktop. "What's the fastest way I can get to the city?"

"What city?"

"Wautangua, the capital."

"Wautangua's more of a town than a city, kiddo," volunteered a petite, dark-skinned woman in a Kansas City

Royals T-shirt. She was standing at the nearby postal desk. "Christchurch is a city. Wellington is a city. Boston is a city, and I'm guessin' that's from where you're about, given your accent and your attitude. But Wautangua . . . that's a town."

Jack turned to the woman. "You're American." He approached her, daring to hope for a quick resolution to his transportation problem. "Finally, someone who speaks regular English."

The woman slipped on a pair of thick glasses that had been hanging from her neck by a fine braided leather cord. "Levora Wilkins Solomon." She offered her hand. Jack took it and she gave his hand two hard pumps that shook his garment bag from his shoulder to the crook of his elbow. "I came to Darwin twenty-five years ago to study the Moriori. I went and fell in love with one of them, and I've been here ever since." She crossed her arms over her nonexistent bosom. "So tell me, son. What brings you to Darwin and how can I help you get to it?"

"I'm here on business."

She stared at him, clearly waiting for him to elaborate. "It's confidential."

She stood frozen a moment longer, but then tossed her hands up. "Good enough. Come on." She started for the exit, waving Jack along behind her. "My business here is finished, so I can ride you into Wautangua."

Jack offered a silent prayer of thanks as he fell into step beside Levora. They exited the terminal to see that the chicken was still kicking up a ruckus. Several laughing young boys darted after it in half-hearted pursuit, but the chicken always skipped out of reach, stopping just short of crossing the wide dirt road. Then it turned and ran erratically, skidding to a stop beneath the goat-drawn cart. The devilish-looking goats spooked and took off in a cloud of dust, clattering wheels and terrified bleating.

Mindless of the scene before him, Jack scanned the area for the practical four-wheeled vehicle he imagined Levora would drive. "Where's your car?"

"That was it." She pointed to the goat-powered speck disappearing into the horizon. "BeBe and CeCe don't like chickens. Never have, never will." Levora began walking in the direction her goats had taken.

Jack's shoulders fell. He stared at the sky, seething as he contemplated the nature of God, man and just how much pleasure he would take in sucking J.T. Marchand dry.

"Hey, you." Levora, her hands on the hips of her loose-fitting blue jeans, had doubled back for him. "Are you comin' or not?"

He glanced back at the airstrip, but he resisted the temptation to return to the plane and fly right back to Boston. Taking a firmer grip on the handle of his bag, he quickly caught up to Levora. "How far is Wautangua?"

"Mmm, 'bout ten miles." She kicked at a few broken oyster shells with the toe of her worn hiking boot. "Shouldn't take more than a couple hours to walk it. 'Course, we should catch up to BeBe and CeCe long before then. Unless they decide to go all the way home this time."

"Why do you drive a goat cart?"

"You got something against goats?"

"No. I just think it's unusual in this day and age to travel by goat-driven cart."

"A lot of things on Darwin are unusual. It's the nature of the place. Not too many folks drive cars here. We've got ambulances and fire trucks and all, but there was a law passed twenty-some years ago banning most other vehicles. It's never been enforced, really, considering who made the declaration, but most everybody abides by it. The only folks who drive are the ones who absolutely need to."

Jack fished out his cell phone. "I have to call my hotel and let them know that I'll be checking in late."

"Where're you staying?"

"The Hotel Warutara."

Levora slowed her step to closely examine a stand of tiger lilies growing on the side of the dirt road. "That's too bad."

Dread settled in Jack's belly. "Why's that?"

Levora snapped off one of the pale lemonade-colored blossoms. She handed the lovely bloom to Jack, who scarcely looked at it. "It really wasn't that great of a hotel. Of course, that's neither here nor there, since the Warutara collapsed in a typhoon three months ago."

The tiger lily fell from Jack's hand as he scowled and readjusted his bags. Grumbling under his breath, he again fell into step behind Levora, inadvertently crushing the delicate flower under his heel.

Wautangua was more of a village than a town, with no automobile traffic on the roads, which alternated between hard-packed dirt and gravel. Jack allowed Levora to lead him past well-kept, sprawling, single-story stucco homes and smaller, cozy stone bungalows set far from the main road to the center of Wautangua. Foot traffic picked up as they entered Wautangua, and Jack was only mildly surprised to see that Levora seemed to know every person she encountered by name. An even mix of tourists and natives ambled in and out of one-story storefronts with colorful plate glass windows, rough plank market stalls and a single gas station that doubled as a visitor's center. A three-story brick building, the one oasis of urban "civility" on the island, rose on the edge of town.

"This was the factory." Levora sat on the topmost of three stone stairs leading to the long walkway to the building's entrance. She took off one of her hiking boots. Gripping it by its heel, she hung it upside down, pouring sand and pebbles from it. "Back when the North and South were at war in America, they used to make commercial fishing nets here at the Marchand factory. It's been the governor's house, a hospital and a warehouse in the past, but now the place is used for offices. The Marchand family's owned the whole island since Methuselah came off the mountain. Are you here for the tea, Jack?"

Levora had single-handedly kept the conversation flowing during their long trek into town. She had told him all about her childhood in Kansas City, Kansas, her scholarship to Berkeley and the decision to study anthropology, her marriage to Moriori tribesman Errol Solomon, her daughter Louise and son Ben, who were currently enrolled at MIT and Penn respectively, and the small oyster farm her husband currently ran. She hadn't inquired further about Jack's business on the island, so he was more inclined to answer her question. In part.

"I won't say no. But I can't say yes."

"How old would you say I am, Jack? Even if you didn't know that both my babies are in college, how old would you think I was?"

"That's a loaded question, Levora, and you know it."

"Go on and answer. I promise, I won't kill you."

"Well, you've been on Darwin for twenty-five years, and you came while you were working on a graduate research project. Given those facts, I'd guess that you were fifty years old, even though you don't look a minute over forty."

Levora's eyes sparkled, their color rivaling a rich, dark, home-brewed coffee. "I worked for ten years before I started graduate school, Jack. I was thirty-four years old when I came to Darwin. I'll be sixty next week."

Jack studied Levora a little closer. She had maintained a good pace, never once stopping to rest or to catch her breath, even though she had been speaking incessantly. Tiny lines fanned from the outer corners of her black eyes, but only when she laughed or smiled, which had been often. Her teeth were bright, almost too white against her ebony skin. Jack noted a few strands of silver hair at her temples and in her stubby ponytail, but they complemented the twinkle in her eyes. Levora was slender, and she carried herself with such a lively step that it was hard for Jack to believe that she was closer to sixty than forty.

"A lot of people have come here to get their hands on the tea, Jack."

"Is it the fountain of youth? Is that why you stayed on Darwin?"

Levora laughed and tied her bootlaces. "It's just tea, kid." She stood and patted the front of his jacket, raising a puff of road dust. "And I stayed because of my hot island lover. Goodbye, Jack. And good luck with J.T."

As he traveled the lengthy stone path to the front of the building, Jack brushed off his clothes and stamped his feet to remove as much dust from himself as he could before he swung open the lobby doors. He was instantly comfortable in the elegant, if not luxurious, surroundings. Traces of the island were still evident, despite the corporate setting: with her silk blouse and headset phone, the receptionist wore a skirt made of brightly colored, papery Masi cloth.

Jack dropped his valise and briefcase at his feet and leaned over the tall counter wrapping around the receptionist's desk. "I'm from Coyle-Wexler Pharmaceuticals and I'm here to see J.T. Marchand. I had an appointment this afternoon, but I was unavoidably detained at the airport."

Without looking up at him, the receptionist removed a glossy magazine from atop a large appointment book. "Well, let's see here, Mr . . ." Her eyes followed the path of her long red fingernail as it moved down the left side of the appointment book before coming to an abrupt stop. "You must be 'Coyle-Wexler rep.' " She peered at the large clock affixed high on one wall. "You're very late."

Jack scowled, but he managed to suppress the Bostonian instinct to snap, "No kidding, Einstein."

"J.T. is no longer on the premises." The receptionist shifted her gaze from the appointment book to the fashion magazine beside it. "You'll have to reschedule for tomorrow."

The muscles of Jack's neck tensed. "I'm in town for twenty-four hours. I need to see J.T. Marchand *today*. Can you give me a number to call, or a home address?"

The receptionist finally glanced up at him. Her eyes widened for an instant, becoming two deep pools of jet within the terra cotta of her face before her lids dropped, suggestively hooding her eyes. She took the left corner of her lower lip between her pearly teeth and gave Jack a long, leisurely appraisal. "I can give you *my* number. I guarantee that you'll have more fun with me than with J.T. Marchand."

Jack squinted in annoyance and shook his head. He took several long strides back toward the plate glass lobby front. He turned and knocked his head against the surrounding brick as he formed a mental picture of exactly how he would financially keelhaul J.T. Marchand.

The receptionist's voice dragged him from his vengeful reverie. "J.T. has an opening tomorrow morning at 7:30."

"I'll take it." He finally raised his head from the brick.

"Is there anything else I can do for you, Mr . . . ?"

"Yes," Jack snapped pointedly. "I need a place to spend the night."

A feline grin slowly spread across the receptionist's face. Wearily, Jack sighed and rolled his eyes heavenward.

2008 Reprint Mass Market Titles

January

Cautious Heart
Cheris F. Hodges
ISBN-13: 978-1-58571-301-1
ISBN-10: 1-58571-301-5
$6.99

Suddenly You
Crystal Hubbard
ISBN-13: 978-1-58571-302-8
ISBN-10: 1-58571-302-3
$6.99

February

Passion
T. T. Henderson
ISBN-13: 978-1-58571-303-5
ISBN-10: 1-58571-303-1
$6.99

Whispers in the Sand
LaFlorya Gauthier
ISBN-13: 978-1-58571-304-2
ISBN-10: 1-58571-304-x
$6.99

March

Life Is Never As It Seems
J. J. Michael
ISBN-13: 978-1-58571-305-9
ISBN-10: 1-58571-305-8
$6.99

Beyond the Rapture
Beverly Clark
ISBN-13: 978-1-58571-306-6
ISBN-10: 1-58571-306-6
$6.99

April

A Heart's Awakening
Veronica Parker
ISBN-13: 978-1-58571-307-3
ISBN-10: 1-58571-307-4
$6.99

Breeze
Robin Lynette Hampton
ISBN-13: 978-1-58571-308-0
ISBN-10: 1-58571-308-2
$6.99

May

I'll Be Your Shelter
Giselle Carmichael
ISBN-13: 978-1-58571-309-7
ISBN-10: 1-58571-309-0
$6.99

Careless Whispers
Rochelle Alers
ISBN-13: 978-1-58571-310-3
ISBN-10: 1-58571-310-4
$6.99

June

Sin
Crystal Rhodes
ISBN-13: 978-1-58571-311-0
ISBN-10: 1-58571-311-2
$6.99

Dark Storm Rising
Chinelu Moore
ISBN-13: 978-1-58571-312-7
ISBN-10: 1-58571-312-0
$6.99

2008 Reprint Mass Market Titles (continued)

July

Object of His Desire
A.C. Arthur
ISBN-13: 978-1-58571-313-4
ISBN-10: 1-58571-313-9
$6.99

Angel's Paradise
Janice Angelique
ISBN-13: 978-1-58571-314-1
ISBN-10: 1-58571-314-7
$6.99

August

Unbreak My Heart
Dar Tomlinson
ISBN-13: 978-1-58571-315-8
ISBN-10: 1-58571-315-5
$6.99

All I Ask
Barbara Keaton
ISBN-13: 978-1-58571-316-5
ISBN-10: 1-58571-316-3
$6.99

September

Icie
Pamela Leigh Starr
ISBN-13: 978-1-58571-275-5
ISBN-10: 1-58571-275-2
$6.99

At Last
Lisa Riley
ISBN-13: 978-1-58571-276-2
ISBN-10: 1-58571-276-0
$6.99

October

Everlastin' Love
Gay G. Gunn
ISBN-13: 978-1-58571-277-9
ISBN-10: 1-58571-277-9
$6.99

Three Wishes
Seressia Glass
ISBN-13: 978-1-58571-278-6
ISBN-10: 1-58571-278-7
$6.99

November

Yesterday Is Gone
Beverly Clark
ISBN-13: 978-1-58571-279-3
ISBN-10: 1-58571-279-5
$6.99

Again My Love
Kayla Perrin
ISBN-13: 978-1-58571-280-9
ISBN-10: 1-58571-280-9
$6.99

December

Office Policy
A.C. Arthur
ISBN-13: 978-1-58571-281-6
ISBN-10: 1-58571-281-7
$6.99

Rendezvous With Fate
Jeanne Sumerix
ISBN-13: 978-1-58571-283-3
ISBN-10: 1-58571-283-3
$6.99

2008 New Mass Market Titles

January

Where I Want To Be
Maryam Diaab
ISBN-13: 978-1-58571-268-7
ISBN-10: 1-58571-268-X
$6.99

Never Say Never
Michele Cameron
ISBN-13: 978-1-58571-269-4
ISBN-10: 1-58571-269-8
$6.99

February

Stolen Memories
Michele Sudler
ISBN-13: 978-1-58571-270-0
ISBN-10: 1-58571-270-1
$6.99

Dawn's Harbor
Kymberly Hunt
ISBN-13: 978-1-58571-271-7
ISBN-10: 1-58571-271-X
$6.99

March

Undying Love
Renee Alexis
ISBN-13: 978-1-58571-272-4
ISBN-10: 1-58571-272-8
$6.99

Blame It On Paradise
Crystal Hubbard
ISBN-13: 978-1-58571-273-1
ISBN-10: 1-58571-273-6
$6.99

April

When A Man Loves A Woman
La Connie Taylor-Jones
ISBN-13: 978-1-58571-274-8
ISBN-10: 1-58571-274-4
$6.99

Choices
Tammy Williams
ISBN-13: 978-1-58571-300-4
ISBN-10: 1-58571-300-7
$6.99

May

Dream Runner
Gail McFarland
ISBN-13: 978-1-58571-317-2
ISBN-10: 1-58571-317-1
$6.99

Southern Fried Standards
S.R. Maddox
ISBN-13: 978-1-58571-318-9
ISBN-10: 1-58571-318-X
$6.99

June

Looking for Lily
Africa Fine
ISBN-13: 978-1-58571-319-6
ISBN-10: 1-58571-319-8
$6.99

Bliss, Inc.
Chamein Canton
ISBN-13: 978-1-58571-325-7
ISBN-10: 1-58571-325-2
$6.99

2008 New Mass Market Titles (continued)

July

Love's Secrets
Yolanda McVey
ISBN-13: 978-1-58571-321-9
ISBN-10: 1-58571-321-X
$6.99

Things Forbidden
Maryam Diaab
ISBN-13: 978-1-58571-327-1
ISBN-10: 1-58571-327-9
$6.99

August

Storm
Pamela Leigh Starr
ISBN-13: 978-1-58571-323-3
ISBN-10: 1-58571-323-6
$6.99

Passion's Furies
AlTonya Washington
ISBN-13: 978-1-58571-324-0
ISBN-10: 1-58571-324-4
$6.99

September

Three Doors Down
Michele Sudler
ISBN-13: 978-1-58571-332-5
ISBN-10: 1-58571-332-5
$6.99

Mr Fix-It
Crystal Hubbard
ISBN-13: 978-1-58571-326-4
ISBN-10: 1-58571-326-0
$6.99

October

Moments of Clarity
Michele Cameron
ISBN-13: 978-1-58571-330-1
ISBN-10: 1-58571-330-9
$6.99

Lady Preacher
K.T. Richey
ISBN-13: 978-1-58571-333-2
ISBN-10: 1-58571-333-3
$6.99

November

This Life Isn't Perfect Holla
Sandra Foy
ISBN: 978-1-58571-331-8
ISBN-10: 1-58571-331-7
$6.99

Promises Made
Bernice Layton
ISBN-13: 978-1-58571-334-9
ISBN-10: 1-58571-334-1
$6.99

December

A Voice Behind Thunder
Carrie Elizabeth Greene
ISBN-13: 978-1-58571-329-5
ISBN-10: 1-58571-329-5
$6.99

The More Things Change
Chamein Canton
ISBN-13: 978-1-58571-328-8
ISBN-10: 1-58571-328-7
$6.99

Other Genesis Press, Inc. Titles

A Dangerous Deception	J.M. Jeffries	$8.95
A Dangerous Love	J.M. Jeffries	$8.95
A Dangerous Obsession	J.M. Jeffries	$8.95
A Drummer's Beat to Mend	Kei Swanson	$9.95
A Happy Life	Charlotte Harris	$9.95
A Heart's Awakening	Veronica Parker	$9.95
A Lark on the Wing	Phyliss Hamilton	$9.95
A Love of Her Own	Cheris F. Hodges	$9.95
A Love to Cherish	Beverly Clark	$8.95
A Risk of Rain	Dar Tomlinson	$8.95
A Taste of Temptation	Reneé Alexis	$9.95
A Twist of Fate	Beverly Clark	$8.95
A Will to Love	Angie Daniels	$9.95
Acquisitions	Kimberley White	$8.95
Across	Carol Payne	$12.95
After the Vows	Leslie Esdaile	$10.95
(Summer Anthology)	T.T. Henderson	
	Jacqueline Thomas	
Again My Love	Kayla Perrin	$10.95
Against the Wind	Gwynne Forster	$8.95
All I Ask	Barbara Keaton	$8.95
Always You	Crystal Hubbard	$6.99
Ambrosia	T.T. Henderson	$8.95
An Unfinished Love Affair	Barbara Keaton	$8.95
And Then Came You	Dorothy Elizabeth Love	$8.95
Angel's Paradise	Janice Angelique	$9.95
At Last	Lisa G. Riley	$8.95
Best of Friends	Natalie Dunbar	$8.95
Beyond the Rapture	Beverly Clark	$9.95

Other Genesis Press, Inc. Titles (continued)

Other Genesis Press, Inc. Titles (continued)

Daughter of the Wind	Joan Xian	$8.95
Deadly Sacrifice	Jack Kean	$22.95
Designer Passion	Dar Tomlinson	$8.95
	Diana Richeaux	
Do Over	Celya Bowers	$9.95
Dreamtective	Liz Swados	$5.95
Ebony Angel	Deatri King-Bey	$9.95
Ebony Butterfly II	Delilah Dawson	$14.95
Echoes of Yesterday	Beverly Clark	$9.95
Eden's Garden	Elizabeth Rose	$8.95
Eve's Prescription	Edwina Martin Arnold	$8.95
Everlastin' Love	Gay G. Gunn	$8.95
Everlasting Moments	Dorothy Elizabeth Love	$8.95
Everything and More	Sinclair Lebeau	$8.95
Everything but Love	Natalie Dunbar	$8.95
Falling	Natalie Dunbar	$9.95
Fate	Pamela Leigh Starr	$8.95
Finding Isabella	A.J. Garrotto	$8.95
Forbidden Quest	Dar Tomlinson	$10.95
Forever Love	Wanda Y. Thomas	$8.95
From the Ashes	Kathleen Suzanne	$8.95
	Jeanne Sumerix	
Gentle Yearning	Rochelle Alers	$10.95
Glory of Love	Sinclair LeBeau	$10.95
Go Gentle into that Good Night	Malcom Boyd	$12.95
Goldengroove	Mary Beth Craft	$16.95
Groove, Bang, and Jive	Steve Cannon	$8.99
Hand in Glove	Andrea Jackson	$9.95

Other Genesis Press, Inc. Titles (continued)

Other Genesis Press, Inc. Titles (continued)

Last Train to Memphis	Elsa Cook	$12.95
Lasting Valor	Ken Olsen	$24.95
Let Us Prey	Hunter Lundy	$25.95
Lies Too Long	Pamela Ridley	$13.95
Life Is Never As It Seems	J.J. Michael	$12.95
Lighter Shade of Brown	Vicki Andrews	$8.95
Love Always	Mildred E. Riley	$10.95
Love Doesn't Come Easy	Charlyne Dickerson	$8.95
Love Unveiled	Gloria Greene	$10.95
Love's Deception	Charlene Berry	$10.95
Love's Destiny	M. Loui Quezada	$8.95
Mae's Promise	Melody Walcott	$8.95
Magnolia Sunset	Giselle Carmichael	$8.95
Many Shades of Gray	Dyanne Davis	$6.99
Matters of Life and Death	Lesego Malepe, Ph.D.	$15.95
Meant to Be	Jeanne Sumerix	$8.95
Midnight Clear (Anthology)	Leslie Esdaile	$10.95
	Gwynne Forster	
	Carmen Green	
	Monica Jackson	
Midnight Magic	Gwynne Forster	$8.95
Midnight Peril	Vicki Andrews	$10.95
Misconceptions	Pamela Leigh Starr	$9.95
Montgomery's Children	Richard Perry	$14.95
My Buffalo Soldier	Barbara B. K. Reeves	$8.95
Naked Soul	Gwynne Forster	$8.95
Next to Last Chance	Louisa Dixon	$24.95
No Apologies	Seressia Glass	$8.95
No Commitment Required	Seressia Glass	$8.95

Other Genesis Press, Inc. Titles (continued)

Other Genesis Press, Inc. Titles (continued)

Revelations	Cheris F. Hodges	$8.95
Rivers of the Soul	Leslie Esdaile	$8.95
Rocky Mountain Romance	Kathleen Suzanne	$8.95
Rooms of the Heart	Donna Hill	$8.95
Rough on Rats and Tough on Cats	Chris Parker	$12.95
Secret Library Vol. 1	Nina Sheridan	$18.95
Secret Library Vol. 2	Cassandra Colt	$8.95
Secret Thunder	Annetta P. Lee	$9.95
Shades of Brown	Denise Becker	$8.95
Shades of Desire	Monica White	$8.95
Shadows in the Moonlight	Jeanne Sumerix	$8.95
Sin	Crystal Rhodes	$8.95
Small Whispers	Annetta P. Lee	$6.99
So Amazing	Sinclair LeBeau	$8.95
Somebody's Someone	Sinclair LeBeau	$8.95
Someone to Love	Alicia Wiggins	$8.95
Song in the Park	Martin Brant	$15.95
Soul Eyes	Wayne L. Wilson	$12.95
Soul to Soul	Donna Hill	$8.95
Southern Comfort	J.M. Jeffries	$8.95
Still the Storm	Sharon Robinson	$8.95
Still Waters Run Deep	Leslie Esdaile	$8.95
Stolen Kisses	Dominiqua Douglas	$9.95
Stories to Excite You	Anna Forrest/Divine	$14.95
Subtle Secrets	Wanda Y. Thomas	$8.95
Suddenly You	Crystal Hubbard	$9.95
Sweet Repercussions	Kimberley White	$9.95
Sweet Sensations	Gwendolyn Bolton	$9.95

Other Genesis Press, Inc. Titles (continued)

Sweet Tomorrows	Kimberly White	$8.95
Taken by You	Dorothy Elizabeth Love	$9.95
Tattooed Tears	T. T. Henderson	$8.95
The Color Line	Lizzette Grayson Carter	$9.95
The Color of Trouble	Dyanne Davis	$8.95
The Disappearance of Allison Jones	Kayla Perrin	$5.95
The Fires Within	Beverly Clark	$9.95
The Foursome	Celya Bowers	$6.99
The Honey Dipper's Legacy	Pannell-Allen	$14.95
The Joker's Love Tune	Sidney Rickman	$15.95
The Little Pretender	Barbara Cartland	$10.95
The Love We Had	Natalie Dunbar	$8.95
The Man Who Could Fly	Bob & Milana Beamon	$18.95
The Missing Link	Charlyne Dickerson	$8.95
The Mission	Pamela Leigh Starr	$6.99
The Perfect Frame	Beverly Clark	$9.95
The Price of Love	Sinclair LeBeau	$8.95
The Smoking Life	Ilene Barth	$29.95
The Words of the Pitcher	Kei Swanson	$8.95
Three Wishes	Seressia Glass	$8.95
Ties That Bind	Kathleen Suzanne	$8.95
Tiger Woods	Libby Hughes	$5.95
Time is of the Essence	Angie Daniels	$9.95
Timeless Devotion	Bella McFarland	$9.95
Tomorrow's Promise	Leslie Esdaile	$8.95
Truly Inseparable	Wanda Y. Thomas	$8.95
Two Sides to Every Story	Dyanne Davis	$9.95
Unbreak My Heart	Dar Tomlinson	$8.95

Other Genesis Press, Inc. Titles (continued)

Uncommon Prayer	Kenneth Swanson	$9.95
Unconditional Love	Alicia Wiggins	$8.95
Unconditional	A.C. Arthur	$9.95
Until Death Do Us Part	Susan Paul	$8.95
Vows of Passion	Bella McFarland	$9.95
Wedding Gown	Dyanne Davis	$8.95
What's Under Benjamin's Bed	Sandra Schaffer	$8.95
When Dreams Float	Dorothy Elizabeth Love	$8.95
When I'm With You	LaConnie Taylor-Jones	$6.99
Whispers in the Night	Dorothy Elizabeth Love	$8.95
Whispers in the Sand	LaFlorya Gauthier	$10.95
Who's That Lady?	Andrea Jackson	$9.95
Wild Ravens	Altonya Washington	$9.95
Yesterday Is Gone	Beverly Clark	$10.95
Yesterday's Dreams, Tomorrow's Promises	Reon Laudat	$8.95
Your Precious Love	Sinclair LeBeau	$8.95

Order Form

Mail to: Genesis Press, Inc.
P.O. Box 101
Columbus, MS 39703

Name _____
Address _____
City/State _____ Zip _____
Telephone _____

Ship to (if different from above)
Name _____
Address _____
City/State _____ Zip _____
Telephone _____

Credit Card Information
Credit Card # _____ ☐ Visa   ☐ Mastercard
Expiration Date (mm/yy) _____ ☐ AmEx ☐ Discover

Qty.	Author	Title	Price	Total

Use this order form, or call 1-888-INDIGO-1	Total for books	_____
	Shipping and handling: $5 first two books, $1 each additional book	_____
	Total S & H	_____
	Total amount enclosed	_____

Mississippi residents add 7% sales tax